Book 4 - Remote Heroes
Written & art directed by: Vlane Carter
Illustrations by: John Buurman
www.BIO-Sapien.com

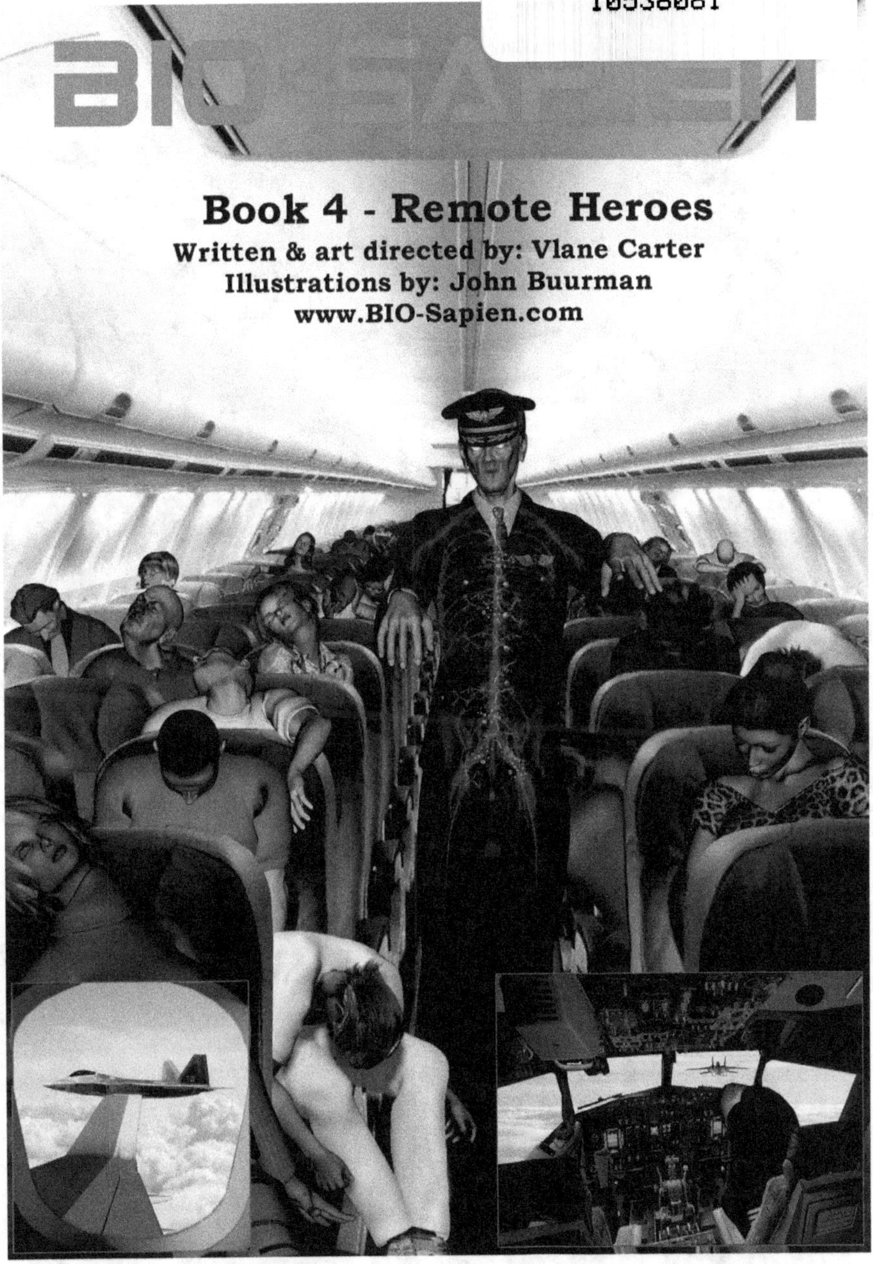

Comics, seasoned burgers, Anime, cosplay, sci-fi movies, meetup.com groups, free old school video games (NES, Xbox, xbox 360 WII U), liquor milkshakes, beer and amazing food.

Take a 360 video tour of Action Burger:

Action Burger's latest music video on youtube:

BIO-SAPIEN 101

JADEN'S HUMAN BODY BIO-ENGINEERED WITH ALIEN NANOTECHNOLOGY.

CONTROL YOUR BODY LIKE A STAR TREK ENTERPRISE SHIP.
CAPTAIN OF BIO-SAPIEN HOST: Jaden Marino. 5'10-6'1 155LBS.
SECOND OFFICER IN CHARGE: AI – (A1SCAN) Artificial Intelligent Synthetic Crystal Andromedian Nanobot.

CREW MEMBERS: NANODRONE'S (+1000 Quintillion) PCBO.ALF communicate hi-speed with pro-gravity and magnetic Nanodrones in feet. They also communicate with anti-gravity Nanodrones in kidney/lower spine. Allows host to walk on walls or ceilings and feet as if he is walking on the ground.

– Prototype Carbon and Biochemical-based Organic Alien Life Forms. Also known as organic Nanobots.

LEFT ARM
– Atom Ripper Nanodrones embedded in skin; based on plasma fusion technology.

SPINAL CORD AND BACK
– Energy shield generating Nanodrones storage area. Brain controls RPM speed and direction of energy shield outside of body. Energy shield is base on plasma fusion technology and Neutrino energy. It retrieves most of its energy from replaced digestive system area.
– Magnetically charged Nanodrones enhances intervertebral disc of cartilage.

SKELETON
– Reconstructed Cancellous and Compact bones. Nanodrone webs of organic fiber proteins. 500 pounds per square inch of force needed to break a bone.

JOINTS
– Enhanced synovial joints around body. Magnetic energy between Nanodrones in joints makes the joints 10x stronger and flexible.

PENIS
– Multiple joints added to penal shaft for controllable directional curving.

"EVOLVE YOUR IMAGINATION"
WWW.BIO-SAPIEN.COM

COPYRIGHT 2010 BY: VC IMAGINATION FACTORY
Illustration by: John Moriarty
Creative art director: Vlane Carter

BRAIN
- Rostral anterior cingulate cortex – Unknown signals transmitted when host feels pain or becomes angry.
- Instant on internal forward moving one layer energy shield, that extends around the skull.

EARS
- Enhanced equilibrium in inner ears. Nanodrones in ears communicate hi-speed with pro-gravity and magnetic Nanodrones in feet. They also communicate with anti-gravity Nanodrones in kidney/lower spine. Allows host to walk on walls or ceilings and feet as if he is walking on the ground.

ARMS
– Specially modified cells and tissue to accept high-energy forces.

RIGHT ARM
– Gravity shockwave Nanodrones embedded in skin.

MUSCLES
– Myostatin protein in muscles cells modified. MSTN gene decoded.
- On demand muscle strength equivalent to 2-4HP.
- Musculoskeletal - Nanodrones enhances muscle fibers strength and coordinate with skeleton system.

RIGHT KIDNEY
– Internal tissue removed. Nanodrones doing the same job in the blood around body. Kidney replaced with quadrillions of Anti-gravity Nanodrones.

NERVOUS SYSTEM
- Nanodrones in brain bypasses chemical messages during Nanotime. They transmit hi-speed collective signals at 8000 feet per second to Nanodrones at nerve endings.

FEET
- Pro-gravity and magnetic Nanodrones; works directly with equilibrium in ears.

LEGS
- Enhanced muscles enables host to run and average between 20-30Mph.
- Host can jump an unlimited height with anti-gravity Nanodrones support.

4

BIO-SAPIEN 101
JADEN'S HUMAN BODY BIO-ENGINEERED WITH ALIEN NANOTECHNOLOGY.

CAPTAIN OF BIALIEN HOST: Jaden Marino.

SECOND OFFICER IN CHARGE: AI (AISCAN) Artificial Intelligent Synthetic Crystal Andromedian Nanobot.

ALIEN NANOTECHNOLOGY:

NANODRONES (+1000 Quintillion) PCBOALF – Prototype Carbon and Biochemical-based Organic Alien Life Forms. Also known as organic Nanobots. - Varies in size.
- Communicate in an atomic digital level 3 collective.
- Split into trillions of communities to perform millions of different duties in organic host.
- Nanodrones are loyal to the DNA of one host.

BRAIN
- New multitasking matrix area in the brain.
- RPM control area for forward and reverse energy shields.
- Artificial nicotine cigarette stimulation. Reconfigured Dopamine areas of the brain.
- 200 billion enhanced neurons.
- Neural code decoded. Neurotransmitters enhanced.
- Total brain usage 60-100%; up from 7-10% average Homosapien.
- Nanotine accelerates the communication speed in the brain. Time dilation reroutes to different parts of the brain. Nanodrones create artificial neurons, artificial synapses and axons. Host witnesses everything happening outside the body in slow motion. Nanotine ranges from 1x to 100x. 1x is the slowest speed and host can see a bullet approaching. Negative side is Nanotine puts a strain on brain and lasts only seconds; can lead to seizures.

LUNGS
- Nanodrones double lung capabilities. 30% more carbon dioxide leaves lungs from added oxygen breathing Nanodrones in skin.
- Instant on internal forward moving one layer energy shield, that extends through the rib cage and around heart.

DNA
- 10,000 compressed DNA memo groups in various locations around body.
- Encoded DNA. Built in anti-cloning prevention. DNA strips away when it leaves host.
- Modified DNA and RNA genetic code.
- Advanced protein folding.

BLOOD
- Reprogrammed white and red blood cells to accept Nanodrones.
- Artificial stem cells regeneration capacities. Rapid injury repair system.

- Turn the human host into a powerful offensive and defensive weapon.
- Enhanced rods and cones behind eyes.
- Jaden's eyes command screen. Nanodrones reports body's actions, energy updates, statistics, energy shield RPM and navigation info, defense weapons, energy status, energy updates.

They pass through and scan any matter. They transmit sound, smell, vision and taste to host. They can also carry trillions of Nanodrones to do remote tasks, also help to return gravity shockwave and atom ripper Nanodrones back to host.

- Artificial orbital hybridization web binds with skin cells; also known as Nanodrone nanotubing organic fibers.
- Self cleaning skin - Bacteria and dirt deposits around body pulls into skin and manually transported securely in blood stream by skin and manually transported securely in blood stream by
- Advanced photosynthesis in skin. Sunlight provides carbohydrate energy into blood stream. Host does not have to eat for days. When combined with water can produce oxygen
- 100% filtered oxygen absorbed through pores and injected into the blood stream. Host can hold breathe for 20-30 minutes. 30% carbon dioxide leaves Nanodrones can also reproduce air temperature molecules to match body heat
- Light reflecting Metamaterial Nanodrones embedded around skin.

STOMACH, SMALL AND LARGE INTESTINES
- Unnecessary organs, removed. Replaced with: Nanodrones energy storage areas, Atomic Solar Recharge fusion area and sub-atomic particles smashing areas.
- Nanodrones protect every outer cell in area from radiation energies.
- Nanodrones can do the same job the digestive system does in a fraction of an inch. Vitamins, minerals, salts, water, carbohydrates, amino acids from proteins, H2O, and fats from food. Filter in seconds directly into the blood stream from the throat area. The rest redirects into the buttocks area for storage.
- Nanodrones redirect and duplicate chemical messages to let the brain know the organs are still there.

NANODRONE GOALS
- Remove and replace unnecessary body parts/organs.
- Evolve the BIO body to its maximum capabilities.
- Avoid alien metamorphosis. - Defend and protect host.
- Defrag and recalibrate the brain configuration for ultimate performance.
- Avoid technological singularity.

EYES
- 1 terapixels of resolution in each eye, zooming capabilities.

- Programmable matter capabilities.

NANOSCANNERS
(Six Nanoscanners created from Nanodrones made for BIO host) Nanodrones made for BIO host) Autonomous alien molecules that vary in size.

SKIN
- Skin will evolve to be stronger than Kevlar.
- Nanodrones to throat area.
- signature

COPYRIGHT 2010 BY: VC IMAGINATION FACTORY
Illustration by: John Moriarty
Creative art director: Vane Carter

WWW.BIO-SAPIEN.COM

5

VC IMAGINATION FACTORY PRESENTS:

BIO-SAPIEN VOLUME I (BOOKS 1-6).

A SCI-FI, SPACE, ACTION, ADVENTURE & ROMANCE NOVEL

PROLOGUE

An average teenager Jaden Marino discovers a UFO landing one evening in upstate NY. The government is also looking for the mysterious UFO in the area. The government eventually follows him to it while trying to kill him. He hides inside of the advanced nanotechnology UFO while the government tries to take it away to Area 51 on a trailer. His mind goes into a comatose state and he has an out-of-the-body experience. The spaceship translates his English language from his mind into its language, enabling him to control the UFO with his mind. As he tries to fly away, the government sends all of their best and top-secret aircraft to intercept this very advanced spacecraft. Jaden quickly learns what this spaceship is capable of and goes against the best pilots in an intense chase over NY. Eventually he leaves Earth and travels 2.1 million light-years into the Andromeda Galaxy. He learns of an advanced alien species called Andromedians, who are 70,000 years ahead of humans. The Andromedians are peaceful explorers and their thinking is very far ahead of our own.

Jaden comes back to Earth eighteen years later and is aware of an alien conspiracy that is about to take place on Earth. He tries to warn people, but everyone thinks he is crazy. They lock him up in a mental ward. Society, relationships, values and technology has changed on Earth. He has a microscopic artificial intelligence alien companion in his mind helping him along the way, called AI. His body begins developing its advanced alien nanotechnology weapons system to work on Earth. After the government and citizens do not listen, he tries to help the people he cares about while the government places him on a terrorist list and uses their full military forces to kill him. He goes against the government's future weapons, Motherdrone (a super computer that controls all UAV drone crafts), super exoskeleton soldiers, SWATbots, thermobaric weapons and himself. At the same time, a bad alien race, called Darclonians, are implementing their silent planned strike on humans. An energy knight is the Darclonians new powerful weapon that can manipulate dark energy. Unbelievable movie style action sequences throughout the book and an ending you won't stop talking about. Jaden Marino's adventure of a lifetime begins.

BIO-SAPIEN SERIES (Formally known as the BIAlien trilogy.)

VOL I PROFESSIONAL BOOK REVIEWS

NOTE: Book reviews are based on all six books to volume I series.

"Science fiction fans unite! If the title doesn't say it all, I don't know what will! To preface this review, all of you naysayers out there who shake their heads at sci-fi should remember that, back in the 70's, the names R2-D2, C3PO, Chewie...you get my point, here...were unknowns. Now they are as much a facet of popular literary culture as is Mr. Darcy. Jane Austen, Henry James, Dickens, etc., were beautiful storytellers, but sci-fi has amazingly imaginative beauty surrounding it as well. And this author, Vlane Carter, knows that for a fact....

...there are A LOT of scenes that the reader gets to experience. From the military battle with the UFO, to the alien shark attack on another planet (which is really cool, by the way), this author offers a never-ending parade of amazing creatures and locations that will, perhaps, one day be logged into popular literary culture right beside old C3PO and his little beeping buddy......There are two factions out there in America - Star Wars vs. Star Trek - and I am definitely on the side of George Lucas having the more creative concept. So hats off to this writer, Vlane Carter, who may someday join those Lucas ranks if readers and sci-fi fans everywhere band together and realize that the force really MAY be with this one." – **FEATHERED QUILL REVIEWS.**

"....the bialien trilogy is not your typical sci-fi novel. Think of a comic book that uses words instead of illustrations and you might come close. One thing that the writer certainly has is imagination. It is written very visually....

.....you may tell by his style that Vlane is very passionate about his writing. It takes time and effort to envision and write a novel of this length without losing the energy throughout it. Bialien is his first novel, and, from his marketing material and website, certainly not his last. It is always interesting to see the first story written and how writing styles evolve from book to book. Let's see where Volume Two takes us." –**TOP BOOK REVIEWERS.**

"A Sci-Fi series set on exploring concepts of the deep future, "The Bialien Trilogy" is for the Science fiction fan who likes to be amazed at what the future holds...." - **MIDWEST BOOK REVIEWS**

-"Vlane Carter first novel is a huge "tome" of a book. There is lots of action and adventure as our main character, Jaden, meets a host of aliens from across the universe, engages in a host of battles as well as doing some "fun" stuff. There is a lot of "things" in this book to cause the reader to pause and ponder. For the adventurous reader who likes long novels make sure you put this close to the top of your Must Read list.—**STEVEN FIVECATS, EDITOR. YELLOW30 SCI-FI REVIEW.**

"…the first thing readers will notice about this book is the author's manner of storytelling. It's different and can take some getting use to. That said, if you adjust your thinking to the author's way of telling the story, you'll find that it works! He achieves his goal of making the story read as if you're seeing it on the big screen, as an action packed movie. Also worth mentioning, is that to complete the entire scope of the story, Vlane has placed visual images throughout, as well as a book sound track, creating an entirely new dimension to the meaning of author/story/reader interaction….

….Outside of the book itself, this author takes great care to interact with his readers and has a website that includes free chapter plus loads of information about the series. Inside the book, he takes just as much care, and it's clear he has put his entire being into each and every word. Real knowledge can make or break a book, and this author definitely knows his technology. ….

....Give this book a chance and you won't be disappointed by the in your face, non-stop action that leaves you on a roller coaster ride that thrusts you up and down, side to side, both thrills and chills, and then rockets you out of this world..."
-New Reads Underground. Rachel M. D'aigle, NRU Head and Author of YA Fantasy Series The Journals of The Jacoby Odyssey

....This book crosses many topics, from government conspiracies, alien technology, nanotechnology, world domination, love, female empowerment and religion... All which take the reader into new realms of thought and possibility, allowing for outside the box thinking and discussion amongst readers.....

....Sci-fi and fiction enthusiasts will have a hard time putting this book down. Vlane Carter succeeds in his unconventional storytelling style, drawing readers into his vast creation, while the plot twists keep you riveted and guessing until the books final page. Or, make that the final word...." **-M. Penny Harmon, Review SIP "ReviewSIP" (Salt Lake City, Utah)**

BIAlien - Rise of the BIAliensapien: Human Evolved book 1,2 & 3 (vol I)

BIO-Sapien books 1,2,3,4,5,6 (Vol I)

TO ALL READERS AND BOOK CRITICS PLEASE NOTE:

BIO-Sapien was written in present tense for the following reasons:

1. So the reader can read and experience the novel as if they were watching a movie.
2. Nanotime.
3. Detailed action sequences.
4. Movie soundtracks inserted into different parts of the story.
5. Telepathic communication and talking to another personality.
6. Mind reading and answering questions inside of a conversation.
7. Have the reader experience the story as if they are right with Jaden at all times.

"….Author, Vlane Carter, has created a story told in a unique and unconventional writing style, keeping the action in the present tense, so as to keep the reader feeling as though they are experiencing the action as its happening. It can be akin to reading a script, or make you feel as though you're watching a movie. It is a writing style that can, at first, be jarring and difficult to understand. But if you give it a few chapters it will not only grow on you, but draw you in. And then you suddenly cannot imagine the story written any other way. And, quite possibly, it could be the first book that includes its own music recommendations (to listen to while reading)….." - **M. Penny Harmon, Review SIP "ReviewSIP"**

Single quotes ' ' are used in the book when:

To show main character Jaden communicating with his alien friend Al (located in his mind).
High-speed telepathic communications.

WHAT HAPPENED IN "BIO-Sapien 1 & 2?"

PLOT/SYNOPSIS

The evil Darclonians (formerly known as Robogods) used to be an all robotic species, but have been using organic bodies for the past 150,000 years in search of the perfect host for their experiment. The robotic droids scanned millions of solar systems to find a planet the right distance from the Sun that could support life. Over 100,000 years ago a droid fired small comets filled with sextillions of Nanomoles towards Earth. Reaching the lower atmosphere, the comets had exploded and dispersed Nanomoles which sought out organic and intelligent life. Undetectable, the parasites have since been sitting in their host's brains learning the biology and recording the human experience from generation to generation. They have been awaiting a signal from a mothership which will activate an 84 hour, three stage countdown.

The good Andromedians (from the Andromeda galaxy) needed a purpose for humans as well. They are peaceful explorers and have been in several battles with Darclonians over the years. Their dilemma is their Biomechanical bodies would be destroyed in their ships when they use Optic-warp to exit the Milky-way's center super massive blackhole in subspace. They have been monitoring a lot of Darclonian activity in this galaxy and needed a way to investigate it. They used one of their older class ships with Artificial intelligence on it to seek out an intelligent human being on Earth, to see if the body can make it to their Galaxy in one piece. This is when Jaden Marino finds the UFO.

On a cold winter evening in 2000, Jaden Marino, discovers a UFO near his home in upstate NY. The government detects it and swarms the area on a full-scale UFO hunt. Unable to find the now invisible UFO, the government follows Jaden to it after listening to him excitedly disclose it to a friend on the telephone.

On the run from the persistent government wanting him for "further questioning," he hides inside of the UFO made of liquid metal nanotechnology. Meanwhile, the government tries to take the craft to Area 51. Inside the ship, Jaden's body goes into a comatose state, and he has an out-of-the-body experience. The spaceship translates his English language and math capabilities from his mind into its alien language, subsequently enabling him to control the UFO with his mind.

Jaden manages to pilot the ship, escaping the government. As he gets used to controlling the ship by pure thought, the government sends all of their best and top-secret aircraft to intercept and destroy the spacecraft. Jaden uses microscopic autonomous alien eyes, called nanoeyes, which allow him to see outside the ship in dozens of directions, as well as smell, taste, and feel. The nanoeyes transform into nanoscanners when they detect a threat. Nanoscanners can scan through any non-shielded aircraft and learn its defenses in seconds.

Jaden quickly learns the capabilities of the UFO and engages the best government pilots in an intense chase over New York. Jaden outruns missiles and can actually see bullets moving past the UFO. The intense chase creates dozens of powerful sonic booms, the impact of which breaks windows and causes citizens' ears to ring. Jaden rescues an SR-71 Blackbird aircraft that flies past its maximum ceiling height. Jaden's quick thinking activates a tractor beam in an attempt to stop the SR-71 Blackbird from crashing into a house.

Jaden races a top-secret Blackbird from New York City to Chicago at Mach 7, just missing an airliner that was about to land. Jaden realizes he is at the maximum speed on Earth and is trying to explore the speed of light engines. He overrides the light engine controls in an attempt to outrun the Blackbird. The engines of the UFO charge to 0.1% the speed of light and Jaden is over North Korea in a split second. Jaden loses control of the ship and it flies on autopilot away from Earth's orbit. The UFO accelerates and takes a quick thirty-minute ride to Jupiter, where it explores the inner layers of this giant planet. Jaden's mind is blown away when he sees Jupiter up close.

The UFO then explores Jupiter's moon Europa and Jaden has his first alien encounter with thousands of species of alien sea life. The glow-in-the-dark animals are intriguing to Jaden at first. Jaden then encounters intelligent, coordinated alien sharks that greet him by biting different parts of the UFO. Being integrated with the UFO,

Jaden's body feels what the ship feels. Eventually the ship tries to leave the moon Europa, but not before being swallowed by a mother shark and taking her to the surface of the moon with the ship.

The UFO sets a course towards the sun. The craft travels through space by using an advanced space traveling method called optic-warp. This system allows the UFO to travel in subspace after being broken into a quadrillion molecules, which allows the ship to pass a light-year every 7-90 seconds.

The UFO eventually sets a course to planet Xenos (Andromedian's home planet), they are captured by a Darclonian colony in the Andromeda Galaxy, 2.1 million light-years from Earth. His body was experimented on and the Darclonians realized there is some value in humans. This sets off a chain of events for Earth and a mothership is dispatched. Jaden and the ship are later rescued by an elite Andromedian biomechanical team lead by BELLONA.

Bellona, Marco and Bomani, who range in age from 50,000-69,000 years old, make their debut appearance. Marco and Bellona show off a few of their superhero skills and advanced weapons as they take on an army of blisters, cubfighters and skelborgs. Bellona fights at super speeds with her anti-hydrogen energy sword while dodging a hail of meteorites hitting the ground around her. Marco also shows his stealth and advanced weaponry skills. These highly skilled, peaceful warriors are shocked when they see a new threat to their galaxy. The dark energy knight makes its first appearance. They hit it with dozens of torpedoes from their ships and then leave to return Jaden to their home planet.

Jaden wakes up discovering he is on another planet called Xenos, and is in a virtual under water city in an artificial body. Bellona informs Jaden of everything that has taken place and Jaden learns about a chain of events that is unfolding for Earth.

While on Xenos, Jaden plays in the Andromedian's futuristic gravity games; flies around the planet without a body by using nanoeyes; observes the planet's gravity tides; wars; joins a space team; races in exoskeleton intergalactic spaceships (EIS) and plays a virtual game of chess with alien pieces.

Bellona befriends Jaden and is his personal escort while he is a guest on Xenos. Bellona unintentionally develops a special interest for Jaden (Bellona used to be a carbon life form in her past life). She tries to understand his Catholic beliefs and explains her people's long history on religion, technology and why he is there.

Even though ten years has passed on Earth, Jaden's human body has only aged a few weeks. He misses his family, friends and girlfriend back on Earth. Jaden's travel to the Andromeda Galaxy sets off a chain of events for Earth. Jaden learns of a Darclonian mother ship leaving from another part of the Milky Way Galaxy and heading towards Earth. There are conflicts in the Andromedian elder council on whether it is too dangerous for Jaden to return to Earth by himself. Jaden later proves himself worthy to one elder.

The Andromedians pack Jaden full of prototype organic nanotechnology called nanodrones. The nanodrones run Jaden's body like crewmembers on the Star Trek Enterprise. The quadrillions of nanodrones modify his brain and DNA for optimum performance.

BIO-Sapien book 3

Book 3 starts off with Jaden returning to Earth in his upgraded EIS, eighteen years later by earth time.

His bio-engineered body is slowly evolving into superhuman levels. His mission is to help scientist locate the Nanomole in humans and then deactivate it, before the Darclonian mothership enters broadcast range. When a Nanomole is activated and is in the correct stage, it can control a human body. It would need to synchronize with a Bio-parasite for a permanent takeover of the human mind (Bio-parasites are Darclonians in microbe form).

BIO-Sapien book 4 – Remote Heroes

(This chapter contains sexual references and romance scenes. If you are under 13 please skip this chapter).

Chapter 16: 3x Terminal Velocity

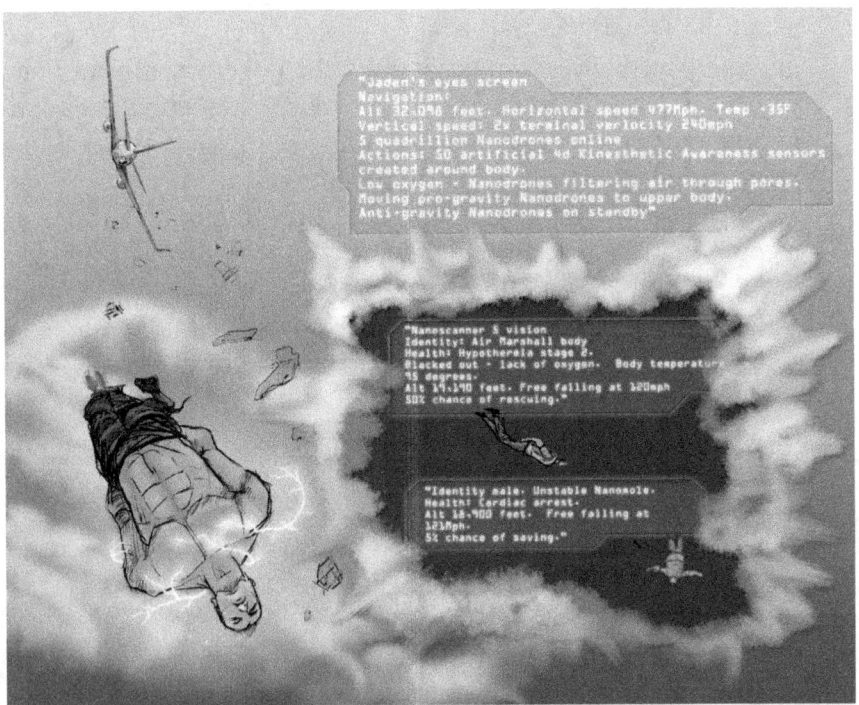

Jaden arrives at the airport. He pulls into the long-term parking area. Security cameras are all around recording license plates and pointing in different directions recording activity. There are people walking around and pulling luggage.

'I need to change my appearance and change my clothes. Use the nanoscanners to check every car in this parking lot for any clothes around my size. Most likely they will be in a suitcase and trunk of a vehicle. Also check to see if there is wireless Internet in the airport,' Jaden says.

'Yes sir.'

Jaden pulls into a parking space on the fourth level. He is facing a brick wall. Jaden turns the car off with the keys. He closes his eyes and switches to the nanoscanner's vision.

'There is free wireless Internet in the terminals. I'll use two of the nanoscanners to continue downloading more of the information we will need. The other four are checking vehicles on each floor. So far I found a suitcase with suits in it around your size,' AI says.

'No, keep looking. I can't walk around in a suit,' he says.

'Yes sir.'

'I need to do something about my facial structure. I'm thinking about the facial recognition scan done to me when I first checked into the psychiatric hospital. I know the government uses that as a way to identify people. Look up more info about that on the Internet and have the nanodrones analyze my face to see what can be modified,' Jaden says in a confident voice.

'I just checked eight websites, the government does facial recognition scans at all transportation sites throughout the country to catch criminals and fugitives,' AI says.

A security guard walks up behind the car. He stops for a second then walks towards the driver side of the vehicle where Jaden is sitting with his eyes closed.

"Excuse me sir, is everything okay here," the guard asks while looking at broken glass still stuck in the frame of the window seal.

Jaden opens his eyes startled and looks at the guard. He quickly thinks of something to say, while he sees the guard's eyes on the broken glass all over the place inside the car.

"Everything is fine, sir. I was out partying last night at a club, and someone broke into my car last night. I didn't have time to get it fixed because I have to pick up my parents at the airport this morning," Jaden says.

"Sorry to hear that sir. What did they steal from your car?" The young man asks.

Jaden continues to look the guard in the eyes, as he thinks of something to say.

"They stole my Walkman and some music cassette tapes," Jaden says.

"Don't you mean Blu-ray music disc or holographic disc? What is a Walkman?" The guard asks.

AI quickly pulls off the Internet gadgets young people use in 2018 and displays it on Jaden's eye screen.

"I'm sorry sir, I meant an I-PCphone second generation was stolen and a holographic disc with over 150 movies on it," Jaden says.

"Oh okay. I came over to you because you are parked in a non-electric car zone. On the other side of the roof is a free electric car plug," he says.

"Thank you sir," Jaden says while starting the car.

"I have some plastic to put over the window if you need it."

"No, I'm okay. Thanks anyway. I won't be long here, goodbye," Jaden says.

He backs up and drives forward.

'Thanks for the help, AI. That was close. I didn't know all these cool gadgets are out. Three hundred high definition movies on one holographic disc? That's crazy. One mini Blu-ray music disc plays over 15,000 hours of music?' Jaden asks in a surprised tone.

'I found a SUV on the roof that has luggage and clothes around your frame type. Someone just parked their car up there,' AI says.

'Okay.'

Jaden pulls into a parking space with an electric outlet. He sees other cars and SUV's with solar panels on their roofs and hoods. The roaring of airplanes taking off and landing are all around. Jaden can see the security guard is checking with the police department about the car he was driving, downstairs in the office.

Jaden gets out of the car and goes invisible. Glass is falling from his legs and backside. He walks over to the SUV three cars away. The rear of the SUV is by a five-foot concrete wall. He looks over the concrete wall and sees the street. He turns towards the trunk of the SUV. Shield energy goes around his right hand as he destroys the rear lock of the trunk. He lifts the trunk hatch with his other hand. The vehicle alarm goes off. The horn honks and a voice comes from the SUV's loudspeaker, "A theft has broken the back window! Calling owner's cell phone and notifying Offstar!" It continues to repeat itself.

Jaden removes the luggage in the middle and closes the trunk hatch. The nanodrones begin moving around the luggage as well, making it go invisible with his body. Jaden walks towards the stairwell as more security guards run towards the alarm going off. He walks down to the second floor and crosses a walkway into the airport. Jaden avoids walking into people since they don't see him.

'Jaden, I have a way to change your facial and body appearance. It is going to be painful, but I researched on what muscles, glands and tissues in the face can be moved around. The first face transplant was done in 2006, and the second in 2010. There is a lot of info on face lifts and face repairs on the Internet,' AI says.

'Okay, there is a bathroom straight ahead inside the building on the right side coming up. I'm going to walk in there to change, and you can work on my face,' Jaden says as he goes visible again. There are people all around walking in different directions.

He walks inside the airport building and walks towards the bathroom. A man with his kid walks out of the bathroom. Jaden walks inside and goes in a toilet stall. He quickly closes the door with his small luggage.

'Okay, start changing my face,' Jaden says.

Jaden opens the small luggage over the toilet.

'Outer space bags?' Jaden asks, while reading the label of the plastic bags.

The clothes are in vacuumed sealed plastic bags. He opens the compressed plastic bag and looks for the clothes he wanted to wear. Several men are coming into the bathroom and using the urinals. Urinals are flushing and the sink water is running. He puts on his new clothes. A navy blue button up silk shirt and a cream pair of dress pants. He puts on a black blazer and some black dress shoes. Jaden remembered seeing a small CD in the inside compartment from the nanoscanner. He looks inside and sees a holographic disc. Jaden puts it in his pocket along with his belongings from his jeans. He puts his old clothes back in the luggage.

Jaden looks at himself through a nanoscanner in front of him.

'Okay, this guy has some nice clothes and knows how to dress,' Jaden says while he pushes the luggage under the toilet stall and into the next stall.

Jaden begins to groan and moan as one hundred billion nanodrones begin working on different areas inside the skin of his face. The men using the urinals look at the stall Jaden is in. They think he is trying to unload something big.

"Don't push too hard in there!" A man yells while walking out of the bathroom without washing his hands.

The four nanoscanners are in front of Jaden's face recording different angles. Jaden sees on his eye screen: TEMPORARY DISABLING NERVE ENDINGS IN FACE, SAVING FACE DISTANCE STRUCTURE 85%, MODIFYING FAT TISSUE 47%, ANALYZING BONE STRUCTURE 80%, STRETCHING BONE DENSITY IN LEGS AND HIPS.

Jaden's face feels numb as his jawbone and cheekbone crackle. He feels a burning sensation in his nose as the cartilage structure is changing. The nanoscanners go out and look around the bathroom. He sees many more words passing on his eyes: REDUCING

CARTILAGE IN NOSE AND RESTRUCTURING, CHEEK BONE MODIFYING, REDUCING 20% OF MELANIN PIGMENT IN EPIDERMIS AROUND BODY, MODIFYING DNA IN HAIR FOLLICLES AND ACCELERATING HAIR GROWTH 1500%, CHANGING EYES AND EARS STRUCTURE.

Jaden feels his skin around his body tingling. His hair is falling off his head as he leans over the toilet. He feels completely bald as his hair begins to quickly grow again. Jaden notices airport police officers are walking towards the bathroom door. He can hear their radios above the urinals flushing.

'How much longer AI?" He asks.

'Less than a minute, the nanodrones are ninety-five percent finished.'

The officers open the door and start looking around the mid-sized bathroom. They look at the three guys by the urinals and one washing his hands. He notices none of them resemble Jaden.

"Excuse me; we are looking for a fugitive. Has anyone seen this young man? He was last seen coming into this bathroom," the older police officer says.

'Damn, I knew I should have stayed invisible all the way in here,' Jaden says while his face is still bubbling.

The men in the room shake their head and say no. They quickly try to leave the bathroom.

"Hold on a second, before you gentlemen leave," the officer says.

A younger officer starts pushing open the toilet stalls. He pushes open the other two to the right of Jaden. He gets to Jaden's cubical.

"Excuse me sir, are you almost done?" He asks.

"I'll be out in a minute," Jaden replies with an English accent.

"Sir, if you have some ID on you that would be sufficient and you could finish your business," the young officer says.

Jaden ignores him while he flushes the toilet. The older officer opens the other stall to the left of Jaden. He sees the stolen suitcase from the SUV sitting in the open cubical by itself.

"I found the suitcase," the older officer says while pulling it out.

The younger officer bangs on Jaden's door again.

"Some ID, sir," he asks.

Jaden opens his cubical door and looks the officer in the eyes. The officer looks at Jaden's face.

"Good morning officer," Jaden says with an English accent.

"Good day to you sir. I'm sorry to bother you, but we are looking for this fugitive," the officer shows Jaden's picture from the hospital check in.

"No, I haven't seen him. But he is a handsome fella," Jaden says.

"Have you seen someone in the next cubical put this suitcase down and maybe change his clothes?" The younger officer asks.

"Yes, someone sat down there, used the bathroom and left the suitcase on the floor five minutes ago. He didn't even wash his hands that nasty American bastard."

Jaden walks over to wash his hands at the sink.

"You American buggers are still the most overweight country in the world and you wash your hands the least. Do you know how many germs are out here in the world?" Jaden asks.

"No sir."

"I can see little bacteria on your face and hands right now. They are crawling around and moving as we speak. When I was using this john, which might I say was very dirty compared to my city in London, I noticed only two out of six people actually washed their hands. Also what kind of a bathroom doesn't have mirrors…" Jaden is interrupted.

"I'm sorry to hear that sir, but we are trying to find someone. Thank you for your time," the younger officer says.

"Excuse me sir," the older officer asks Jaden.

Jaden stops in his tracks and slowly turns around. He keeps his cool and looks the officer in the eyes. A young kid walks by and bumps into Jaden.

"Watch where you are going, you 90210 wanna be!" The kid yells.

"Yes sir?" Jaden asks in his American accent.

'Oops.'

He responds again with his English accent as the officer stands in front of him, "Yes officer?"

"Why did you have tears in your eyes when you came out of the toilet stall?" The officer asks.

"I was crying a little while ago because I just found out my R.F.E.C. unit was stolen from my house back home. Some bloody bugger took her a few hours ago. She was my best friend, she cooked, cleaned, took care of me in the bed at night; my father got her for me for graduating from Harvard. I also didn't have insurance on her and my father is still making payments on it," Jaden says.

They look at Jaden with a strange look.

"Us British people are emotional people," Jaden adds.

"Okay sir, have a good day," the officer says.

Jaden walks out of the bathroom. His nanoscanners are still in the bathroom monitoring the officers. One radios in the findings of the luggage.

"Man what is going with this generation of young kids, crying over a metal non-human object and even having sex with it. A father buys their son a robot instead of a car? What is this world coming too?" The older officer asks.

"At least he is having sex with something that looks like a female. I thought he was gay or something," the younger officer says.

"Yeah, he looked a little like one of those guys I arrested years ago, who was having sex in a public bathroom with other men," the older officer says.

"I'm glad that doesn't happen anymore. Now they do it at *Adult World* online. So sick."

"That is sick. I could have sworn his hair on his head grew another inch before my eyes."

Jaden walks downstairs. He uses his nanoscanners to look at his face.

'Wow, I'm a handsome white guy with blond hair. Cool. I can't believe my skin color is pale white, I feel like another person. Those officers were right, I do look gay. My face feels so tight,' he says.

'Jaden, why did you spend so much time talking to those officers about irrelevant things?'

'I'm sorry AI; I was practicing my acting skills. I was also trying to annoy the police officers like most European men do when they want to complain about something here. Also in movies, the bad guys always talk more to the officers to throw them off.'

'I understand. What is the plan now?' AI asks.

'I'm going to try and book a plane ticket to North Carolina,' Jaden says while walking by different airline counters. The nanoscanners are looking at different departure screens throughout the airport. The arrival and departure screens are floating over each airline check-in area in 3D.

'I found a departure from Jetgreen Airline going to Raleigh at 9 AM,' AI says.

'That sounds close enough, we have twenty minutes before it takes off,' Jaden says.

He walks up to an automated self check-in. Jaden clicks on the screen.

'I doubt if we will have enough money to pay for this ticket,' AI says.

"Welcome, do you have a ticket, or would you like to purchase your ticket now. Press or say your choice," the female voice computer says.

Jaden clicks on have a ticket. AI is confused as to what Jaden is doing. Jaden types in a last name.

"Please identify yourself, you can insert ID or credit card or other," the computer says.

Jaden presses OTHER on the ten-inch touch screen.

"You can use: fingerprint scan, voice scan verification, facial recognition scan, or eyescan ID. Please select your two other ID verification methods."

He chooses two.

'AI run the saved Ruffo's voice profile.'

Jaden feels his throat stinging and his Adam's apple tingling.

"Please speak into the mini microphone to the right and read the following on the screen."

"I pledge allegiance to the flag of the United States of America, and to the republic for which it stands, one nation under God, indivisible, with liberty and justice for all," Jaden says in Ruffo's voice.

"Thank you, voice confirmed. Please standby for second verification."

'AI, change my eyes…'

'I'm already ahead of you. The nanodrones are modifying the iris, pigment color cells, texture and patterns in your eyes as we speak.'

"Please insert eyes into the above viewer. Thank you."

Jaden inserts his face into the viewer as a green light scans his eyes.

"Sorry match not confirmed. Please try again. Another invalid verification and the authorities will be notified."

'AI what is going on? It isn't working.'

'He was wearing contacts. Try it again, I've adjusted the pigment color and verified the pattern distances. These machines only need seventy percent verification,' AI says.

"Please insert face. Please insert face."

'This better work or the police will be all over me. We only have fifteen minutes before the flight leaves. We still didn't go through the checkpoint,' Jaden says.

Jaden inserts his face into the eye viewer. It quick scans his eyes again. There is a pause.

'Shit, it's not working,' Jaden says while getting nervous as the green light goes out.

A few seconds go by, "Thank you, verification complete. Good morning Dexter Ruffo. Your flight leaves today for Cancun at 4 PM."

Jaden clicks on change flight to Raleigh for 9 AM. He clicks first class.

"First class would be for one-way. Round trip would be an extra $300."

'Why not just fly coach and get a round trip?' AI asks.

'I never flown first class and I remember airlines usually hold the plane for first class people if they just purchased a ticket. I also doubt if I'll be flying back,' Jaden says.

"Do you have any bags? A bag over thirty-five pounds will be an extra fifty dollars. If you weigh over 240 lbs it is an extra seventy-five dollars."

Jaden clicks no for bags. A small platform comes out from under the machine.

"Please step on scale for weight verification."

He steps on the scale.

"Verification complete, congratulations Mr. D. Ruffo you lost 105 lbs."

'I can't believe they charge for overweight people now. Man I lost weight; I'm at 155 lbs now,'

'I removed a lot of unnecessary body fat,' AI says.

The screen shows an extra hundred dollars to change to another airline.

'Shit, I still have to pay. Man, these airlines are rip-offs in the future. I know the price to Cancun coach costs more than a one-way trip to North Carolina first class.'

"How do you want to pay today?" The computer asks.

He sees Paylife at the bottom and clicks on it.

"Is this Paylife device yours or a friend's?"

He clicks on a friend.

"Please note fraudulent activity will be reported to authorities. Unauthorized use of a Paylife device is a federal felony. The owner of the Paylife will be notified within seconds of this purchase. Clicking yes means you agree to these terms."

'I hope she knows it's me and doesn't rat me out,' he says while clicking yes.

The nanoscanners copy the saved magnetic information from Chan's Paylife card to the nanodrones in Jaden's left hand. He feels a tingling sensation in his left hand as his nerves feel the magnetic impulses.

"Please swipe device by the Paylife logo below."

Jaden swipes his left hand.

"Thank you, your friend is being notified by phone and brain text. Have a good day. Your boarding pass is printing out now, please hurry to gate five. Flight 104 leaves in eight minutes."

Jaden grabs the boarding pass and quickly walks to the security gate. He sees his other face on the screen above as a wanted fugitive. There are a lot of police walking around the terminal.

'Take off your shoes,' AI says.

'Why?'

Jaden gets to the gate and goes to the left where only two people are at.

"Please take off your shoes and put anything metal through the scanner on the right," a female security personnel says.

'What is this, Russia or Israel?'

He takes off his shoes and puts them on the x-ray machine belt. He walks through the full body scanner. A male and female behind a computer screen tell him to put his hands up. He puts his hands up and they look at Jaden's naked body through the machine.

They whisper to each other and Jaden overhears.

"He has a good sized penis, but I know he is gay, look at his flat ass," the security lady tells her co-worker and they chuckle.

Jaden sees himself naked from the security people's screen.

'What the hell? They are laughing at me.'

'The machine is releasing a small amount of radiation around us, we can use and convert this radiation,' AI suggests.

"Turn around sir!" The female yells.

Jaden's nanodrones leave his body and quickly spin around his body. They see a swarm of microscopic particles moving around Jaden on the screen. They have a surprised look on their face as the images on the screen become distorted. The radiation is being drained and the machine automatically increases the power. The machine quickly turns off and they signal Jaden to walk through. He walks over to the security officers.

"Everything okay back there?" Jaden asks in Ruffo's voice, while grabbing his shoes and putting them on.

"Yes, there was a malfunction in the system," the lady says.

"You know you two don't look so hot naked either," Jaden looks at the female. "Your clit ring is buried in the valley of seal blubber. You sir, your hemorrhoids looks like an unborn fetus."

They look at Jaden with shocked looks on their faces.

He jogs to gate five. Jaden notices men and women are looking at him smiling. Police dogs and officers are patrolling. There are hundreds of cameras all over the place. Jaden sees through the nanoscanners that the plane is eighty percent full in coach and half-full in first class. The plane is waiting for him. Jaden notices the 737 airplanes have wing tips that point upwards.

He reaches the gate and gives the airline guy the boarding pass at the gate.

"Thank you sir, have a nice flight."

"Thank you," Jaden says.

'AI change my voice back from that sick bionic dick pervert.'

Jaden walks down the tunnel and steps onto the 737. The jetliner has two seats on each side of an aisle.

"Good morning sir," the flight attendant says.

"Good morning to you also," Jaden replies in his normal voice.

He walks to the left in business class and finds his seat. He takes off his blazer and sits over it.

'There are 131 people in coach, eight people in first class, three flight attendants and two pilots on this plane,' AI says.

'Thanks for the info AI. Did you finish downloading the information you need?' Jaden asks while sitting down.

'Yes, I've downloaded another fifty-five terabytes of information. Bringing the total to 155 terabytes of downloads and website information,' AI says.

Jaden feels very comfortable in his leather seat and ten-inch LCD on the headrest in front of him. The flight attendant talks to everyone about airline safety. Jaden tunes it out.

'So tell me all I need to know. Any questions I think about you can answer them while you are talking,' Jaden says while the airplane taxis on the runway.

'The dopamine neuron signals in the frontal lobe of your brain have been changing and being manipulated by unknown forces. I can't detect what or where the energy forces are coming from. The frontal lobe of your brain controls long-term memory, judgment, morals and decisions on future actions. Your judgment was being suppressed and you were having feelings of doing evil or bad things without consequences for your actions. When you were feeling pain, you were getting more angry. There are strange chemical and energy imbalances coming from different areas of your brain. It affects my synthetic brain in calculations and other operations. No, the nanodrones aren't affected by this for some reason. I tried that, I have tried to disable certain nerves sending pain to your brain. The pain signals are still getting to your brain somehow. I have to run more diagnostic checks on different parts of your brain when you are sleeping. I will use some special nanodrones smaller than .002mm to check and analyze all your 150 billion neurons in your brain. This may take a few days. Yes, the average human brain has an average of one hundred billion neurons, but your brain neurons are modified to reproduce like stem cells. The additional neurons are mostly for multi-tasking, enhancing your current neurons and nanotime.

Nanotime is when your brain is speeding up, but everything around you feels as if it is slowing down. A cluster of suprachiasmatic nucleus cells in your brain have been modified and tweaked. Time dilation in different parts of your brain is rerouted when nanotime is activated. Neurons are nerve cells that send chemical signals to and from different parts of the brain. The neurons in the part of your brain that controls the central processing is enhanced with artificial neurons. Nanodrones temporarily bypass chemical signals in the spinal cord and nerves, by sending their own wirelessly. This increases the nerve's transmission speed from 200 mph up to 8000 mph. The muscle fibers accepting the faster transmission signals will suffer a bottleneck, resulting in a delay in how fast you can move. I help with the processing so that your brain doesn't get overloaded or go into shock. The nucleus of the neurons has been reprogrammed to temporarily accept this high speed of transmitting. Everything has to be closely monitored. This requires a lot of energy to create and is only temporary. Some tissues and cells will need to be repaired, because scarring happens. Nanotime is on a timer and can last anywhere between ten to thirty seconds. It's on a timer to protect your brain and nervous system from being overloaded. Your mind wasn't made for this type of high-speed communication. Your body movement speed will need time to adjust with your faster thinking speed. Time meaning maybe days,' AI says.

'That's cool, about the frontal lobe thing. I have been feeling a lot different; the pain has been making me think evil things. When the lady in the car almost ran me off the road hitting me with her car, I wanted to pull her out while it was moving. When I found out what Ruffo did to his family members, I had no respect if he lived or died. Something is changing in me and I feel as if I'm fighting with myself on decisions when I'm angry. I'll try not to get angry until we figure this out. I would hate to lose you my friend,' Jaden says.

'I have never been another species' friend. A friend is a person attached to another by feelings of affection or personal regard.'

'Exactly; what did you do, download the entire dictionary?' Jaden asks.

'Yes.'

'If something happened to you, who is going to tell the nanodrones what to do and give me superhero powers?'

'In theory, you should be able to do everything I do for you. What your mind is fully capable of is still unknown. Your organic brain is capable of things mostly computers are geared towards,' AI says.

The plane quickly accelerates to take off. Jaden can see the plane taking off from outside the plane at different angles. Jaden sees the aircraft's speed and altitude on his eye screen.

'This is an awesome view. The engines are so loud outside and a perfect take off at 205 mph and 158 feet. This is a realistic view. I can even see inside the jet engines. How fast can these nanoscanners made for a human body go?' He asks.

'Speeds vary, they move faster in the sun and slower at night. Now they are riding in the wake of the plane. The nanoscanners for our Gravhawk can move fifteen percent faster than the speed of light in space. The nanoscanners working with your body are still in the experimental stage.'

The plane turns a few times and then sets its bearings south. It continues to climb in altitude.

'Looks as if we were the last plane to take off,' AI says.

'What do you mean?' He asks before changing nanoscanner.

The first nanoscanners are floating midair not moving. The second pair is in the airport terminal reviewing the flight boards. Jaden sees inside the airport that all the flights are cancelled due to an ongoing police investigation. Police locked down the entire airport and is DNA scanning everyone. Jaden is happy he lucked out and had excellent timing.

'How am I able to see inside the airport?' Jaden asks. 'We are over thirty miles from the airport and at 9081 feet.'

'I've connected two together. The first nanoscanners in the airport are sending their information to the nanoscanner midway. Then the first one slingshots back into the other, giving it enough momentum to reach the aircraft,' AI says.

'Cool. Very cool. The Internet has helped us out a lot I see. Anything new with the nanodrones?'

'Yes, reversing the polarity of the pro-gravity nanodrones in your feet will create a strong magnetic field. They attract the Earth's natural magnetic energy that is all around us. Meaning you can walk on something metal easier in any direction, and it won't use your bodies pro-gravity energy or anti-gravity energy. They will then be called magnetic nanodrones,' AI says.

'That sounds good. For some reason I keep thinking about Chan. I have feelings towards her already. This is weird, I keep thinking about everything I learned about her in such a short period of time. I feel as if I've known her for quite some years. I keep thinking about her likes, dislikes, where she likes to be kissed and about her personality traits. I know all the activities she likes to do and I care for her already. It feels strange and confusing. Do you think she feels the same way?' Jaden asks.

'I'm still learning about human emotional feelings and relationship bonding. She learned the same things about you when you two were connected to each other by your minds. Her logic might override her emotions. Her logic can also override all the info she learned about you traveling to another galaxy and coming back here to help save Earth. I guess time will tell.'

'I hope she feels the same way. I think she does so far, since she didn't report the Paylife stolen. Did you find anything out about my parents and friends?' He asks.

Jaden sits by the window and stares out it. The sunlight energizes his body. His leg is near the electrical outlet on the floor slowly draining electricity from it.

'There is a good chance your father is living in or around Halifax, North Carolina. I searched many records and they point to down there. I believe your mother lives in London with her family. Your parents were divorced since 2002 records show. Your father had prostate cancer, but it was treated. I don't know if it is best to contact your parents, especially with the government probably having phone lines tapped,' AI says.

'Yeah I know. Can you tell me something about my friends?' He asks.

'Your friend James lived or lives in New Jersey. According to his Myfacebook page, he has hit the lottery twice. He opened his own studio and started producing music for people recently. He was married and has kids.'

'Next time you get on the Internet leave him a message on his page, saying I'm back,' he says.

'Okay.'

"Sir would you like something to eat or drink?" The young Hispanic flight attendant asks.

A menu shows up on the screen in front of Jaden. He has a choice of breakfast, lunch or dinner.

'Jaden you need something high in protein, your body needs natural nutrients. Choose the dinner,' AI says.

"Yes, I will. I'll take the roasted half chicken meal and some white wine," Jaden says while smiling at the flight attendant.

"Yes, sir. I'll bring your white wine out now. The food will take a few minutes. I'm Terry, if you need anything just turn your light on above," Terry says.

Jaden smiles at her while she walks away.

'My logic still doesn't understand what you are getting out of looking through women's clothes with a nanoscanner. These women's bodies all look the same to me, similar to looking at an animal's body or a human male's body,' AI says.

Jaden's wine arrives and she places it next to him.

'It is a sexual thing with men; we want to know what is underneath the clothes. For example, look at this good looking, mixed Asian and white flight attendant named Pam serving drinks to fliers in coach with a skirt to her knees. She has a hairless body with very smooth looking skin. She even has a thong on under her skirt. I can smell everything around her body. That is a turn on. Now look at this other blonde hair, firm hips, white flight attendant named Kate. Her hips are perfect for conceiving a child. Her silicone breast implants are perfectly implanted, no scars. Between her legs, long and silky, I travel north. She moves quickly serving drinks on the food cart and the nanoscanner stays between her legs like a basketball being dribbled in someone's hand. They slowly travel up her legs to see what pretty image lies at the top of the one-eyed vertical basketball hoop. What do we have here? Are these, are these, are these little mountains? What the hell?'

'She has some kind of sores. The medical encyclopedia downloaded in my memory banks indicates the flight attendant as having herpes. There is a vaccine for it, but no cure for people who have it already,' AI says.

'Yuck, that was nasty. The image is stuck in my mind. I feel like throwing up,' Jaden says while switching back to his eyes.

"Here is your food sir," Terry says while she places the tray over his lap.

"Um.. thank you," he replies.

'AI I keep seeing this lady's sore mountain bumps. Can you do something about those disturbing images?' Jaden asks.

'Sorry, friend. You're going to have to live with those images for now. I've learned the saying is, you are getting what you deserve,' AI says.

'You are learning too much human culture, Mr. AI. Come on, I want to eat my food. These images are too enhanced,' Jaden pleads.

'Pervert: a person who practices in sexual perversion or man who looks at naked women without permission, correct?' AI asks.

'Yes, but that is only for guys looking at women in dressing rooms or peaking through a female's house window. This is like looking at a nice looking lady in a porno magazine or movie. I'm observing the art of a beautiful woman's body,' Jaden says.

'AI?'

'AI?'

'Friends try to help friends with a problem, correct?' AI asks.

'I don't need your help and I don't have a problem. I'll block the images out myself,' Jaden says while cutting up his meat and chewing it. He shoves some vegetables and wine down his throat.

'See, I don't need your, I don't need your…'

He sees herpes sores on his chicken and vegetables. Jaden puts his hand over his mouth and puts the tray on the empty seat next to him. He quickly walks to the small lavatory and closes the door. He begins to throw up into the toilet.

'You see AI, now I'm losing proteins and nutrition.'

'I already drained the proteins and nutrients out of the food when it went down and back up.'

'Okay, AI you win,' he says while clearing his throat and spitting.

'It is bad enough women are looked at like sex objects and are still fighting for equal pay with men. Women are exploited enough and deserve respect from their male counterparts. They cherish their naked bodies…'

'Okay, enough with the speech. I get the point, you sound like a lesbian equal rights protester giving a speech on a college campus.'

WASHINGTON, D.C. VICE PRESIDENT'S OFFICE 9:41 AM

Vice President Robinson is looking at a computer screen talking with special FBI agent Andrew Mcright in charge of apprehending Jaden. The agent is at the airport using a BlueberryPC phone with a camera in it. He also sees Robinson's face. Agent Mcright is a white male in his late 50's with a full head of salt and pepper hair. He is of medium build and has been with the FBI for the past fifteen years.

"I know a lot doesn't make sense and you think he is still hiding in the airport somewhere. Listen Mr. Mcright, this young man is not human. He got away in a UFO and now he is mysteriously back on Earth eighteen years later. He has found a way to escape our security several times. I believe he has taken someone else's body as an identity. I believe he is part of some conspiracy to kill many Americans. This thing is not considered human and needs to be destroyed," Robinson says on an image phone.

"Sir, doesn't he need to be interrogated and questioned if he is apprehended?" Mcright asks.

"Interrogated? Interrogation is for humans, citizens and non-alien personnel. This alien, Bialien, bisexual alien or alien experiment can be here to kill us all. He is a threat to this country and planet. Didn't you learn anything from *War of the Worlds, Independence Day*, and *V*?"

"Sir, I'm not comparing movies to real life. This could be a serious situation we have here with these unknown energy waves coming from deep space, affecting millions of people at night. He could be here to help us. We could probably learn from whatever advanced technology he possesses. He can manipulate his DNA for starters and disappear. A member on your team said he could be here to help us, and possibly protect us from a pending unknown attack," Mcright says.

"Who told you that?" Robinson asks.

"I'm not at liberty to say. The point is we need to get to the bottom of what is going on and so far he looks as if he is trying to help us in some way. I think arresting him and interrogating him is the best option. I read the anonymous blog left from the computer at the state psychiatric hospital. Those coordinates were precise and only top government officials knew. I also read the encoded information from the unknown space source. Microscopic nanomoles in our brains that could take over our minds. The things to do to block the signals of the nanomoles. A possible pending attack."

Robinson shakes his head in disagreement. His face gets red as he gets upset.

"Listen agent, we didn't find any nanomoles in anyone's brain yet. We have our top scientists looking for this protein in people's brains. So far this could be a hoax."

"Have you begun creating the special helmets or materials to block these signals on a massive level?" The agent asks.

"We produced a few hundred signal blocking helmets and some materials to put in a helmet for our military personnel only," Robinson says.

"Only a couple hundred? Military scientists already proved that the newly created helmets bring people out of a comatose state at night. The material being used over the head stopped future involuntary episodes in people."

"At night, only one percent of the population is affected. In the morning, they are fine. Mostly people at high altitudes are being affected," Robinson says.

"Sir, it could get worst. It could start happening in the daytime and it could start to affect more people. You grounded all flights at night and so did other countries for this reason. Sir, something big could be about to happen. We need to take this seriously. The other day there was hundreds of thousands of car accidents around the world when everyone passed out for thirty seconds. It wasn't a fluke, something like that has never happened before."

"Listen agent, don't worry about other problems or bigger problems. You need to worry about catching this little half alien boy running around killing people," Robinson says.

"He *allegedly* killed the security guard, we are still investigating that."

"If you can't do the job, then I will personally. This kid is a terrorist and he must be killed," Robinson says.

"How do you consider him a terrorist?"

"He downloaded over one hundred terabytes of information on how to build nuclear bombs, advanced energy manipulations, everything about our planet, security profiles, rocket science, our computer systems and everything we know about space. He downloaded entire encyclopedias, medical information and looked up thousands of people. He is a threat and part of this conspiracy taking place," Robinson says.

"That is what we need to find out. We need to keep an open mind. He could have downloaded all that information for himself or the aliens may be trying to help us. Sir, have you notified other countries and is the President aware of this latest information?" The agent asks.

"This is top-secret United States info only. No, she isn't aware of this latest info, she is busy in New York at the World Trade Center II grand opening event. I will let her know when I feel she should know. We don't need weak decision making now. I'm done with your questions Agent Mcright; find the suspect and kill the son of a bitch, or I'll find someone else who will. Goodbye," Robinson says.

Robinson hangs up the video phone on his desk. The phone rings again and it shows Peters' face on the screen. He answers it.

"Do you have some good news for me General Peters?"

"Yes sir. The CIA concluded their instant investigation. It turns out Jaden Marino stole an older woman's car by breaking the window while she was driving, one mile from the hospital. They assumed he was running at the speed the car was moving. Then he drove to the airport parking lot, where a security guard noticed he was driving a car with a broken window and was parked in the wrong place. He moved the car and parked on the roof. Then he stole a suitcase from a SUV. He disappeared from security cameras and was shown walking into the bathroom in the airport. He wasn't

36

seen coming out of the bathroom. But this person here on video could be him. This unknown man was not seen going into the bathroom. His face doesn't show up in any databases."

Robinson sees that the guy is a white male with a different looking face.

"He is a totally different person, with blond hair, taller and different nose. How can it be the same person?" Robinson asks.

"The guy used the automated self check to use the dead officer's bio identifications to exchange a plane ticket."

"Bio identifications? Which ones?" Robinson asks excitedly.

"He used the eye and voice identifications."

"Unbelievable; I told the FAA there should be four required bio identifications needed instead of two," Robinson says.

"Sir, no one has ever been able to beat the bio identifications at airports. Maybe one, but never two. However, he then used Dr. K. Chan's Paylife device."

"Who is Dr. Chan and how is it possible he used her Paylife device? Was she there too?"

"Dr. Chan was the suspect's doctor at the hospital. She was investigating the then John Doe's unusual DNA and amnesia. She was sent home yesterday evening to Virginia for alleged sexual contact with a patient. She also used her same Paylife device in Virginia thirty minutes before it was used in New York."

"Holy Mars shit, this just gets better and better. This guy is seducing women, probably to make alien babies. She is probably working with him," Robinson says.

"There is more, sir. It turns out Jaden Marino's ex-girlfriend Amy Patterson came to visit him yesterday. She claims her 17 ½-year-old daughter Sabrina Patterson is his."

"Holy space monkey shit," Robinson says while laughing.

"We are monitoring Dr. Chan. The CIA is going to bring her in for questioning," Peters says.

"No, don't do anything yet. Just monitor her for now. Did Chan report her Paylife card as stolen or any unauthorized use?" Robinson asks.

"No, she didn't."

"Great, an accomplice, aiding and abetting, excellent," Robinson says while smiling.

"What about the ex-girlfriend, um, Amy?" Robinson asks.

"We can't locate her yet, but we believe she is driving back home to North Carolina. We will try to locate her by satellite once the skies clear," Peters says while showing an image of the new Jaden on the screen.

"We believe this gentleman is Jaden Marino and he is on flight 104 heading to Raleigh, North Carolina now. We have an army of agents, SWATbots, and twenty-third generation exoskeleton suited soldiers on their way to the airport. The plane is over south New Jersey now and is fifty-five minutes away from landing. We notified an armed air marshal onboard the flight to watch the suspect. The pilots are also aware of the situation," Peters says.

"Good work General Peters. Keep me updated. I also want live feed to the surveillance and SWATbots' cameras at the airport in North Carolina."

"Yes sir."

FLIGHT 104 JETGREEN AIRLINES
SOUTH NJ 33,012 FEET 579 MPH 9:49 AM

Jaden just finished eating two dinners, a few milks and two wines. The flight attendant removes the trays of food.

"Would you like anything else, sir?"

"No, I'm okay. Thanks. I'm going to take a nap for now," Jaden says while moving towards the window seat.

'I researched what you were talking about earlier, about thinking outside the box and getting me away from normal logical thinking,' AI says.

'Yeah,' Jaden says while closing his eyes and relaxing.

'Well, my intelligence level and synthetic crystal nanobot molecules are very obsolete according to other artificial intelligence nanobots on Xenos. I'm the oldest generation that is why I was able to come to Earth. My materials are different than biomechanical bodies and other AI nanobots Andromedians used for the past thousand years. I believe I was part of the experiment also. If I were ever captured by the enemy, my technology wouldn't be close to the standard AI nanobot. Maybe this is why my thinking is so logical and linear.'

'Your point is?' Jaden says while yawning.

'I'm going to program myself to evolve and think more randomly. I'm going to also try to be open-minded and create an artificial imagination vortex. This is going to require your help and it might take a little time. Out of thousands of intelligent species I've encountered, yours is the most interesting and unique, in regards to imagination, random thinking, open mindedness and the way your brain sees things. Violent, primitive, barbaric, and very religious is something I've seen on many other planets,' AI says.

'Thanks for the compliment. I'm here to help you buddy,' Jaden says.

'Did you know gay marriages are legal in twenty-five states and civil unions are legal in fifteen. Why do same sex humans choose to be together in a relationship? They can't reproduce, isn't that the main purpose of being human?' AI asks.

'I have no idea. Things have changed a lot since I've been on Earth last. I think some men and women are born into liking the same sex. I think the environment they grow up in sometimes affects their decision to like the same sex. There are many animals born liking the same sex. Organic creatures evolve differently. I don't have anything against gay people, I think people should have the right to choose what they want,' Jaden says.

'Homosexual marriages have a higher success rate over heterosexual marriages,' AI says.

'Good for them. This doesn't really interest me since I'm not trying to be homosexual any time soon. Tell me about something useful,' he says.

'There is a man in coach behind us in the front row and he keeps staring in our direction. He could be a terrorist or a possible hijacker. He has a gun on him, 9mm Glock with a fingerprint safety. Fingerprint safeties are the safety measure on all government issued guns. The gun can only be fired with the person's fingerprint registered with the gun.'

Jaden looks with a nanoscanner and sees the fully loaded gun and stun gun in his waistband. He controls the nanoscanner to go into the suspicious person's mind. The randomly moving electronic signals just show images of Jaden's face there. He then checks his wallet for ID. The Hispanic man in his mid-40's with brown hair and a full beard continues to stare at Jaden. He is wearing blue jeans and a white and blue three-button shirt with a soft collar.

'Federal Air Marshal 4091, Fredrick Lopez,' Jaden says while looking to get the flight attendant's attention walking by.

"What are air marshals and what are they doing on airplanes?"

"Air marshals are undercover federal agents that began riding on airlines after the September 11th terrorist attacks. One agent usually rides on random flights undercover. Why do you ask sir?"

"The air marshal behind me, in the middle aisle, is making me nervous. I didn't know people were allowed to have guns onboard an airplane," Jaden says.

"How do you know he is an air marshal? He looks like a regular passenger to me."

"I can tell, I have x-ray vision," Jaden snaps as the wine hits his bloodstream.

"Oh okay, well will there be anything else sir?"

"Yes, why do women have these small devices near the base of their spines? A very small white devices about a fraction of an inch."

"I don't know what you are talking about, sir."

"Come on, good looking. You have one in your lower back also," Jaden says.

She stares at him with a confused look.

"Excuse me, sir," she says while walking away.

'Why did you tell her all of that?' AI asks.

"Dr. Chan had one of those things in her lower back; I wanted to know what it was. I'm always a jerk when I drink," Jaden says aloud while another first class passenger turns around to look at him.

'Jaden, you said that aloud. I'm going to remove some of the alcohol from your bloodstream. It seems that since you don't have a working stomach more alcohol is going into your bloodstream. Okay, you will get sober in a few minutes.'

'Thanks AI; you are the coolest artificial intelligence supercomputer friend I know.'

'Feeling better?'

'Yes, I do. Thanks.'

'There is a guy in the back of the plane acting strange. He is talking to himself very loudly,' AI says.

Jaden uses his nanoscanner eye to get a closer view to what AI is talking about. A muscular white man in his thirties is yelling aloud to the flight attendant. The man stands at 6'2" and 280 lbs.

"They are in my head. They are coming. Arrggghhhhhh!" The distressed passenger yells.

40

"Sir, if you don't calm down, you will be arrested when we land," Pam says nicely while all the other passengers turn to see all the commotion.

The undercover federal air marshal stands up and looks towards the back at the commotion.

'I think something is happening here. Thirty percent of the passengers are sleeping, but their eyes are opening and closing. Their nanomoles are online and are open. I think the high altitude is giving their nanomoles a better signal. The Darclonian's ship is getting much closer,' AI says.

'Maybe, thirty percent isn't that bad, they will wake up when the plane lands,' Jaden says.

'That may or may not happen. It could get worst,' AI says.

Jaden switches back to his eyes and closes his eyes to take a nap.

'That man panicking in the back could set off other passengers to panic. We should do something,' AI suggests.

'Let the air marshal dude handle it. That is his job and the taxpayers' money at work,' he says while dozing off.

'Jaden stay awake, something could be affecting you also,' AI says.

The disturbed man screams again and the federal agent gets out of his seat and walks down the aisle. Everyone on the plane is looking back towards the commotion. The passengers that are half-asleep stay in their current position without budging towards the commotion. They are in a deep sleep. The second flight attendant, Kate, stands by the middle of the airplane where the food trays rest, talking to the pilots by microphone.

"You are not taking my brain. I'll die first!" He yells while getting out of his seat.

"Sir, please sit back down in your seat," Pam says

"I want off this plane! Let me off this plane!" He yells at the top of his lungs, while shoving the flight attendant out of his way.

Jaden can hear the crazy man from where he is.

'Now he should be in a psychiatric hospital in a straitjacket,' Jaden says while chuckling aloud.

The seat belt light turns on. The agent approaches the hysterical man screaming and holding his head. The screaming man walks towards the rear emergency exit.

"Sir, I'm a federal agent. Please come with me and step away from the emergency door," Agent Lopez says while pulling out handcuffs.

'Jaden this hysterical man's nanomole is unstable. If you can touch his head, we can deactivate it.'

'Did you do something to keep me awake AI?' He asks.

'Yes, the nanodrones created artificial caffeine in your bloodstream,' AI says.

'Okay. I'm feeling awake now. This is a job for Bialien man!' He yells while he takes off his seat belt.

"Sir, the seat belt light is on, you can't move from your seat," Terry says.

"Yeah, yeah, I'm here to help in the back," Jaden says to her while walking down the aisle.

'I have a bad feeling about this,' Jaden says.

The out of control man puts his hands on the rear emergency door handle. Pam puts her hands up to her mouth and begins to cry behind the air marshal as she gets scared.

"Sir, get your hand off that handle. You don't want to open that at this altitude," the calm agent says about six feet from him.

"Don't get any closer to me, I'll jump! Stay back! I want off this plane!" He yells and begins to cry, "You aliens aren't taking my brain. I feel you inside of me trying to take over!"

Jaden reaches the middle of the aircraft where the second flight attendant is.

"Sir, you can't leave your seat. You can't go back there," Kate says while standing in front of Jaden pushing him to go back.

"Please don't touch me, Miss Herpes," Jaden says.

"Excuse me?"

"What you have between your legs, has cleansed my perverted ways! I've seen the bumpy light!" He yells with a preacher's voice.

"I beg your pardon!" She yells.

"You are having a herpes outbreak. Get out of my way, you walking infection. Miss Nice and Smooth on the Outside, Bumpy and Contagious Underneath."

"How did you know that?" She asks with a shocked look on her face, "It wasn't my fault; I caught it from a used R.M.E.C. unit I bought from Zbay."

"Shame on you, for buying a robotic man online. It should have used a condom. Looks like you got your money's worth from Zbay, freak," he says while pushing her to the side.

Jaden wipes his hands on the cushion headrests as he quickly walks down the aisles.

The co-pilot begins running from the cockpit through business class.

"Don't come any closer!" The crazy man yells while he begins to put pressure on the handle of the emergency door.

The man's nanomole is making him stronger for some reason. The man fights the pressure of the aircraft and slowly turns the handle.

"Must get off!"

The agent pulls out his gun and aims it at the man.

"Don't turn that anymore, I will shoot you right here!" Agent Lopez yells, while pulling out another device from his waist with his left hand.

Jaden walks faster and everything slows down as he is eighteen feet away from the door.

The man keeps turning the handle. Suddenly the agent fires a Taser gun with his left hand and it hits the man in the chest, electrocuting him. The long wire is stuck in his chest. The man begins to holler and scream. The agent puts away his gun, drops the Taser and rushes towards the man grabbing his arms. Jaden continues to walk towards them. The emergency exit door pulls inwards and then outwards to the right. There is a loud rush of air. Both men fall out the door screaming. Emergency oxygen masks open over the passenger's seats. Jaden's brain speeds up and goes into nanotime instantly. Loud rushing air sounds rush through the entire aircraft and sucks air towards the door. His ears begin to pop and nanodrones seal his ears as everything goes silent around him. He can hear his heartbeat slowly thumping every five seconds. The loud sounds of the jet engines flood the cabin area.

'I can do this, I can do this, I'm increasing my courage, reducing my fear. I have no fear, I have no fear. Save a human life, you know what you have to do Jaden Marino. I have the confidence and the courage to rescue these people. I am unstoppable,' Jaden says while everything is moving in slow motion. His adrenaline rushes around his bloodstream. Nanotime goes off and everything around speeds up to normal time.

Two nanoscanners quickly follow the two screaming and falling bodies. Jaden quickly moves towards the open door. The plane begins to dive out of control. Jaden loses his balance and falls towards the left. Jaden sees the co-pilot approaching behind him. Very cold air speeds through the airplane as air is being sucked out. Passengers are screaming putting on their oxygen masks. The passengers in a comatose sleep state still sit there unmoved by what is going on around them. The awake passengers put oxygen masks on the sleeping passengers next to them.

Pam inches towards the door holding on to passenger seats with a tight grip. Jaden stands back up and continues towards the open door. The co-pilot grabs Jaden's shoulder to pull him back. But Jaden shoves the co-pilot and the he falls backwards. Pam holds on to a handle with her right hand and reaches out into the freezing cold to close the door with her left hand. The captain steers the airplane to the right in an attempt to lose altitude. Everyone leans and falls to the right of the airplane, as the plane tilts seventy degrees. Pro-gravity nanodrones go online in Jaden's feet and penetrate his shoes. ENHANCING PROPRIOCEPTION is displaying on Jaden's eye screen. Gravity disrupting nanodrones quickly move around his body, enabling him to stand up straight. Pam is holding on to the handle with both hands, as her body dangles in midair, horizontal to the floor. Debris continues to fall out of the door.

The Superman theme begins to play in Jaden's mind. He runs upwards as if he is running up a wall. The G-forces are fighting with the nanodrones quickly passing around his body. He runs towards the door as paper trays, plastic forks and soda cans hit his back. He gets to the edge and leaps upwards as if he is jumping off a diving board. Jaden quickly departs from the airplane as he feels the roar of the jet engines to his right. The freezing winds hit all around his body. The nanodrones stop moving around his body and they go into his back. The instant cold shocks his body, as nanodrones override some of his natural initial body responses. Goose bumps quickly form all around his body.

The sun shines brightly on his body. His body stops ascending upwards and Earth's gravity pulls his body down. The low oxygen makes his clothes shutter minimally as he falls headfirst. The 737 airplane can be seen still banking behind him. His blonde hair waves in the wind and he has a serious look on his red face. His eye screen shows -35°F degrees, 32,098 feet, 477 mph horizontal speed, and 100 mph vertical speed. His lungs feel as if they are freezing and not getting enough air. He stops breathing and holds his breath. Nanodrones in his skin are quickly moving around creating internal heat and filtering oxygen into his pores. His eyes display CREATING 50 ARTIFICIAL 4D KINESTHETIC AWARENESS SENSORS AROUND BODY. Jaden doesn't really care what that means.

The airplane levels out and the co-pilot helps the flight attendant to close the door. The door slams shut and air pressure slowly returns. The flight attendant collapses on the floor and lays unconscious.

Jaden knows what he has to do. The nanodrones are reacting on their own around Jaden's thoughts. AI is doing calculations while paper napkins and left over airplane food passes by Jaden. He can see the clouds far below him. He changes his arms from being spread out to placing them to his side. He places his legs together and increases speed. Everything is quiet around him as he concentrates on the direction of the two men. He reaches two times terminal velocity at 29,091 feet. The nanoscanners show that both men are passed out due to a lack of oxygen and are slowly rotating about two miles below him. The crazed man is unconscious at 18,098 feet. The frozen Taser wires still stuck in his chest dangle upwards towards the Taser being pulled down by his heavy body. The air marshal at 19,190 feet has blacked out from the low oxygen and his extremities are freezing. His lifeless body continues to fall with his legs and arms spread out.

'The air marshal's body is going into hypothermia stage 2 according to the medical encyclopedia. My calculations are telling me you have to increase your vertical speed down in order to reach them before they hit the ground,' AI says.

The air marshal's body reaches 16,091 feet and begins to slow down due to the increased oxygen.

'How am I going to do that? What is the condition of the fat mental patient?' Jaden asks while his body continues to free fall. His hair has frosted and is motionless.

'He is in pretty bad shape, the Taser made him unconscious as soon as he fell out of the plane. He too is suffering from a lack of oxygen, the freezing cold and he is going into cardiac arrest. I'm going to figure out what we can do to increase your speed,' AI says.

'What are my odds of rescuing them?'

'You barely have enough energy to rescue yourself now. Nanotime drained a lot of energy and running up the plane drained quite a bit of your gravity energy. Nanodrones are using energy as you can see from your eye screen. Five percent chance of rescuing them both. Fifty percent chance of reaching the federal agent before he hits the ground. Thirty percent chance of safely rescuing both of you before hitting the ground at over 120 miles an hour,' AI says.

Jaden takes over as if he is the captain of a *Star Trek* ship.

'I have an idea. Stop the nanodrones from heating my body and stop them from injecting oxygen into my pores. Just do it, charge more anti-gravity nanodrones in my back. I'm going to take off my shirt off so you can use direct sunlight energy on my back. I'm also going to hold my breath until we get to breathing altitude. Move the pro-gravity nanodrones in my feet to my head and upper body,' Jaden says while taking off his shirt and wrapping it around his right leg. His hands and body are freezing. The skin around his body is dark red, while its temperature drops three degrees. The skin on his back changes from red to a glowing yellow as nanodrones absorb sunlight like a solar panel.

'Okay, there won't be enough from your feet, but I can quickly program other nanodrones to do the same job. I'm trying to keep your pain level down, so it doesn't mess up my calculations and system's functionality,' AI says.

Jaden continues with his head in a downward position while increasing speed. He is directly over the agent. The pro-gravity nanodrones in his upper body and head are increasing his G-forces downwards. Jaden can feel himself being pulled down faster. His head and body feel the friction against the air, making him feel warmer. His eye screen shows +3X TERMINAL VELOCITY as he reaches 18,091 feet. He is less than a mile and a half from the federal agent.

Suddenly Jaden feels his body slowing down. The oxygen is increasing around him. More anti-gravity nanodrones go into Jaden's upper body to combat the slowing down.

'What is the condition of the crazed man?' Jaden asks.

'He's dead, he died a few minutes ago. His body is falling through the clouds now at 125 mph.'

'Shit, I hope he doesn't land on someone.'

'The federal agent is beginning to breathe, but he is still unconscious and is in hypothermia stage 2.'

'Hey AI, I'm breaking wind,' Jaden says.

Jaden continues to torpedo towards the Earth at 361 mph. He can see the air moving out of his way through the nanoscanners. He is less than half a mile from the air marshal. The agent looks like a dot from his eyes, which is getting bigger and bigger. Jaden passes through some broken up clouds. He can see the ocean and land. Jaden estimates being somewhere around Washington or Virginia.

The federal agent's lifeless body is around is around 7000 feet. The agent's clothes are flapping like a flag in the strong wind. Jaden is at about 9000 feet and quickly closing in. The heat slowly begins to cook Jaden's head and hair. His hair begins to fall out. A small energy shield goes around his head. Jaden is determined to reach the agent as he gets closer and closer. The ground is getting closer and closer. Jaden reaches 3189 feet and the agent is at 2709.

'You are cutting it close, we might just have to save ourselves. You are coming in too fast,' AI says.

'Don't worry, I almost got him,' Jaden says while he slowly stretches his arms out.

Jaden quickly comes up behind the federal agent facing downwards. He spreads out his legs and arms to quickly slow himself down. The pro-gravity nanodrones in his upper body go offline. Jaden slows down considerably as if he just opened a parachute. He grabs the agent's cold body from behind and the agent suddenly wakes up. They begin to spiral together out of control in circles. The agent begins to scream as he looks down at the ground and doesn't know who is grabbing him. Agent Lopez tries to push Jaden away from him as they reach 1391 feet.

"Calm down! I'm trying save us!" Jaden yells in his ears as he counters the centrifugal forces.

"How are you going to do that? We don't have any parachutes," the agent yells while staring at the quickly approaching ground.

'Can we make towards the ocean?' Jaden asks AI.

The nanodrones come out of his back and quickly spin around both men, creating glowing particles. They reach 969 feet at 115 mph.

'We are five miles from the coastline. We can't glide there at this low altitude. Your weight and the agent's weight are 325 lbs. We aren't going to be able to create a powerful enough upwards force once we are in a zero gravity environment. You have to let him go,' AI says.

A low thumping sound is heard as the other man hits the ground. ZERO GRAVITY OBTAINED shows on Jaden's eyes. The nanodrones quickly move down and back up creating an upwards force. It begins to slow them down to 73 mph at 488 feet.

'We are going to have to try, I'm not letting him go. AI try to think random, think of an outside the box solution,' Jaden says.

'I've done the calculations using human advance calculus and Andromedian's advance calculus. The energy we have available, speed, distance we can only hold an extra fifty pounds plus your weight. Jaden if you hit the ground at a speed greater than 18 mph you are going to have injuries that will require hours to repair. A speed greater than 40 mph you are going to have serious injuries that are catastrophic,' AI says.

'What does that mean?'

'You might explode on impact. Just like the crazed man that just exploded on impact.'

'Oh God, we are going to need a miracle,' he pleads.

'God? How is an imaginary spirit going to help this situation?'

'AI if you want to think more human, you need to have a little faith.'

Agent Lopez is in shock and is hyperventilating. He is disorientated as he sees the ground getting closer and Jaden's arm around his back without a shirt on. The federal agent begins to pray and holds on to the cross on his necklace.

"Calm down and stop moving or we are both going to die," Jaden yells again.

Jaden hears a propeller plane from a distance away.

The agent closes his eyes and holds on to Jaden tightly. They continue downwards feet first at a steady 65 mph.

'Shit, at least we are doing the speed limit,' Jaden snaps.

'Jaden, let him go, we are at 130 feet. If you die, I have to return back to the Gravhawk and destroy your body, then return back to Xenos.'

'That would suck. I can't let this guy go. He has a family and was just doing his job. Us humans always try to beat the logical odds. A little faith and luck can go a long way, even if it isn't logical,' Jaden quickly says.

'Okay.'

A low flying airplane approaches about a quarter of a mile away from them going in another direction. A light bulb flashes in Jaden's head. He quickly sends two pairs of nanoscanners towards the two person personal airplane, flying at 700 feet. Jaden makes them scan the materials on the plane.

'There is no time to explain. Just reverse the polarity in the pro-gravity nanodrones and the extra ones we were just using. Make them go in the skin of my back and rear legs. Quickly! This has to work,' Jaden says as he reaches ninety-eight feet.

Jaden turns his and Mr. Lopez's body horizontal to the ground.

"What are you doing? I don't want to die on my face!" Lopez yells

"Trust me!"

They reach fifty-six feet as the wind continues to hit their faces. The magnetic nanodrones in the skin on Jaden's backside begin to strongly attract any metal behind him. The anti-gravity, upward energy forces and magnetic nanodrones are all working together. They both begin to slow down considerably as Jaden's skin is being stretched causing him great pain. He begins to bleed through his pores on his back. Lopez's eyes are wide open as he sees a miracle taking place before his eyes. Jaden increases his grip around Agent Lopez. Jaden's body is pulling him towards the small airplane's direction. They reach 35 mph and then 23 mph. Jaden screams in pain as they reach 8 mph at thirteen feet. The magnetic nanodrones go offline as their bodies turns vertical to the ground and they land on their feet.

Waffle Sundae Quad

**Four layers of warm Belgium waffles, 3 layers of: Nutella, Syrup, vanilla ice cream & bacon.
Layer 1: Vanilla ice cream, Nutella, syrup, bacon.
Layer 2: Vanilla ice cream, Nutella, syrup & bacon.
Layer 3: Crushed Sweet tots, syrup & whipped cream.**

Chapter 17: The Miracle Halo

Jaden drops and rolls, and so does the agent. They land in a wooded area. They are on their backs looking upwards and breathing heavily. The sounds of wilderness are all around them. Officer Lopez begins to rub his hands and kisses the cross around his neck repeatedly. He begins to kiss the ground and rub his hands together. Jaden takes his navy shirt from around his leg and puts it back on.

'Whoa! We did it, AI.'

'AI? Buddy?'

There is no response. The medical nanodrones begin to repair the skin tissue in Jaden's stretched and bleeding skin. Jaden ignores the pain as he wonders why AI isn't responding. They also repair some frostbite in his numb fingers. Jaden's energy is very low. He thinks maybe because his body's energy is low AI isn't responding. He thinks about where he can get a powerful source of energy from.

"Sir, do you have another Taser on you?" Jaden asks.

"No, just my gun. How did you do that, land us without a parachute? Who are you?" Officer Lopez asks.

"I'll answer that when I get back," he says.

Jaden uses all the nanoscanners to locate where the crazed fat man landed. He finds the guy's remains about fifty feet to his left and focuses in on the Taser still looking as if it is in good shape. Jaden quickly runs over there to see if it is working.

"Where you going?" The agent asks while he follows.

Jaden reaches the exploded body area. He tries to watch where he steps.

'AI?'

He finds the Taser and picks it up. Jaden walks out of the death zone.

"The wires already recoiled, cool. I guess it's still working," Jaden says while he pulls the trigger on himself and shoots himself in the stomach.

A powerful jolt of electricity channels into his abdomen. He drops to his knees as the electricity weakens him. Jaden drops the stun gun.

"Buddy, what are you doing?" The agent asks while looking at Jaden with a confused look. The skin on Jaden's back finishes healing and he stands up.

"Are you okay sir?" The agent asks while picking up the stun gun.

"Yeah I'm fine," Jaden says.

'I'm fine too,' AI says.

'Your back buddy? I thought I lost you. What happened to you?' Jaden asks excitedly.

"Sir, what is going on here? I remember falling out of the airplane and then you rescuing me without a parachute. None of this is making any sense," the agent says.

'I don't know, your pain level went off the chart, then I shut down. My systems really took a hit. I'm checking my synthetic crystals now. The unknown energy that came from your mind started to go down your arms and hands. Did you feel anything strange?' AI asks.

'I felt a lot of pain all over. Listen, I'm getting a strange feeling that the flight we were on is in some kind of trouble.'

"Sir, I'll explain in a few. I think the airplane we were on might be in trouble. I'm going to need your help. Can I use your cell phone?" Jaden asks.

"Sure."

Officer Lopez pulls out his cell phone from his pocket and gives it to Jaden. He dials Dr. Chan's cell phone. The phone rings and she picks up.

"Hello?" She asks.

"Dr. Chan, it's me."

"Where are you? What is going on? Are you okay?" She asks.

"Yes, I'm fine. Listen, I'm going to need your help. First, I need you to check the status of Flight 104. Second, I'm going to send you the coordinates to where I am, I need you to pick me up. Make sure you aren't followed," Jaden says.

"There is a strange van outside my apartment window downstairs. But I have an idea," she says.

"Thanks, call me back at this number if you hear anything about the flight. Thanks a lot," Jaden says.

"You're welcome sweetie," Chan says while hanging up the phone.

Jaden walks up to the agent, "How do you text on this phone?"

"I can send encrypted text messages through this phone, what would you like me to text?"

"Text the number I just called these coordinates lat=37.931472, long=-76.774878," Jaden says.

"How did you know the coordinates to where we are?" Lopez asks.

"I memorized the coordinates for the entire world and all the maps," Jaden replies.

The agent gives Jaden a strange look. He sends the text to her phone. His phone beeps back instantly. Lopez reads the text message out loud.

"Flight 104 is in trouble. My superiors are trying to contact me. The airplane is on autopilot and no one is responding on the flight. I have to inform them I'm on the ground," Lopez says.

'I knew it. I knew something was wrong with the flight. I want to try to reach the aircraft somehow,' Jaden says.

"No, don't do that. That won't be a good idea. You can't let them know you are on the ground, when you are supposed to be on the aircraft," Jaden says.

"Why not? You are a suspect I was told to watch on the flight. Who are you anyway?" He asks while pulling out his gun pointing it at Jaden.

'We could zap his brain with some nanoscanners, or hit him with a gravity shock wave, or reflect his bullets with an energy shield,' AI suggests.

'I'll handle this the non-violent way.'

"Air Marshal Fredrick Lopez, believe it or not, I'm half human and half something else. I'm here to help the people on this planet from a pending attack. I don't think it is fair for you to point your gun at me, after I risked my life to save yours. If I were a bad guy, I would have let you splat on the ground like that hungry, hungry hippo over there and saved myself. The government wants me so they can do some experiments on me. You know how the government likes catching little E.T.'s and sticking probes up their asses. So that's why the government wants me. You just landed on the ground safely after falling over 33,000 feet without a parachute. That should be enough proof to prove I'm a good guy. Now lower your weapon, so I can try to help those people left on the airplane," Jaden says confidently.

Lopez thinks for a few seconds.

"How are you going to help those people on Flight 104 a state away?" Lopez asks.

"Mr. Lopez you believe in God and miracles, right?"

"Yes."

"Today is a day of miracles, and I have an idea. Follow me," Jaden says while walking away.

"What if this doesn't work? I could get in trouble for not reporting to my superiors," he says while putting away his gun.

"Do you have a better idea on how to save a plane full of people from where you are now? How are you going to explain to your superiors you fell out of an aircraft and survived without a parachute?" Jaden asks.

He doesn't respond, but continues to follow Jaden to an open grassy area.

"I need you to shoot me with the stun gun," Jaden says.

"Excuse me?" He asks while pulling it out.

"Less questions and more action. Time is very important here," Jaden says while taking it from his hand.

'AI I want to fill the nanoscanners up with as many nanodrones as they can carry and then get them to connect to each other, like you showed me when we took off from the airport. Do you think they can make it to the airplane from here?'

Jaden changes the stun gun to maximum power and shoots himself with 100,000 volts in the abdomen. He gets on his knees, drops the stun gun and Lopez looks at him as if he is crazy.

Jaden gets up, picks up the stun gun and continues walking to the open grassy area as if nothing happened.

'They might be able to, but it would take too long to reach the airplane at the speed they travel at. They are going to need a boost. I calculate the airplane is over 130 miles from here,' AI says.

'How about an atomic solar recharge?' Jaden asks while standing in the open grass area looking in the sky.

'That won't work, the nanoscanners might go in the wrong direction or too far out. We can use a powerful gravity shock wave and they can ride it out at breakneck speeds. They can drop off one by one at the proper distances in between,' AI says.

Lopez observes Jaden zoning out.

"Sir, are you okay?" Lopez asks. "You just took over 150,000 volts of electricity in the past five minutes. You can drop an elephant with that much electricity."

"Yes, I'm fine. Heroes always take pain to save others. I'm calculating distances and getting ready to remote into the airplane. Do you have another cartridge for the stun gun?" Jaden asks.

"Yes, just this last clip," he says while handing it to Jaden.

Jaden loads it and shoots himself with another 100,000 volts. This time he doesn't drop to his knees. The gun recharges and recoils.

"I'm getting used to this, almost like taking a needle at the doctor's office," Jaden says.

"I just received another text, that the Air Force is going shoot down Flight 104 in the next twenty minutes, if no one responds from the airplane. They are assuming an act of terrorism has taken place," Lopez says.

"That's not good, stand back some."

'The nanoscanners are fully loaded with nanodrones. They are all in your right arm,' AI says.

Gravity shock wave nanodrones are 150 feet in diameter circling around Jaden's body. The quickly spinning nanodrones are creating white smoke where the circle is. The nanodrones speed towards Jaden from all directions taking the gravity forces at ground level with them. The grass folds flat like dominoes tumbling. They quickly reach Jaden's body and travel out his right arm at an incredible speed. At the same time he extends his arm outwards towards the direction of Flight 104. Lopez falls back towards the grass as his legs buckle from the increased gravity traveling under his feet. The energy quickly moves through the air, creating a loud sonic boom.

'Wow, that was the most powerful gravity shock wave I've ever fired. It's moving about 3500 miles an hour,' Jaden says as he sees the nanoscanners quickly moving through the air.

'It will slow down and the nanoscanners will get out before the shock wave changes direction back towards Earth.'

'I was monitoring the neurons in your brain when you came up with the idea to use the metal in the small airplane going by with the pro-gravity nanodrones. The chemical signal just connected with another neuron at random,' AI says.

'Yeah, human brains are still a mystery,' Jaden says.

Lopez stands and looks in the direction the invisible force was cruising through the air. One nanoscanner jumps out of the shock wave at thirty miles out.

"Shit, that was amazing. I've never seen anything like that. What was that?" Lopez asks with an amazed look on his face.

"That was a gravity shock wave heading southwest towards Flight 104. Hopefully it will reach the airplane in less than ten minutes," Jaden says while he shoots himself with the last stun gun charge.

"Okay, I'm ready," Jaden says.

"Ready for what?" Lopez asks.

"To remote into the airplane, to see what is going on, and if I can wake someone up. Would you like to have a front row seat?" Jaden asks.

"Sure why not," he says.

"Lay down in the grass here with me. I'm going to see if you can see what I see, through the nanoscanners," Jaden says while laying flat on his back over the grass.

'Why are you telling this officer everything and why are you going to let him see through the nanoscanners?' AI asks.

'Who is going to believe him?' Jaden asks, 'He might be able to help us with the airplane, if we need help landing it,' Jaden says.

They lay on the grass two feet from each other.

"Close your eyes and relax," Jaden says, while putting his left hand over Lopez's eyes.

Nanodrones create a small bridge behind Lopez's eyes to his optic nerves. The nanodrones keep the resolution at 500 megapixels.

"Make sure you keep your eyes closed, or you'll get double visions and it will overload your brain giving you a serious headache," Jaden says.

"Okay, are you sure you know what you're… Wait a second! I see something, I see clouds quickly moving by, but the image is upside down," Lopez says.

There is a flash and the view changes right side up for him. The nanoscanners break off one by one at approximately thirty miles each. They connect and communicate with each other.

"Is that better?" Jaden asks.

"Yes, this is amazing. I feel like I'm flying in the air without a body."

"Don't worry you'll get used to it. You aren't going to be able to hear any sounds though."

"That's cool, I see something coming up. I see the airplane," Lopez says while the nanoscanners zoom in from miles behind.

"There is something... There is something behind the 737 aircraft, two bright lights exhausting fumes," Lopez says as the scanners analyze the best views, removing light particles.

The nanoscanners change the view to heat and molecule radar. A 3D image is shown of two jet fighters behind the 737 airplane.

"That is a sixth generation Stealth F-22 Raptor on the left behind Flight 104 and a Predator drone on the right. Shit, they are using visual stealth technology," Lopez says excitedly, while the nanoscanners get closer and zoom out.

AI pulls up information on what a UAV Predator drone is and how the next generation Predator drones works with Motherdrone.

"What is visual stealth technology?" Jaden asks.

"I've heard about it, but have never seen it. It is top-secret. Outside the body of the Raptors and Predators are light diode and fiber-optic panel technology. They flash bright lights around their body, making the jet fighters look invisible against the bright sky. The government is going to shoot down the 737 aircraft and any witnesses from the ground will say it just exploded by itself. Even the missiles have the same technology. They are going to make it look like an accident. We have to do something quick," Lopez says while the nanoscanners pass through the jet fighters.

'I don't like this human. He is saying "we" as if he is actually doing something,' AI says.

'Don't worry about it AI buddy, it is good to make him feel as he is a part of something. His help might come in handy, he can be on our team for awhile,' Jaden says to AI.

"Yes, *we* are going to save the people on this airplane, Mr. Lopez," Jaden says.

"What are all of those periodic table images and small words passing by on my eyes?" Lopez asks.

"Those are the materials the jet fighters are made of. The alien eyes you are seeing through are called nanoscanners. When they pass through a material they identify what they are passing through," Jaden explains.

The nanoscanners slow down and enter the rear of the 737. The passengers are all laid out unconscious. The vision quickly falls all the way behind the aircraft as the fourth scanner sits midair at another thirty miles. The last two remaining nanoscanners quickly look around the airplane. Everyone is unconscious as the co-pilot and Pam lay near the rear of the airplane. People still have the oxygen masks on their faces.

'It appears every human is in a neutral nanomole stage 2,' AI says.

A nanoscanner scans down the aisle towards the cockpit, while the other scans bodies.

"What is wrong with them? Why is everyone sleeping and unconscious?" Lopez asks, while he sees Jaden switching between nanoscanners.

"They are in stage 2. There is going to be a sophisticated alien attack on Earth in the next few days. I've been trying to warn the government. I'll explain to you later, but now we have to land the plane safely," Jaden says.

The pilot is laying face down on the floor of the business class section. The cockpit door is wide open. Inside the cockpit, the airplane is on autopilot at 17,098 feet and 412 mph.

"Looks like the pilot fell out after leveling out the aircraft and leaving the cockpit to check on the other passengers," Lopez says.

'Do you think we can override one of the pilots' brains and control their bodies similar to how the nanomoles will in positive stage 3?' Jaden asks.

'It is possible, but the nanomoles have been in the pilots' brains for years and know the unique electrical impulses and random codes in the motor cortex of the brain. That information is encoded in the nanomoles. The signals travel down the spinal cord to alpha motor neurons near muscles... I have an idea, we can wipe out the brain's information completely and run our own electrical impulses from the brain down the spinal cord to the muscles. The negative side will be the human mind will be brain dead beyond repair. We have less than ten minutes before the next nanoscanner has to get into its thirty mile connection distance,' AI says.

'I have an idea, do you think we can quickly access both pilots' brains and nanomoles, so I can decide who will have to be sacrificed,' Jaden says.

'It would be faster to just choose a pilot now,' AI says.

'I can't do that. I have to know who has a family before I can do such a thing to a human. Pilots always sacrifice for the passengers on their airplane. I need to choose which one.'

AI quickly scans both pilots' nanomoles and brain cells.

"What is going on, why are we inside of the pilots' brain?" Lopez asks.

"I'm determining which one has to be sacrificed, so that I can try to control their bodies to land the plane. The airplane has fingerprint scan to deactivate the autopilot. Sacrificed meaning when the other people on the airplane wake up this pilot will be brain dead forever," Jaden says.

"Is that the only way?" Lopez asks.

"Yes."

"You can't connect into the electronics of the airplane to land it?"

"No, I wish," Jaden says.

Information is quickly being accessed in both pilots' brains. Jaden sees images from both nanoscanners.

"Okay, the pilot, named Richard, is fifty-eight, has four kids, none are in college, and he is divorced. His child support payments are fifty percent of his $105,000 a year salary. His ex-wife remarried. His ex-girlfriend was caught cheating on him while he was piloting and came home early. His alimony is another fifteen percent of his salary. His kids don't love him and his oldest daughter is pregnant at eighteen and dropped out of college. His oldest son is twenty years old and addicted to *Third Virtual Life Adult World* and doesn't work or do anything. His second oldest daughter is sixteen and married to a thirty-four year old man. The youngest ran away from his ex-wife's house. Man, this guy needs to be put out of his misery," Jaden says to Lopez.

"Shit, you are right. I thought my kids and separation was bad," Lopez says while agreeing.

"The co-pilot, Stan, is forty-five, has two adopted kids, and he has a husband at home. He has had a civil union for four years. The kids are nine and ten from the Philippines..." Jaden is interrupted.

"Get rid of the co-pilot, use him to land the plane," Lopez quickly says.

"Why is that? I didn't even finish," Jaden says.

"I don't like gay men. I was in the Marines for ten years and the government kept changing their don't ask, don't tell policies.

Sixty percent of the Marines in my platoon were gay or bisexual. Twenty-five percent of them getting blue discharges every year. Some straight men were saying they were gay to get out of combat in Afghanistan and Iraq. I've seen more and more homosexual acts in the military over the years. Men sleeping with men and orgies behind closed doors. No safe sex, and then the soldiers go home to their wives. To me those aren't real soldiers..."

'Jaden we have to hurry, three minutes left before the fifth nanoscanner has to get into position,' AI says.

"...A real soldier is a robot soldier or the soldiers in the Vietnam War, Korean War, WWII, WWI, Civil War... Those were real soldiers..." Lopez continues talking in the background.

'Scan the pilot's short-term and long-term memory. I want you to save any information regarding flying an aircraft and landing an aircraft,' Jaden says to AI.

"...Even when Bin Laden was killed in 2011 and the war was over...."

"Mr. Lopez your opinion is greatly appreciated, but I'm going by who has more to live for. Sexual preference is not my concern. Maybe when these bad aliens attack Earth, and we can't stop them, maybe they can reconfigure these gay men to have babies somehow. They can transform men's penises into a vagina. Then sexual preference won't matter, will it? Lesbian women can have transformed vagina penises. Who knows what they have in mind for us humans... But I'm choosing the senior pilot. The pilot/captain is always first to sacrifice themselves for everyone. This guy would probably be better off being put out of his misery, instead of losing sixty-five percent of his salary plus taxes every two weeks. He has good life insurance. I'll be doing him a favor," Jaden says.

"Okay, Mr. Half Alien Dude," Lopez says, while his phone vibrates.

Jaden takes his hand from over Lopez's eyes. Lopez leans up and squints his eyes from the bright sunlight to look at the new text message on his phone.

"They are going to shoot down the airliner in six minutes, unless someone responds. They probably want the airplane pieces to land over a lake or a non-populated area in North Carolina. The aircraft just passed Henderson, North Carolina," Lopez says while laying back down, closing his eyes.

Jaden puts his hand over his eyes again. Jaden looks at the images from the pilot's memories. Lopez also sees the images. He sees him learning to fly a plane from his father at sixteen and getting his license by seventeen. This information is being recorded and sent to Jaden's mind. He skips past some images in his twenties. Memories of him learning to fly a commercial plane in his early thirties and being a co-pilot. Jaden sees memories in his fifties as a flight instructor.

"Okay, the instructor memories are more useful for flying and landing," Jaden says.

Information on how to land a commercial aircraft is being saved and what buttons to press.

Images of Sully, the hero pilot, keep coming up and repeated images of an airliner landing on a river in New York City flash by.

'AI, zap his brain and run our impulse electrical signals with the nanodrones.'

'Yes sir.'

The fifth nanoscanner releases millions of nanodrones in the pilot's brain, then the scanner quickly leaves. The fifth nanoscanner quickly stops midair exiting the aircraft at the thirty-one mile mark.

'That was close. All five nanoscanners are connected at ninety-nine percent efficiency . Transmitting at one hundred nanoseconds,' AI says.

The sixth and last nanoscanner begins to quickly spin around the primary motor cortex of the brain destroying neurons. The energy created also destroys short-term and long-term memory cells. The pilot's body begins to shake as if he is having a seizure. Nanodrones are quickly being attacked by white blood cells in the blood as they move down the spinal cord creating checkpoints in the nervous system. The nanodrones defend themselves destroying white blood cells with microscopic iron-oxide particles. They reach the arms and spread out. The pilot stops shaking and begins sneezing. His fingers shake and then begin to move. His legs begin to shake and then move regularly.

"Who is this hero pilot Sully?" Jaden asks Lopez.

"Where have you been? On another planet? Everyone has heard of Sully..."

"Yeah, I have been on another planet," Jaden snaps.

61

"...He landed an airplane over the Hudson River in New York City back in February 2009 with no engines. Geese were sucked into both of his engines. He did a perfect landing without destroying the plane. Another pilot tried the same thing in 2012 over a lake near Michigan, but wasn't successful. The plane broke into three pieces, ejecting people all over the lake," Lopez says.

"Yeah I see, this pilot watched that landing hundreds of times. It was all over his memory. That is amazing. What does Sully do now?" Jaden asks.

"He flies for one of the private spaceship companies," Lopez says.

"Cool. Private spaceship companies? That is interesting. I guess MASA couldn't monopolize space after all," Jaden says while watching what is going on. He hears a beeping sound coming from the cockpit.

"I hear a beeping sound coming from the cockpit," Jaden tells Lopez.

"They are probably firing warning shots at the plane. You have to hurry, the Air Force is about to fire upon the airliner," Lopez says.

The pilot stands up on his feet, but quickly falls over an overweight female passenger sitting in a big business class seat. Her oxygen mask falls from her face and the pilot lands on his back in front of her legs between a row of seats.

'Something is wrong with his equilibrium and coordination cells,' AI says.

Jaden can see outside the pilot's eyes. He is looking up the big lady's skirt without panties.

"Shit!" Jaden yells.

"Holy shit!" Lopez yells.

"This is what I get for looking through all those women's clothes the last few months," Jaden says.

"What am I looking at?" Lopez asks.

"Just close your eyes, the pilot fell between a passenger's legs," Jaden says while the nanodrones attempt to fix the problems.

"I can't! My eyes are closed! I still see it!" Lopez yells.

The pilot stands up, but holds on to the headrest on the right.

"Man up soldier, I know you saw worse in Iraq. You mean to tell me you have never been with or dated a heavy girl?" Jaden asks.

There is silence.

"Come on, this is America where the average women's size is still a fourteen," Jaden says.

Lopez is quiet and doesn't respond. The pilot walks very slowly, step-by-step holding on to headrests and arm rests. The nanodrones are firing impulse signals to each other at different parts of the pilot's body getting him to walk. He walks like a zombie towards the cockpit door.

"Why is he walking like that and so slow?" Lopez asks.

"His white blood cells are constantly attacking my alien soldiers trying to control the movements in hundreds of muscles around his body in the correct order," Jaden says.

"Oh okay. The comment you made about being able to look up women's clothes, is that true? You were able to look through women's clothes and see them naked?" Lopez asks.

"Yes, I'm still able too. But trust me, I learned my lesson with that. Sometimes you don't always want to see what a woman looks like without any clothes on," Jaden says.

"I could never get tired of seeing women without any clothes on. Man, I wish I had x-ray vision," Lopez says.

"I used to think the same thing. But when images of periods, herpes, STDs, hair everywhere, and bad smells stay stuck in your memory, it isn't a good sight."

"I didn't think of all of that, I don't want to see those things. But that is probably less than ten percent of women right?" Lopez asks.

"More than you think my friend, more than you think," Jaden says.

Goose bumps run down Lopez's arms as eerie thoughts pass through his mind.

'AI change my face, body and pigment color in my skin back to my old self when you get a chance. I want to be myself and I'm sure the government knows this face already,' Jaden says.

'Yes sir.'

WASHINGTON, D.C. 10:25 AM

"Fire at will on Flight 104, Raptor 16," Robinson gives the order from the situation room. He is looking at the live video from the Predator drone's 3D imaging cameras and satellite. A computer screen has a trajectory path that the airliner's debris will land in a lake and forested area outside of Wake Forest, North Carolina.

On Jetgreen Flight 104 Fifteen seconds later.

The pilot crawls up the stairs and into the cockpit after trying twice to walk up the two stairs. His eyes are wide open like someone on drugs.

"Someone please answer. The Air Force has been cleared to fire upon you. Please answer the radio," the cockpit radio says.

"You going to have to hurry, Jaden," Lopez says.

The Raptor F-22 pilot falls a mile behind to fire at the huge airliner. It locks on to Jetgreen's fuselage and chooses the missile. He puts his hand on the red trigger button and slightly touches it.

The pilot is still trying to pull himself into the chair. Jaden is trying very hard to control the body movements by thought. Nanodrones go into his throat and vocal cords. Suddenly red lights begin flashing again. The F-22 pilot fires his first missile then he fires a different missile a few seconds later. Jaden finally gets the body in the small seated area. There is a heads up display (HUD) screen in between the pilot and the airliner's front window.

"Grab the yoke!" Lopez yells.

"Yoke?" Jaden asks while groaning.

"Yoke is what the steering wheel is called on an aircraft," Lopez says frantically.

"It's a steering wheel today!"

Jaden moans and groans as he struggles to get the pilot into the seat. He feels as if he is trying to lift his own body into the seat. The pilot reaches up and grabs the steering wheel with both hands. The autopilot goes off and a female voice is heard, "Welcome back Richard Craigwell."

Jaden gets the pilot to turn a hard right, while pressing the rudder pedal. The aircraft leans and banks a hard right.

'This is Pilot Richard Craigwell. Call off the missile fire,' Jaden says through the pilot's voice. The voice sounds low and broken up.

The F-22 pilot sees the airliner banking a hard right and presses the self-destruct button on the first missile.

"Raptor 16 call off the strike, I repeat call off the strike. Detonate missiles," the base orders.

The missile explodes fifteen feet behind the left engine. Debris and fire flies into the rear of the left engine and on the wing. Some debris also hits the side and rear of the airplane in all directions. The second missile extends out small wings and slows down. The F-22 goes over the second missile and two arms grab it. The missile turns off and goes back into the jet fighter. Flight 104 loses its left engine and the left wing is damaged. The fire quickly goes out. The F-22 continues to fly behind the aircraft. A trail of smoke is coming from the left engine.

"Mr. Craigwell what is going on and what is the condition of the crew?" The air traffic controller at Raleigh Airport asks. He repeats himself a few seconds later.

Jaden is searching the memory of the pilot to remember where everything is and what to do next. The airplane straightens out, but is leaning. The pilot presses the button on the microphone.

The pilot automatically reaches to press a lever overhead to increase the thrust in the right engine.

'Shit, I thought the pilot was waking up and doing things himself for a second,' Jaden says, 'Thanks AI.'

'That is impossible. The pilot would be lucky to be a vegetable by the time the nanodrones and nanoscanners leave his body. He would probably catch any bacterial infection or cold, now that his white blood cells are destroyed. Those white blood cells are no match for alien technology,' AI says.

'Poor guy. I see you are deactivating Officer Lopez's nanomole. Good work AI,' Jaden says.

'I'm also halfway done changing your face and body back to your old self,' AI says.

'I can feel it. I'm trying to ignore the pain, good work. Excellent multi-tasking,' Jaden says.

Jaden's eye screen shows in small letters the status of changing his face and body back to the old Bi-racial Jaden: SAVING FACE DISTANCE STRUCTURE 85%, ADDING ORIGINAL FAT TISSUE 76% DONE, REBUILDING CARTILAGE IN NOSE AND RESTRUCTURING, ADDING 20% OF MELANIN PIGMENT IN EPIDERMIS AROUND BODY, REGROWING ORIGINAL DNA HAIR FOLLICLES GROWTH 1100%, ADJUSTING EYES AND EARS STRUCTURE.

"Pilot Craigwell what is the condition of your crew?" The air traffic controller asks again.

"I'm hurt, I feel as if I'm on some kind of drugs. Everyone on, everyone on the flight is unconscious. Some sort of cosmic energy from space has put everyone to sleep," Jaden says through the pilot's voice. The pilot breathes very heavily cutting off his words.

"This man is suffering some serious delusions," the air traffic controller says to the people in the room with him.

"Did you suffer any damage from the missile detonation?" The air traffic controller asks.

"Yes, left wing and engine received damage, but I still have control of the plane."

"Roger that Craigwell, what happened earlier on the flight where your emergency door opened?"

Jaden thinks, he was going to say passengers fell out, and then the government will be looking for him on the ground. Jaden's brain is working overtime. He is using some of his multi-tasking brain cells. AI is controlling the pilot's right hand to push buttons and levers to fly towards a lower altitude. Jaden is controlling the left hand on the steering wheel.

'This is cool, you are controlling the right hand and I'm controlling the left,' Jaden says.

"I'm not sure, I wasn't back there. But the emergency door is closed now. My passengers and crew are breathing, but in a deep sleep. I need an emergency runway to land," Jaden the pilot says.

"Is the dangerous suspect we notified you about earlier still on board?"

'Yeah! The dangerous suspect is talking to you now, you big dummy!' Jaden snaps.

"I'm not sure," the pilot says in a low voice.

"Can you circle around to runway nine?" The air traffic controller asks.

'We only have ten miles before the nanoscanners are out of range. Runway nine is too far to the south, we would have to circle around to land there and the nanoscanners would be out of range. The airport is eleven miles from here, I can extend each nanoscanner at most, 1000 feet each. This is dangerous, if we lose the connection to the nanoscanners in the pilot's brain we are not going to be able to recover that nanoscanner and the nanodrones in his body,' AI says.

Suddenly the right engine power goes down fifty percent. A beeping sound is heard. The pilot's eyes are wandering around as if he is sleeping with his eyes open, until Jaden is looking out of them.

"Can you confirm runway nine, Flight 104?"

'What happened?' Jaden asks.

'The right engine was also damaged from the missile blast. This is bad,' AI says while the plane leans again.

"Air traffic, I just lost fifty percent of my thrust in my right engine. We need a direct runway in our direction. We need to land right away," the pilot says.

The pilot's right hand is pressing buttons and levers all over. The airplane is slowly changing course towards the airport ahead.

'Let them know we are dumping fuel now,' AI says.

"You are cleared to land on runway six. There are two jet fighters behind you to escort you in. There will be fire department and emergency personnel here when you land. Good luck to you Flight 104."

"Thank you air traffic. I am dumping fuel," Jaden says through the pilot's voice.

AI makes the pilot's hands and feet press different levers, buttons and pedals.

ON THE GROUND - FALLS LAKE STATE PARK, NC
2020 FEET BELOW 9 MILES FROM AIRPORT

Boy Scouts are in a log cabin eating breakfast, while one young boy is outside thirty feet away trying to make a fire with a bow, wood tinder, hand socket and a wooden drill. He is quickly drilling a sharp stick into the wood.

"Johnny, you still didn't light the fire?" The older Boy Scout leader asks while walking out side.

"I almost got it scout leader," 7-year-old Johnny replies while kneeling on one knee holding on to the hand socket and quickly turning the bow connected to the wood drill bit.

"Okay, hurry. You've been at it for twenty minutes. Your breakfast is getting cold," the teenage scout leader says while walking back inside the cabin.

Thirty seconds goes by, Johnny runs towards the cabin door. A sprinkle of liquid rains all around as the little boy opens the cabin door.

"I created the fire. I did it! I did it!" He yells while running out of breath.

"Good job, good job, let's see what you did. You earned your merit badge," the scout leader says while walking towards the door.

"It wasn't supposed to rain this morning," the scout leader says while looking at liquid falling on the windows of the cabin.

The scout sees fire spreading from Johnny's wood tinder in all directions. The jet fuel from Flight 104 soaks the area with jet fuel.

"What did you do Johnny?" The scout leader asks while closing the door.

The fire quickly spreads to the grass, trees and log cabin.

"Everybody run! Run out the back door!" He yells.

The twelve scouts begin to scream and run. They drop their breakfast as fire is burning through all the windows. They run out of the back of the log cabin and towards the lake. A scout still has his breakfast in his hands eating and running. The fire spreads behind the scout leader as the kids run in front. They all jump in the lake as the log cabin is on fire. They swim in the lake away from the burning shore and watch the log cabin go up in flames.

"Do I still get my merit badge?" Johnny asks.

FLIGHT 104 MILE 8 FROM THE AIRPORT 1919 FEET 201MPH

'AI, this is going to be impossible to land this way and we can't straighten up the leaning to the left. The rudders are turning very slowly... The airplane is at 1903 feet. We are losing altitude and air speed rapidly. AI what are you showing me?' Jaden asks while he sees images.

'A simulation of the airplane crashing at a leaning angle before the runway, after stalling and bursting into flames. We should get the nanodrones, nanoscanners and get out before the fireworks,' AI says.

'Fireworks? That is a good one, very funny. AI we can't give up now, remember what you are learning about humans?' Jaden asks, 'Don't give up faith, random thinking, or random ideas. Did you try a forward-slip, sideslip, or counter balance approach?'

'The forward-slip won't work. That mostly works with strong winds and one fully working engine. A sideslip might work, but we need more lift and speed. The left side is dragging and we are losing altitude quick. I'm thinking randomly, and using some, using some imagination,' AI pauses for a few seconds, 'I have a random idea. I can use the anti-gravity nanodrones in the five other nanoscanners. We filled the nanoscanners with programmable nanodrones earlier. The nanoscanners can fire them into each other inside the high-speed microscopic communications pathway. Then we can use the anti-gravity nanodrones on that side of the plane. But I don't know if that will be enough. I would need to do some advance quick calculations.'

'Man, if you could breathe AI you would have said all of that in one breath. That's a good idea, now you are thinking. Go ahead and do it, quickly,' Jaden says.

Beeping sounds are heard.

'We are stalling!' Jaden yells while moving the steering wheel forward.

The nose of the plane tilts down more.

The first nanoscanners sitting midair thirty miles from Jaden and Lopez lying on the grass quickly spin around. They fire millions of nanodrones into the communications pathway to the next pair of nanoscanners sitting midair sixty miles away already spinning. This continues four more times until one hundred million nanodrones reach the nanoscanners in the pilot's brain within seconds. The nanodrones quickly increase in size and get to work.

'AI we need to lift the nose of the plane first, we are going forward too fast,' Jaden says.

"Flight 104 increase your speed, you are coming in too steep, you are not going to make the runway, over," the air traffic controller says.

The one hundred million nanodrones quickly spin around the nose of the airplane, disrupting the gravity forces in the front of the plane. They spread out ten feet behind the pilot and around the outside of the aircraft. The aircraft's nose lifts up and the airplane slightly increases speed.

'We need to send the pro-gravity nanodrones and all my anti-gravity nanodrones to help the aircraft. The left wing needs help, it is still leaning,' Jaden says.

'That is a very bad idea Jaden, that is all the nanodrones capable of pro-gravity, anti-gravity, your gravity shock wave weapon and shield system drones. It will be too many for the nanoscanner to fire back through the communications pathway if the plane lands and we might go out of range. I've already stretched the first two nanoscanners,' AI says.

'Shit, we are less than two miles from the airport and 402 feet up. We can't give up, now and we are still leaning, let me think for a second,' Jaden says while quickly thinking, 'Can the nanodrones and nanoscanner hide inside of the pilot's body and we pick them up later?'

'That is possible, but that many can be detected by your government with microscopes and radiation detecting machines...' AI says before being cut off.

The nanodrones fill up in Jaden's brain and quickly fire themselves towards the first nanoscanner 30.2 miles away in the communications pathway. One billion nanodrones continue at a slow 750 mph towards the first nanoscanner.

"Flight 104, you are still leaning on your failed engine side. Please correct," the air traffic controller says over the radio.

'Why are they moving so slow?' Jaden asks while the plane reaches 260 feet and two miles from the airport.

'We didn't have any nanoscanners here left to accelerate them. They will speed up once they reach the first nanoscanner. Each nanoscanner is spinning and ready to accelerate the nanodrone particles like a particle accelerator machine,' AI says.

'Okay, I hope this works,' Jaden says.

'It is a great risk leaving them in the pilot's vegetable body. Your body will be left defenseless, Jaden. We will have to do a manual scan with the nanoscanner once we drive down to Raleigh Airport with Dr. Chan. The nanoscanner left in the pilot's body will be offline.'

'Okay.'

"This is Craigwell to air traffic control. Air traffic control come in," the pilot says.

"Go 104," air traffic control says.

"I need the F-22 behind me to fly over my left wing, over," the pilot says.

"Repeat?"

"I need the F-22 behind me to fly over my left wing within fifty feet," Jaden says through the pilot's voice.

"104, how will that help you land?" The air traffic controller asks.

"Listen I don't have time to explain, there has been strange things happening today on this flight, and I need you to trust me. Can you relay the message to the F-22 pilot?" The pilot asks.

"104, that is impossible to help your situation, please straighten your landing," the air traffic controller says.

"Are you a robot? Or a jackass? Traffic controller? All these passengers on this plane are going to die, unless that F-22 flies over my left wing, right now! Do you want these dead passengers on your conscious? Just do it," the pilot yells.

"Standby, 104."

They reach 148 feet still leaning hard to the left. The nose of the plane is slowly falling downwards as the gravity forces increase fighting with the anti-gravity nanodrones spinning around the nose. AI makes the pilot press the levers for the landing wheels.

'Shit, the nanodrones have to reach that first nanoscanner faster,' Jaden says.

"What did I miss?" Lopez asks while waking up with Jaden's hand still over his eyes.

Jaden responds, "You fell asleep? I'm still trying to land the plane. Hold on a second, enjoy the landing or the crash on Jaden's vision."

"Flight 104, the FAA and the pilot of the F-22 agreed to fly one hundred feet over the left wing. The F-22 pilot said he is afterburning out of there once you land or crash. He said your nose is still too low."

"Okay, over," the pilot says

"Godspeed, to you pilot Craigwell."

"Oh my God. The airliner is about to, is about to crash. The stall lights are on," Lopez says.

Flight 104 reaches ninety-five feet over the beginning of the runway. Fire trucks are lined up on the side of the runway. The stalling lights continue to flash while emitting a loud beeping sound. The right engine is at its maximum thrust of fifty percent. The F-22 pilot flies over the left wing at a slow 160 mph. The nanodrones reach the first already spinning nanoscanner and quickly accelerate through the other five, reaching the airplane in seconds. The pro-gravity nanodrones quickly go into the left wing and spread out. The anti-gravity nanodrones go into the nose of the plane to assist the other anti-gravity nanodrones. The nanodrones spinning around the nose quickly create a bright white halo ring. The nose of the craft begins to lift again. The nanodrones in the left wing quickly reverse their polarity on both sides, magnetically bonding to the wing and creating a strong magnetic force over it. The left side of Flight 104 begins to straighten out as the F-22 pilot feels a downward force pulling on his jet fighter. The F-22 is pulled down to seventy-five feet and then fifty feet as he begins to stall. The pilot doesn't know what is happening or why he is being pulled towards the airliner's wing. He quickly activates his afterburners, slowly pulling the left wing of Flight 104 with it. The nanodrones in the wing reduce their magnetic forces as the rear wheels touch down on the runway. The F-22 quickly accelerates over the runway at a fast speed. The front wheel lands on the runway and the glowing halo disappears. The brakes are applied and smoke comes from the wheels. The right flaps on the airplane go up as the left side does not.

'Shit, we don't have any braking flaps on the left side, there is a malfunction. We are heading to the right of the runway,' Jaden says while the airplane reaches 131 mph.

'Sir, we are almost out of range!' AI yells.

"Use your brakes Flight 104," the FAA person yells.

AI reverses the polarity of the nanodrones in the left wing. The pro-gravity nanodrones move to the bottom of the wing and creating a downward pulling force to the ground. The end of the runway comes in sight. Fire trucks, police and FBI cars are racing behind the airliner as it reaches the end of the runway at 40 mph. The images begin to show static on Jaden's eyes, as the nanoscanners reach the maximum range. The pilot's head falls over the steering wheel and the brake releases. Flight 104 continues to cruise at 26 mph. Jaden's vision through the pilot's eyes are completely blank. Jaden takes his hands from around Lopez's eyes and stands up. He removes his shoes, socks and runs barefoot south.

"Where are you going?" Lopez asks, "Wait a second, who was that guy? Where did the white guy go?"

'AI, keep controlling the pilot to stop the plane! Concentrate on his feet and that brake pedal!' Jaden yells while running over the grass.

He runs faster and faster as static returns to his eyes. The images are going out and in on his eyes. Jaden reaches a dirt road and continues running to keep the nanoscanners connected to the pilot. His feet leap over dirt, rocks and pebbles as dust goes airborne behind him. He ignores the pain in his feet. The pilot's head lifts up and Jaden can see a pond approaching the front of the airliner. The pilot's foot begins to press down on the brakes again, while Jaden reaches 28 mph running on foot. His heart and blood pressure is accelerating and he has a determined look on his face. He has a look of a hero who isn't giving up.

'Slam it AI!'

The front wheel of the airliner dips downwards near the declining bumpy pond area. There is a loud tumbling smashing sound and the pilot's head jerks back and forth like a drunk person. His head continuously bangs the yoke.

The airplane reaches 20 mph and then 10 mph and gently glides into the pond. The front wheel slowly sinks in the pond. The airliner stops completely while tilting downwards.

'We did it AI!' Jaden yells while slowing down as he approaches a gate.

The nanodrones around the airliner quickly go inside the pilot's slumped over body. His eyes are left open and look like a person who just died. The basic functions of the pilot's brain continue to send signals to his heart and lungs to breathe. A wheezing sound can be heard coming from his mouth as the nanoscanner in his brain turns itself off. The furthest nanoscanner midair flies into the other four and heads back towards Jaden. Jaden turns around and jogs back towards Lopez a quarter of a mile away. The five nanoscanners quickly go back into Jaden's body for diagnostics.

'We did it AI! We saved the airplane, we are superheroes. Don't you feel good inside?' Jaden asks while jogging back onto the dirt road.

'Yes we did. I do feel good, that was beyond calculations. That was a miracle and I don't believe in miracles. Everything worked out, even though the odds were against us,' AI says.

'You did good with the last suggestion, to reverse the polarity on the nanodrones in the wing. Good random thinking, you are learning,' Jaden says with a smile on his face.

'Yes, that was unexpected of me. I'm so used to doing things by the numbers and not taking risks,' AI says.

Jaden jogs up the dirt road and sees Lopez walking down the dirt road looking for him.

"That was amazing, I've never seen anyone run that fast before. Dude are you the same guy? Your face and skin color changed!" Lopez yells with a surprised look.

"Yes, I'm the same person. I changed my face and body back to the way I originally look," Jaden says, while Lopez looks at him. Lopez stops and walks along side of Jaden.

"Wild man, are you an angel or something?" Lopez asks.

"No, just human with some good alien technology in my DNA and a helpful artificial intelligent friend," Jaden says while walking to the open grass area.

'Thanks sir, you called me friend again,' AI says.

"Did you land the airplane safely? Are the passengers on board okay?"

"Let's just say I've pulled a 'Sully' of a landing. Yes, they are all safe. I had to keep up the connection to my alien friends, which is why I had to run like that. You are going to need an excuse to tell your superiors. Tell them you fell off the airplane trying to stop a passenger from opening the door. Then you landed in a lake, and miraculously survived. You just woke up not too long ago, and didn't get the messages on your phone," Jaden says.

"No one is going to believe I survived that fall," he says.

"You have a better idea?" Jaden asks. "When the passengers on the plane wake up, they are going to tell the authorities what they last remembered."

"I'll think of something. Oh yeah, your girlfriend called while you were running down the road like Action Jackson. She was a few minutes away," Lopez says.

"Oh, that's not my girlfriend, she's my friend," Jaden says while he picks up his shoes and socks.

He puts them back on and a SUV stops on the small dirt road behind them. A nanoscanner goes up to the SUV to see who is inside of it. Jaden sees it is Chan, as more scanners automatically leave his body.

'Wow, she is looking good, with her hair back and blouse on,' Jaden says to AI.

'No pervertism today right?' AI asks in a sarcastic tone.

Jaden laughs to himself and smile.

'No, I'm not going to do that...now. Thank you for curing me of my guilty conscious.'

Dr. Chan sees him on the grass talking to Lopez about fifty feet away. The SUV turns off the dirt road and goes up a small embankment. The four-wheel drive kicks in while propelling dirt and grass from the rear of the wheels.

"That is a nice truck," Jaden says while it gets closer.

"That is a Hydrogen Escalade, 2015. Wow, that is a 100,000-dollar SUV. Your girlfriend is doing good to afford this," Lopez says.

"Friend! Not girlfriend," Jaden repeats while walking to the right side as she pulls up.

'If she was my girlfriend I'd be looking at her naked now... That would be okay, right AI?'

'Yes, sure.'

"You okay Jaden?" She asks while smiling and happy to see him.

"I'm fine, Dr. *Kimberly* Chan. Thanks for coming. You sure know how to drive this machine, I see," Jaden whispers to her in the window.

"Yes, I have those men driving skills. I see that you figured out my first name, kudos to you. I thought you were on an airplane to North Carolina. What happened?" Chan asks. "Get in."

"Do you need a ride, Lopez?" Jaden asks while getting into the passenger front seat.

"Well sure, can you drop me off at a gas station. I'm going to call from a video pay phone," Lopez says while opening the rear passenger door and sitting down behind Jaden.

She makes a U-turn on the grass and the SUV barely shakes or rocks over the uneven terrain.

Mexican Cheese Fries 3

Double fries or double tots, double bacon, double onions, double jalapenos, double cheddar, double pepper-jack, Action Sauce & sour cream.

Only at Action Burger.

Chapter 18: Shoot me Again with that Gun and…

"I saved this air marshal from the airplane. This crazy passenger opened the emergency exit. This guy fell out at 33,000 feet with him and I had to save this brave federal air marshal," Jaden says.

"Wow, that's amazing," she says.

She drives with her left hand and extends her right arm back towards Lopez. She drives down the small two-foot high embankment with one hand and everyone leans forward.

"Hi, I'm Kimberly," she says.

"Hello, nice to meet you Kimberly. I'm Air Marshal Fredrick Lopez," he says while shaking her hand.

Jaden lays back and relaxes.

"Man, these seats are comfortable," Jaden says.

"Your seats have a built in massage feature, if you want to use it," she says while pointing to the button on the dash in front of Jaden.

He presses the button, and the seat begins to massage his back up and down the leather. Jaden speaks in a vibrating voice, "Oh this feels good for my back, after stretching the skin on my back like a pregnant woman."

"That's what was making that stretching sound behind me?" Lopez asks while laughing.

"You heard that?" Jaden asks and laughs.

Kimberly chuckles while pressing a button on the steering wheel.

"Nearest gas station," she says aloud.

"Nearest gas station is 1.8 miles away, two minutes, continue on road…" the GPS system says.

'Massage me magic leather seat,' Jaden mumbles to AI while his eyes are closed and head is against the headrest.

"I'm glad you are okay, though I was worried," she says while looking at Jaden and putting her right hand over the back of his head.

"Are you sure you two aren't boyfriend and girlfriend or husband and wife?" Lopez asks while turning his head to look at both of them.

"No," they shout at the same time.

'I just finished scanning the entire area to see if she was followed,' AI says.

'Good work. Thanks AI,' Jaden says while relaxing.

'I'm going to continue working on your weapon systems' calculations.'

They reach a main road, there an awkward silence as Jaden thinks about everything that has just happened. Some soft music begins to play on the radio

"I want to thank you again, for saving my life Jaden. I owe you one," Lopez says.

"Don't worry about it. I will put it on your tab,' Jaden says.

"I can't get over Jaden how you took over the pilot's body to land the aircraft from over a hundred miles away; that was amazing. But I don't understand how I fell asleep for a few minutes," Lopez says.

"Just remember I'm here to help. Oh, you fell asleep because your nanomole was deactivated," Jaden says while they pull into a gas station mart.

"Nanomole? Okay, thanks; and thanks for the ride Kimberly," Lopez says.

"Hey, thanks for the help," Jaden says.

"You're welcome. Where are you going now?" Lopez asks.

"Going to try to warn the government in Washington D.C. and maybe go to the news media. But in a day or two, you are going to know everything you need to know about what is going on. Also, remember don't tell anyone you saw me, okay?" Jaden asks.

"Okay, good luck," Lopez says while opening the door and closing it.

They pull off and Lopez waves.

"Set a course for Raleigh Airport in North Carolina. I have to retrieve my nanodrones and nanoscanner," Jaden says.

Kimberly speaks to the navigation system, "Raleigh airport in North Carolina is the destination, go now."

"Why are they at the airport?" She asks.

"I had to use them in a pilot's body so he could land the airplane. Now they are incubating in his body. Also, can I borrow your phone?" he asks. "I want to call my baby's mother to find the location of my daughter."

"Sure," she says while passing him the phone, "So you've been back on Earth for a few days and have baby mama drama already?"

"Very funny," Jaden says.

"Nanodrones are the organic nanobot parasites in your body correct?" She asks.

"Yes," he says while dialing numbers on her fancy I-PCphone.

"Nanoeyes are merged with nanoscanners for your body. They can scan and see through any material and they work with nanodrones, correct?"

"Yes. Shit, voice mail," he says in a frustrated tone.

"So you are wearing perfume for patients now huh?" Jaden asks while handing back her phone.

Kimberly blushes, "Maybe. But only for special patients."

"Hmmm...you are looking good in your blue jeans and light blue blouse, doctor"

"You are looking good in your dress shirt and creamy dress pants. Where did you get them?"

"From someone at the airport."

"So, I'm glad you were finally able to access the Internet. Did they turn it back on?" She asks.

"No, I had to find it, there was wireless Internet in the basement. Wireless Internet, did you know this was for employees there?" Jaden asks.

"No, I didn't know they had it for employees. This was my first time at that hospital, I'm assuming it was probably allowed on the weekend. Wireless Internet is almost everywhere these days, I didn't think about you trying that," Kimberly says.

"No, when I was last on Earth, Internet was connected through wires only."

'Are you okay, AI buddy?' Jaden asks.

'Yes, I'm fine, just learning human interaction and doing some calculations,' AI says.

"Jaden, what is going on, did you really fall from an airplane? Where did you get a parachute?" She asks.

"Three hours and ten minutes to Raleigh international Airport, 201 miles to destination. Please drive the highlighted route," the robotic female navigation voice says.

"I used my nanodrones and some other drones to disrupt the gravity around me, to land on the ground, to rescue Lopez. I didn't have a parachute. It was very dangerous, but I knew I could do it. I wanted to see what the nanodrones could do also," Jaden says.

"That was dangerous, you are needed for this impending attack on Earth. You can't risk your life like that. What happened to the guy who opened the emergency exit?"

"He exploded on impact, big mess," Jaden says.

"Jesus, poor guy. Listen Jaden, all of this is happening so fast. What you did to me was something I've never felt or experienced before. After I left the hospital and I was driving to the airport, your memories became more real. As the hours went by, I remembered so many more things about you. I heard all the funny jokes you said over the past nineteen years of your life. What is going on with me? I can remember more details about your life than I can remember from my own life. I'm having these feelings as if I've known you for all my life. The feelings feel very real, but the detailed images when you left Earth are confusing. It was like watching a good sci-fi movie. There are conflicts with reality and my imagination. I told my father about what happened. He doesn't believe any of this and was on his way to talk to me at my house, before I left to meet you an hour ago. He wants me to stay away from you. But I had to see you and help you to see if you were okay," she says.

"As long as you believe me, that is really what is important. I've been having feelings for you also. I've learned so much about you in such a short period of time. Things have been a little confusing for me also because in reality I've only known you for only the past three days. I actually saw your birth and watched you grow up. I learned everything you like and dislike. I found out what type of person you are in ten minutes, where as it would have taken ten years to learn all those things about you," Jaden says.

"I think the future of dating might be this way. But I think we should concentrate on what is at hand now and try to save people we care about. Notifying the correct government agencies about these nanomoles in humans' brains should be a priority. I was able to locate what I believe is the alien protein in my office not far from where I live. The microscope I used isn't as good as the prototype 4D atom force microscope in another office that requires special permission. My colleagues will verify my findings and they will forward it to my boss if it is the alien nanomole we have been looking for. My boss will forward it to the proper authorities," she says.

"How long will it take for your colleagues to verify the findings?" He asks.

"Hopefully by Monday or Tuesday," she says.

"Tuesday might be too late, a countdown was started the second you went unconscious at the hospital and I caught you."

"Oh, yeah, the countdown. That's not good."

"I know…on Flight 104, every passenger was in the neutral nanomole state. That was stage 2. None of them were responsive. I think the mother ship is getting closer and closer every day. I need to find my daughter, find my parents, and try to deactivate manually as many nanomoles as possible," Jaden says.

"Okay. I'm scared Jaden. This whole alien attacking thing reminds me of the movies I've watched over the years; *Independence Day, War of the Worlds, The Day the Earth Stood Still,* and *V.* Aliens attacking Earth is really scary, so many people can die."

"Don't be scared; I'll protect you."

"Do you mean that?" She asks.

"Yes I do. These aliens are much smarter than the aliens in those movies. Do you remember the D.E.K. on Planet 455?" Jaden asks.

"It sounds familiar…yes, I do. The dark energy knight that couldn't be destroyed?" She asks.

"Yes. Imagine one of those on this planet. That is a powerful alien enemy you can't find in any of those movies. I would never want to be face to face with one of those creatures. That thing would rip Superman apart," he says.

"Turn right onto I-95 expressway ramp and keep right on highway," the navigation computer says.

"Yes, you have a point there. That thing looked scary. Those eerie dark flames make it seem as if it was on fire, but in another dimension."

"That is the HSCCVL system in the left lane, correct?" Jaden asks.

"Yes, they call it CCL, short for computer controlled lane. Only certain vehicles with that expensive system in their vehicles can drive in that lane. Like for example this vehicle," Kimberly says.

"Drive twenty-four miles south on Interstate 95, then take I-85..."

"Cool," Jaden says.

"From me learning your personality and likes in such a short period of time, you want us to drive in the CCL lane, right?" Kimberly asks.

"You know me, oh so well," Jaden says while smiling as he sees a car quickly passing by at 90 mph in the CCL.

She inches over into the middle lane and then the left. Signs are passing over for entrance to the CCL lane.

"Looks just like a HOV lane," Jaden says.

She drives into the entrance lane, infrared signals go back and forth with her SUV and the highway signs overhead. A small transparent screen shows up on the glass of the windshield.

"HSCCVL system activated, your vehicle will drive in this lane for twenty-two miles, to exit 51. Please relax and enjoy your ride," the navigation system says in the car speakers.

The steering wheel begins to slowly move back and forth by itself. The SUV quickly picks up speed as Jaden looks around in amazement.

"Wow, look at your face. That is the same look you had on your face when your parents bought you your first car two years ago, I mean twenty years ago. Then your father snapped the picture of your face with his Polaroid camera," she says.

"You remember that? Wow. I remember that," he says.

"You looked so cute in that picture," she says while completely turning towards Jaden to give her full attention.

The SUV reaches ninety-seven miles an hour. Jaden looks at the transparent screen as he sees ZZ rated tire pressures, rear vehicle distance 480 feet and front vehicle distance 907feet.

"The steering wheel driving by itself reminds me of episodes of *Knight Rider*. You don't feel nervous keeping your eyes completely off the road?" He asks.

"No. This system is completely safe, I use it all the time. *Knight Rider*? *Knight Rider* started coming on in 2008, how do you remember those episodes if you weren't on this planet then," she says in a questioning voice.

"What are you talking about 2008? *Knight Rider* came on in the eighties with KITT."

"*Knight Rider* came on in 2008, I was in college when I watched the new episodes every week," she says while looking at his eyes.

'Damn, she looks so sexy when she thinks she knows what she is talking about,' Jaden says to AI.

"I watched the new episodes of *Knight Rider* when I was in kindergarten that was in 1982, if I recall. I watched all the episodes," Jaden says.

"Okay we will solve this now, I can look it up on the Internet," she says.

"Well, why don't we make a wager?" He asks.

"Sure, what do I get if I win?" She asks.

They look into each other's eyes.

'Jaden if you are thinking about a kiss from her as the prize for winning this wager, why not just tell her that,' AI asks.

'I don't want to come on that strong, I don't know if she might think that is inappropriate.'

'This is confusing to me, your hormone levels are high, her hormone levels are fluctuating…' AI says.

'It is a timing thing, relationships are complicated with humans. Also, all these new feelings I have for her and the new feelings she has for me are new to both of us. So I think the best decision is to take things at her speed,' Jaden says to AI.

"Well?" She asks, "What do you think the wager should be?"

"How about if I win, you buy me something to eat later. If you win, I'll, I'll…give you a back massage," Jaden says.

'I'll kiss you all over your body, if I win,' Jaden says to AI while chuckling to himself.

'With all those germs on her body? Do you see the bacteria all over her skin?' AI asks.

"Okay, that sounds fair," Kimberly says while pressing the eight-inch LCD screen in the center console.

Jaden chuckles to himself and says, 'AI, you have a lot to learn about humans. You are funny though, now you want me to see her naked again.'

'Looking at trillions of microscopic bacteria on the skin isn't being a pervert.'

'Yeah, yeah. I'll do a good job disinfecting her.'

"Welcome to Voice Goojjletron search engine. Please say what you want to look up," the LCD screen says.

"*Knight Rider* TV show aired on TV when?" Kimberly asks.

"Goojjletron search 0.10 seconds. The original *Knight Rider* aired on TV from 1982-1986 and had ninety episodes..." the female computer voice says.

"You see! I told you!" Jaden yells while clapping his hands together.

"What the hell?" She asks.

"...A new *Knight Rider* series ran in 2008-2009..."

"Ha Ha!" She yells while snapping her fingers, "You see, it did come on in 2008 again."

"I guess we were both right," Jaden says.

'I remember from her memory she watched *Knight Rider*, but I thought she was watching the reruns. I thought she just didn't know what she was talking about,' Jaden says.

"So, can I have my massage?" She asks.

"Sorry the bet was a draw. I believe that is your leather seat's job," Jaden says in a sarcastic voice.

A frown appears across her face, "Are you serious?"

"I'm kidding sweetie, it will be my pleasure. I'll massage your tasty back," he says while she turns around and faces her window.

She turns back around and asks, "What did you say?"

"I said, I can't wait to massage your healthy back," he says with a smirk on his face and she turns back towards her window.

The speed on the windshield reaches 101 mph. Kimberly leans back while Jaden massages her back.

'Jaden, there is a guy sitting in the driver's seat of a SUV about 500 feet behind us and a small woman is on top of him. I think she is stuck, she is making all kinds of noises,' AI says.

'That is good to know,' Jaden says while enjoying touching Kimberly's soft shoulders and smelling her perfume. Her scent and physical contact is arousing him. Kimberly is enjoying the feel of a human hand touching her body.

'Would you like to see this through the nanoscanner Jaden? I think the lady is in trouble. Maybe we can help her?' AI asks.

'Nah, I'm good. How about you record it for me,' Jaden says in a trance.

'He isn't helping her up. She is trying to get up, but she is stuck. She is somehow glued to his skin I believe...'

85

'He is trying to kill her with a deadly weapon between his legs,' Jaden sarcastically replies.

'He is? That isn't good, we have to do something. Batman and Robin?' AI asks excitedly.

'AI, calm down, no need to send more nanoscanners to investigate. They are just having sex, AI, practicing reproducing or reproducing. The same thing I want to do right now, practice.'

'But why would they do this while their car drives in the CCL lane?' AI asks.

'AI, I'll explain it to you later, I'm concentrating here. Go look in my memory and see all the wild places I've had sex at.'

"Okay, that's enough. That was very good, Thanks," Kim says while turning around towards the road.

'Her body is giving off chemical hormone messages!' AI yells.

'I know, I can smell them with my super nose.'

"Manual drive in one mile, manual drive in one mile," the female computer voice says.

"Get some rest, I know you had a tough and long morning," she says.

"Okay," he says while closing his eyes.

Some soft music plays in the background.

'Jaden, your pituitary gland was sending extra chemical hormones around your body as if you were ready to mate. Extra blood was going to your reproductive organ.'

'I can't mate when I feel like it. It's a timing thing, AI. It isn't as simple as with animals. I'm also not trying to reproduce with her, even if I had the chance. I wouldn't mind practicing though,' Jaden says.

'That is a waste of 250 million sperm and is murder on the colony of microscopic organisms. Isn't it bad enough leukocytes in the uterus kill off 249 million sperm?' AI asks.

Jaden laughs out loud. Kimberly turns to Jaden, "What's so funny Jaden?"

"AI is sounding like a mental patient. We are having a conversation about….about science."

"Oh okay, a man to alien conversation, gotcha. Tell him I said hello."

86

'AI, do you hear yourself? Do you hear how crazy you sound? Murdering a colony of sperm, by practicing reproducing," Jaden says.

'Yes, that is worst than genocide of a million humans and worst than 250 million abortions.'

'AI, sperm aren't people or an animal. They are on the level of bacteria or skin cells. 99.99% are going to die anyway, even when it is reproducing time. They are like frontline infantry; they know they going to die and they all aren't going to reach the egg. If they had a brain they would go after the egg only when I tell them too.'

'Look at the billions and billions of them all piled together in your testicles. They can't wait to get out and start the marathon race....'

'I don't care to see, don't show me. If you are so concerned about them AI, why don't you and some nanodrones go down there and reprogram every one of them to race when I give the command?' Jaden asks.

'Maybe I will,' AI snaps, 'I'm in the saving any life-form mood.'

'AI, I think you need to reset your computer brain, you are losing your logic. One of them made it to the finish line eighteen years ago and look at the problems I have now. Eighteen years of child support for one stupid sperm. I want to go back in time and vaporize that lucky sperm. I don't want any more kids now. Us humans practice reproducing most of the time, which is called sex or making love. It is a wonderful feeling to have with the opposite sex or same sex. But I wouldn't know if it was the same with the same sex. I'm assuming it feels the same way for gay men. Okay, I'm confusing myself. The point is, sperm are troublemakers and deserve whatever happens to them. Anyways, I'm done talking about this. Wake me up when we get there,' Jaden says while making the seat recline with the massager on.

WASHINGTON, D.C. WHITE HOUSE 11:45 AM

"Shit! Shit! Shit!" Robinson yells while slamming down the phone.

"What happened, sir?" Peters asks sitting in the seat in front of Robinson's desk.

Robinson opens his desk and opens a package of pills. He swallows some down without any water.

"My hemorrhoids are flaring, my blood pressure is high and this situation has more fairy tale stories than Disney. I've never heard so much bullshit in my forty-five years in the military. I think the government should reinstate lie detector tests for all government, federal and state employees. Someone is on some drugs here. I have government official witnesses saying they saw a halo angel ring around the nose of Flight 104 landing. The F-22 pilot says he was magically lifting the left wing of the plane so it could land. Passengers magically waking up at the same time twenty minutes after the plane lands. The pilot landed the airplane then he goes unconscious and is instantly brain dead," Robinson says in a loud voice.

"Is the FBI analyzing his body?

"No, I have someone from my team there, so there aren't any more screw-ups," he says.

"Who did you send?"

"I sent my Commander-in-chief Max Miles to be in charge of the investigation," Robinson says with a smile on his face

"That guy had three psychiatric evaluations done on him in the last ten years. He has suffered from TBI (traumatic brain injuries) in the past and has gotten innocent civilians killed on duty. This man came back from the Iraq War damaged and unstable," Peters says.

"But he gets the job done and he does exactly what I say."

"Have you notified the President on all of this?"

"No, not yet. She is enjoying the day with her family in New York," Robinson says.

"Are you sure this is wise, sir? The President doesn't like this guy," Peters says.

"Listen Peters, I've known you for a long time. You have always been my most logical, family oriented, intelligent officer, friend and advisor. Trust me on this one, I know what I'm doing. This little cocksucker Jaden Marino is the enemy of this country. I've talked to some friends in the senate, you are definitely going to have enough votes for the secretary of defense position available. So take it easy, go home and be with your family this weekend."

"I'm going to look into this possible alien attack with these clues I keep getting from my military personnel. Just in case something bigger is about to happen," Peters says.

"There is no alien attack happening. Just this alien roach Jaden, that is here to spread his alien babies around and to make me look like an asshole again."

Peters walks towards the door and turns around.

"Do you believe the story that F. Lopez, the air marshal onboard fell off out the emergency exit with Jaden Marino and a third person?" Peters asks.

"That he landed in the water and survived the fall. He witnessed Jaden Marino landing in the woods and dying. But he doesn't know where the third mental patient landed. My team is doing a quick DNA analysis of the area where the body landed. So no, I don't believe his story. Max Miles will be interrogating him soon. He is a walking lie detector," Robinson says, while laughing and General Peters walks out of the office.

Robinson turns on the television and he sees BNN news showing an E-reporter video of a glowing ring around the front of Flight 104.

"As you can see from this amateur photo from a local E-reporter, there is a halo angel ring around troubled Jetgreen Flight 104 today. Sources say it had a damaged left engine and was having trouble landing. The passengers and crew onboard all fell asleep from some mysterious gas. They have all since woke up, while the pilot who landed the plane is reported as still unconscious. Witnesses are saying an angel was around the doomed flight as it looked like it was about to crash. Religious witnesses are saying it was a miracle and a sign from God. Experts are saying the flight was flying at a low 140 mph, which is impossible to keep lift with a aircraft that size..." he turns off the television and closes his eyes.

"Sometimes I wish I could be Professor Xaviar from X-men, so I can control the media and civilians' minds..."

RALEIGH, NC, 5 MILES FROM THE AIRPORT 12:45 PM

A talk radio show is on satellite radio. Kimberly is listening to an ex-politician named Andrew Richards talk about his affair that

89

caused his marriage to end a few years ago. A female interviewer named Tammy Cornwell is interviewing him live.

"Men in general are very likely to cheat in a relationship and marriage. Men like myself with power and money are ninety-one percent likely to cheat on their wives. It's a fact that only fifteen percent of these men are actually being caught. Here are my examples: Look at President Clinton in 1997 with his affair with Lewinsky; Mayor of New York City Rudy in 1999, an affair while he was married; Governor McGreevey of New Jersey cheated with a man in 2000; New York Governor Spitzer cheated with an escort in 2008; Governor Sanford of South Carolina cheated on his wife in 2009; Senator John Edwards in 2007 and professional golfer Tiger Woods in 2009. All these married men were tired of their wives and wanted more sexually. This only represents a fraction of the men with power that actually got caught," Richards says excitedly.

"You have a good point there, retired Senator Richards. Give us women an inside understanding as to why men with power and in general, seek sex outside their marriage," she says.

"My political career is already over, so I'm going to break it down for you and tell you how men think. It's not just men with power, it's average men as well. Most men want a trophy wife at home and girlfriends/flings on the side. The girlfriends/flings usually aren't more good looking than their trophy wife. Let's just say I'm married and I have all this money and power, why should I be stuck having sex with the same boring woman forever? My wife was good for reproducing with and taking care of my kids. Many men, including myself, get tired of having sex with the same woman. They want something new to penetrate and to experience. There is a very strong sexual excitement with a new female. A different female has a different smell, different taste, different vaginal feeling when penetrating the first few times and a different personality. Men's brains are sexually stimulated with a new female. It is beyond exciting for a man to be intimate with someone new, that I can't even attempt to explain to you. Us men want our wives at home and freaks on the side. It is a fact that escorts and hookers get eighty percent of their revenue from married men. This clearly backs up my opinion that men want more. "

"Are you saying it's okay for men to cheat on their wives if they get bored with them?" Tammy asks.

"I'm not saying it's okay to do this, but this is what ends up happening anyway. Sex is everywhere these days; it's on the Internet, on television, in movies, in video games and everywhere we look. Society tells these men that a skinny younger female is sexy. A young trophy girlfriend or wife is what most older men seek these days. Society also tells us that a freaky young female is beautiful and something you must have. My ex-wife got older and bigger and society tells us that is not attractive. Money and power drive our egos, so we make it happen no matter how much it costs. Men like myself love nasty things in the bedroom, things they would never want the mother of their kids to do. Sex was in my face all the time, when I was away from my family fundraising or running for office. Basketball players, football players, rappers, actors and public figures experience this all the time. Most men would risk having sex with a stranger even if it risked their marriage with their wives," Richards says.

"Most would?"

"Yes most, because most men don't think they would get caught. We do it with a clear conscious and think we will get away with it, just like a criminal thinks he will get away with a crime at the time he is committing it," Richards says.

"But you got caught and now you are divorced. Was it worth it?" She asks.

"In the end, it isn't worth it. I wish I could have turned off this infectious sexual disease of wanting another female while I was married. I miss being with my wife and kids."

"But instead of helping to solve the problem and speaking out on men staying faithful and loyal to their wives, you are doing the opposite," she snaps.

"That is correct, speaking out on the problem isn't going to solve anything. Sex is everywhere these days and men will always cheat. Cheating dates back to the biblical times. Cheating is an infectious disease and is more addictive than smoking cigarettes. The goal of men like myself is to get the female into a position where we can get away with our cheating ways. 1. Get them pregnant with kids. This would keep her occupied with the household duties and doing most of the raising of the kids. 2. Keep control in the household, be the main breadwinner. 3. Strip away

91

their self-esteem. 4. Keep her in denial of any wrongdoing. 5. Get her in a position where she can't leave you. 6. LIE. Deny and lie about any accusations she accuses you of."

"That sounds like the recipe for a certified narcissist."

"Does it?" He asks.

"I'm sure there are going to be plenty of men upset with you giving away the universal narcissist game plan."

"This younger generation of men just isn't getting married these days and instead has relationships with technology. They aren't getting themselves in these situations in the first place."

"You know divorce court judges are making mostly men take the fMRI lie detector 2.0 in court to verify if cheating occurred in the relationship," she says.

"There are ways to beat that test."

"Moving on, you and many of your political friends are lobbying congress to pass the 2015 special marriage license?" Tammy asks.

"That is correct. The rules of marriage are outdated and were created before Jesus was born. To solve the problem with infidelity, we are introducing a new bill called Marriage Contract 2015 into congress. The special marriage license would cost $100,000 for five years of marriage and $200,000 for 10 years. When the time is up, each party will have to agree to renew, similar to a lease renewal on an apartment or vehicle. The money goes to the federal government or state as a special tax. Up to ten percent of the husband's salary goes into a special trust fund for the wife and/or kids for the future. That doesn't include normal support of the family or wife. Men are allowed to have another woman or female robot on the side. The wife will be fully aware of this before she gets married. Kids will be covered under a special insurance coverage. Safe sex only is allowed and the wife can sue if she catches a STD…."

"So the Marriage Contract bill is pretty much a hired sex nanny for reproducing kids?"

"Pretty much, yes. Less political shame for the man, family, wife and kids. The mistress can't go public with their affair, because everything will be perfectly legal. The men with this special marriage license can legally sue their mistress for going public. Do you know how many mistresses are paid millions to be quiet about their affairs with these men? They have their own Myfacebook fan base called, 'Paid Mistresses.' These leeches are retiring for life after having these affairs. They also try very hard to get pregnant by these men and that is like a huge bonus payout that last up to twenty-two years. When are these men going to evolve passed this? This same cycle of ignorance has been happening for many years. I say legalize cheating, just like marijuana was legalized and taxed in 2012. Legalizing marijuana helped get the country out of its recession. This Marriage Contract bill will do the same and already has over 8000 men interested in buying the license. Basketball, football, baseball players, R&B singers, politicians, bankers and CEOs make up this quickly growing list. $100,000 times 8000 men would bring in over eight billion dollars minimum..."

Kimberly is driving and shakes her head in disappointment at what ex-senator Richards was discussing in the interview. Jaden wakes up from his deep nap, feeling a sensation on his back and around his body. He looks around and clears his eyes. He sees 1.5 billion nanodrones returned and retrieved on his eye screen.

"Did you hear the conversation on the radio Jaden?" She asks in an upset tone.

"No, I didn't."

"That man is destroying the foundation of marriage. Marriage is suppose to be about trust, honesty, commitment, compromise, love, loyalty and a lifetime connection with one partner. Marriage requires hard work just like a full time job. How dare he try to change the rules because he can't keep his schlong in his pants? How can a child grow up knowing his father is allowed to sleep with as many women as he wants? Where does this end? Technology is already messing up the foundations between men and women. Why can't a single man in his twenties have all the freaky sex he wants with as many women as he wants? Then in his thirties, he gets married, stays faithful and raises a family the way humans were intended too?" She asks.

"What did I miss? I don't know sweetie. I don't see why a man can't be faithful to one woman. Marriage is a serious bond between a man and a woman, the way God intended."

"I'm sorry Jaden, I go on a rant sometimes. I get angry when I hear men trying to excuse their infidelity and blame society for their problems."

"It's okay, don't worry about it. I understand your points," he says.

"I have a solution to solve their infidelity issues. When a man gets married, his sperm should be frozen at a sperm bank. If he is caught cheating on his wife, his penis should be chopped off and frozen. He can urinate through a tube and won't have to worry about cheating again. That will make men want to control their urges and be faithful. Problem solved."

"Wow, that was direct, but painful. I felt your pain and so did my little friend between my legs. Wow Kimberly, that would really make men think before cheating."

"I am a new generation of women and we women need to empower ourselves. It's the year 2018, we deserve respect and honesty. We aren't sex nannies for reproducing. It's been ninety-four years since women won the right to vote in America and we are still fighting for equal pay and not being seen as a sex object!" She yells angrily. Jaden stares at her speechless as she continues, "It's bad enough us females have to freeze our eggs in our early twenties, finish college and have a strong career before we can use those same eggs in our late thirties. Most of us are just going to the fertility bank and using a sperm donor to fertilize our eggs to be single parent!"

Jaden sees how red Kim's face is becoming and how heavy she is breathing. He thinks back to Kim's memories and remembers she froze her eggs 2 years ago.

"I understand your points. Take it easy, take a breath, I respect you. Um… so…on another note, where are we?" Jaden asks while looking out the window.

Kimberly takes some deep breaths and calms down.

"About a mile and a half from the airport on Highway 540. We had to detour around Route 85, there was a forest fire in Falls Lake State Park," Kimberly says.

"I hope no one got hurt," Jaden says.

'AI, what's going on, you found the nanodrones already?'

'Yes, I just found him. I've been looking for the pilot's body for the past hour. They moved him into a truck covered in lead and another strong metal material I couldn't identify. I didn't think to look in the lead truck right away, because it is hard for just one nanoscanner to look through a lead truck.'

"Where should I go, Jaden?" Kimberly asks.

'Why can't one nanoscanner pass through lead? I thought they could pass through anything?' Jaden asks.

'To penetrate that thick lead, these weaker nanoscanners, made to work with your human body, need at least three combined to penetrate something that thick. They also can't do 4D x-ray scans through the lead from the outside of it. Something with the compounds and molecules in that lead. One nanoscanner from the Gravhawk can penetrate lead a few feet thick.'

'Okay.'

"Hello? Earth to Jaden?" Kimberly asks again while smiling waving her hand in front of his dazed eyes, "Are you talking to your AI friend hidden in the multiple personalities area of your brain?"

Jaden multi-tasks while listening to AI's story.

"How did you know I was talking to AI?" He asks.

'So I continued checking the entire airport without finding the body. Then I tried to think more randomly and outside the box. I thought, why would there be a lead truck here and I was curious to what was inside…'

"Your face looks as if you are listening to something and you look occupied," she says.

'…Then I found the pilot unconscious and hooked up to a respirator with a man with an all white body suit covered around his body. It was a similar white suit to the white suits that were around the Gravhawk back on Earth when…'

'AI, keep to the story, I know what an all white body suit looks like.'

"Tell him I said hello for me," she says.

"I'll tell him, it looks like he retrieved the nanodrones and nanoscanner from the pilot's body already. He was telling me the story how he did it while I was sleeping," Jaden says.

"Okay."

'So I activated the nanodrones and nanoscanner in his body, but I couldn't get the nanodrones through the lead. Then the truck began to drive away. I didn't want to lose the truck and the nanodrones. I was too busy calculating how far I could follow the truck. But then I started thinking randomly and outside the box. I used my artificial imagination. I got the nanodrones to go back into their positions in the pilot's body they were at on the airplane. The three nanoscanners had to keep going in and out of the truck to relay the messages back to me, since the communication pathway couldn't penetrate the lead. So I programmed the nanoscanner in the pilot's brain to do this creative task I came up with...'

'Okay, okay, keep going,' Jaden says.

'Can you guess?' AI asks.

'I don't feel like guessing,' Jaden says.

'Humans like to guess things like this, am I correct?' AI asks.

'Okay, I'll guess. You zapped the guy sitting with the pilot in the truck?' He asks.

'No, you told me it isn't good to hurt other humans if you can avoid it. I got the unconscious pilot to jump up screaming, saying he needed fresh air and to stop the truck. He was touching all over the young man like a scary zombie movie. He was also yelling he was claustrophobic, I found that word in the medical encyclopedia,' AI says.

'That is funny, very funny and creative. Good work AI,' Jaden says while chuckling to himself.

'Then the man in the white suit jumped up panicking and radioed to the driver to stop the truck. The backdoor automatically opened and the pilot was walking towards it like a zombie. Then all the nanoscanners made a straight communication pathway to you a few minutes ago. They worked together and fired all the nanodrones back into your body from the pilot's body. The pilot fell backwards onto the man. It was amusing, watching the young man panicking and getting scared out of his mind. He was screaming like a girl and had such a look of terror on his face. I took a photo for you of his face.'

Jaden sees the image of the scared military officer's face and laughs.

'Good job, AI. You see if you change your thinking, how much easier things can be. A little imagination and a little non-linear thinking can come in handy.'

"Can you drive to Halifax, North Carolina?" Jaden asks Kimberly. "Do you think we can make it to a Halifax State Bank before 3 PM?"

"I'll check, most banks usually stay open past 3 PM these days. Halifax State Bank," she says towards the dashboard.

'Kimberly said hello to you AI.'

'Oh okay, tell her greetings,' AI says.

"Halifax State Bank is 89.1 miles northeast. Drive the highlighted area, one hour and twenty minutes is your total driving time," the navigation voice says.

"I'm trying to remember why you have to go to the bank," she says, "I'm remembering, you have to go to the bank because…because your father left money in a safety deposit box for you. You think there could be a message or note inside the safety deposit box and you think he lives in the town somewhere. There is also a chance your daughter and ex lives or is visiting there," she says.

"You are correct. Can I borrow your phone again?" He asks.

"This memory of you is coming in bits and pieces. I feel like I have amnesia and clues are helping me to remember things," she says while passing him the phone.

The phone rings on speakerphone and the voice mail picks up.

"It sounds like she has a pre-paid phone."

Jaden speaks into the phone, "Amy, this is Jaden. Listen I have the money that I owe you. I would like to see my daughter to make sure she is okay. Please call back at this number when you get a chance, I'm in Halifax, North Carolina now, bye."

He passes her the phone back and stretches out to take another nap.

"Relax, sweetie, get some rest," she says.

'I've completed more of your weapons. You now have a counterclockwise shield system, which is also called reverse shields. It has three layers and works similar to the Gravhawk's reverse shield system. The first outside layer slows a fast moving projectile down to a complete stop in a gravity matrix. The second layer is where the projectile or blast particles are analyzed, where it can be recycled into an offensive weapon. Third layer protects the person inside the shield and feels like a solid force. Yes, the second layer works with nanoscanners to determine the material. Forward or clockwise shield was the one you were using at the hospital that destroyed any materials in front of it. But remember, both shields can only absorb so much outside forces at once. The person inside the shield can feel the blunt energy of an object moving fast enough towards it. Yes, meaning the shield doesn't just have to be around you, it can be expanded around a certain circumference around you or another person or object. This and using the outside two layers require more energy. Good question, full body shield is where the shield is fully around your body and around your feet. You will be walking on the inside of the shield like a bubble. The inside will turn and go the direction you are walking and adjust speeds with your mind. In other words, it will feel as if you are on a hamster wheel, but moving in a direction. The nanodrones in the shield will automatically adjust so that it doesn't destroy the ground it is going over,' AI says.

'Interesting.'

'Remember the rpm can be controlled by me or yourself. The faster the rpm the more brain energy and calculations will be needed. I almost forgot. Your left hand will be able to fire an atoms ripper weapon. Yes, I got a little creative with the naming. An atoms ripper is a molecule destroying energy, similar to plasma fusion in the forward shields. Combining the gravity shock wave and atoms ripper can fire a very powerful fast moving projectile...'

Jaden falls asleep, while AI stops talking and continues calculating.

HALIFAX, NC RIGHT SIDE OF BANK PARKING LOT 2:33 PM

The vehicle's door closes as Kimberly gets back in the SUV. A rush of air hits Jaden's body. Jaden wakes up to the familiar scent of food in the air.

"Hey there blue eyes. I got you your favorite. Pastrami on rye, with mustard and cheese," she says while holding a bag towards him.

"How did you....oh okay, I'm still getting used to this new memory thing myself. Thanks," Jaden says while taking the bag and opening it.

"I got you a root beer also."

"Oh thank you sweetie. I haven't had food like this in over eighteen years," Jaden says while stuffing his face.

A few minutes go by. Jaden eats with a smile on his face. The taste from the sandwich is greatly enhanced on his taste buds. He tastes every particle in the sandwich.

"This question was bothering me for the past two days. What is the little device you and other women have at the bottom of their spinal cords?" Jaden asks.

There is silence as Jaden continues eating. He continues to take huge bites while looking at Kimberly blushing.

"Hmmm…shouldn't you know this answer already since you have most of my memories?"

"Certain things I can't remember, like memories that went into your subconscious, certain memories your brain tries to forget or really personal things," Jaden says.

There is a long pause and Jaden asks again, "Well what is it?"

"It is a device that helps a woman have an orgasm. It can be activated remotely or through a cell phone. It is an instant orgasm for some women and others it takes a little time. They work best while having sex. Now you know the answer to your embarrassing question," she says with her head down.

"I'm sorry, I was just curious. Don't be sad," he says while resting his hand on her shoulder.

"How did you know I had that on my lower back?" She asks.

Jaden fumbles his speech, "Um…well…I.. noticed you had one when I was… trying to remove the nanomole… in your brain, back at the hospital. I also checked if you had one in your uterus, because you know they split and wait in the uterus for an offspring," Jaden says nervously.

"Okay, well how did you know other women had one on their lower back?" She asks.

"That is a good question…."

"I think you were using those nanoscanners to look at women and maybe even me without any clothes on," she says with her arms folded.

'You see how looking at women naked can come back and bite you,' AI says.

'Shit, she is doing the arms folded thing. My ex did that. I don't know what to say now,' Jaden says to AI.

"I might have looked at one or two other women without any clothes on, but I would never look at you without any clothes on. I had respect for you from when you first came to my hospital bed," Jaden says while smiling.

Jaden starts to feel a slight pain in his nose.

'AI what are you doing to my nose?'

'I'm stretching it out some, just like Pinocchio's,' AI says.

"That is so sweet for you to say," she says.

'AI, this is not funny, you are behaving too human,' Jaden says while covering his nose.

'Stop it, it hurts.' Jaden demands.

"Are you okay? Do I smell bad or something?" She asks as she sees two hands over his nose.

'Reverse it!'

'You wanted me to act and think more human, right?' AI asks.

"No sweetie, just my nose was hurting a little," he says in a muffled voice.

She rolls down her window some.

"Oh okay, I thought you passed gas and this was your way of warning me or telling me," she says while smiling.

"You aren't hungry?" He asks while drinking his soda and holding his nose.

'You are embarrassing me. Joke over,' he says.

"Nah I'm on a real old school diet, not one of these new anti-fat pill diets and you can eat anything. My father kept texting me and calling me while you were asleep. He wants to know where I am," she says.

"Well I don't want to get you in any trouble with your father," he says while pushing down on his nose.

"He has been overprotective ever since my mother passed away. He is worried about me contacting you, he thinks you are a con artist," she says.

"I'm sorry about your mother dying in the World Trade Center terror attacks," Jaden says.

"Yeah, it's okay. Flight 11 from Boston was the airplane she was on. She was on her way to a client's site in LA. I was living with my parents in New York at the time. Next week will be thirteen years since I lost her."

His nose begins to shrink back to its normal size.

"It sounds like your mother was a good woman, I wish I could have met her," he says.

"She was a great woman. Then my father and I moved to Virginia. He never remarried and told me a good woman you don't try to replace. He loved her so much. They had a special love and he would never cheat on my mother, like these men these days are trying to condone. You should get in the bank before it closes," Kimberly says in a sad tone.

"I was just thinking, I'm going to need some ID right?" Jaden asks while uncovering his nose.

"Banks have bio scan IDs, you can use your fingerprint, retinal scan, DNA scan or voice scan. Some banks require one and some two of these IDs."

"Before I go, I want to finish deactivating your nanomole," Jaden says.

"We have plenty of time for that," she says.

"I just want to get it out of the way now, that thing is very dangerous," he says while her seat goes backwards.

"Just relax, I'm going to put one hand on your forehead and the other near your stomach. You will be unconscious for about ten minutes," Jaden says while placing his hands in those two places.

The nanodrones create an artificial neuron pathway into her brain and uterus area. The pathway looks like layers and layers of spider webs, expanding towards the nanomoles. She feels a tingling sensation as the drones get to work. She closes her eyes and becomes unconscious. A few minutes go by and Jaden removes his hands. He opens the passenger door and stands outside. The warm summer air hits his body. The smell of pine trees engulfs his nostrils. He looks at her before he closes the door. He admires her beauty while she naps in peace. Jaden closes the SUV door and walks to the bank's front entrance. As he enters, a cherry scent tickles his nose hairs. An armed security guard by the door looks Jaden up and down. There are about ten customers in the bank, doing various transactions. There is a line for the teller, but Jaden walks towards the bank officers sitting at the desk. There are three other banking officers sitting at desk in the small bank.

'AI, don't embarrass me like that again. Men have to lie sometimes to save a female's feelings and to not make me look like a pervert. I can't tell her I looked at her without any clothes on. How would that help me to be with her, if she knew I did that?' He asks.

'Okay, I understand. I think I'm evolving a human sense of humor. It's kinda funny, something you would probably do if you were me,' AI says.

"Can I help you today sir?" An older white haired man asks with a southern accent.

"Yes, I'm here to take belongings from a safety deposit box in my name," Jaden says.

'He looks like the KFC Colonel,' AI says.

'AI, enough. Turn the sense of humor program off. I need a straight face now. It is serious time. I don't need to be laughing in this older man's face.'

"Come sit down here, sir. I'm Tom, what is your name?" The bank officer asks while looking at a screen and touching it.

Tom puts a small metal headband around over his head.

"My name is Jaden Marino. I believe my father left a safety deposit box with my name on the account," Jaden says while looking at him confused.

Tom is inputting information into the computer without a keyboard. The screen is facing Tom and Jaden is on the other side of the desk. Jaden uses a nanoscanner to see what he is putting into the screen.

'The device over his head is allowing him to input information into the computer screen wirelessly,' AI says.

'That is amazing, it is reading the impulse signals from his brain. Record the signal wavelength that the device is reading from his brain,' he says.

"Okay, sir I found it. A Tony Marino left a safety deposit box and its contents to a Jaden Marino back in March 2006. The safety deposit box is still here and it has been paid for until the year 2026. Now we just need some ID to prove you are Jaden Marino," Tom says.

"I don't have any plastic ID on me," Jaden says.

"Well, sir let me check in the system to see what other bio ID's are on file here," Tom says while his eyes go back and forth on the screen.

"It shows a Mr. Tony Marino came back in 2012 to update the account with hair DNA and a fingerprint for a Mr. Jaden Marino. We will need two bio ID's. Can you provide these today?" Tom asks.

"Yes sir, colonel sir," Jaden says while thinking about the DNA ID.

'You just called him Colonel,' AI says.

'I know I said that, you have that KFC Colonel comment stuck in my head now. Every time I look at this guy.'

"I'll be right back with the DNA ID machine," Tom says.

'AI, tell me you can duplicate some original DNA from me,' Jaden says.

'That is going to be near impossible. Your DNA molecules have all been modified. Once it leaves your body, they self implode. However, your sperm is modified to last longer outside your body, but it is encoded in open air and not coded inside of a body. Some have built in GPS type of systems and they know where they are at all times.'

'Great, my sperm can give me directions to where the vaginal hole is if I get lost,' Jaden snaps.

'At least you have built in birth control. Your sperm can be turned off from working without any side effects,' AI says.

'What am I going to do? Jerk off in a cup and hope the DNA works?' Jaden asks.

'How about this, I'm going to scan the safe area behind the tellers with the nanoscanners to find out where your safety deposit box is and to see if there is anything inside of it,' AI says.

'Very good idea. It feels good having a creative mind right?' Jaden asks.

'Yes, it makes me feel more helpful.'

"Okay sir, put your thumb in here," Tom says.

Jaden feels the skin on his thumb moving. Jaden puts his right thumb on the ID machine.

'What was that in my thumb?' Jaden asks.

'I had to adjust your fingerprint to your original fingerprint. So humans couldn't identify you,' AI says.

'Okay.'

The machine beeps a green color.

"ID checked out sir, just one more," Tom says.

"Is there any other test besides the DNA test, I can take?" Jaden asks.

"No, your father only left two for this account. If you were here at the time he did it, then you could have put your voice, face or eyes in the system. Hair or cheek swab?" Tom asks.

"Both."

'Jaden you are wasting your time.'

'I'm buying some time to think of something.'

Jaden hands a few pieces of hair from his head and gives it to the bank officer. He rubs the Q-tip in the back of his mouth and gives it Tom. The bank officer puts it in a small machine that is six inches square and looks like a scanner for a computer. Tom looks on the computer screen and sees a probability DNA match of zero percent.

"Sorry sir, verification is not a match. We can't open your safety deposit box today," Tom says.

"Listen sir, the fingerprint scan worked fine. Maybe something is wrong with the machine today. But I am Jaden Marino," he says.

"Do you have a photo ID, passport, birth certificate, Social Security RFID?" Tom asks in an annoyed voice.

'There is money and a note in the safety deposit box inside of the safe. I can't read what the note says from here, it is folded a few times.'

"No, I don't. I told you what I had when I came in here," Jaden says while raising his voice. Customers standing in the teller line look in Jaden's direction. The big guard at the door turns his head in Jaden's direction.

"Then sorry, sir, I cannot help you. Have a good day," he says in a nasty voice while putting the bio ID machines away.

"I'm not going anywhere, until I get the contents of my safety deposit box that my father left me. I want to speak to the manager," Jaden says in a loud tone while hitting the desk.

'Jaden your blood pressure is going high and some of those weird energy particles are coming towards your body and disappearing into your brain. Let's just leave and come back another time.'

'Not now AI,' he says.

"I am the manager, now sir, are you going to leave or I'm going to have to call security," Tom says.

Instantly Jaden's offensive and defensive weapons and energy strengths show up on his eye screen. He looks Tom directly in the eyes. Tom gets nervous and signals for the armed security man at the door while stepping back. Tom begins to sweat on his forehead as Jaden gives him a bad feeling.

"I proved to you who I am and I want what belongs to me," Jaden says in an angry voice while standing and hitting the table. His seat is a few inches behind his legs.

'What are you doing?' AI asks.

'I'm getting what belongs to me, by any means necessary. I'm not letting anything on this planet stop me,' Jaden says to AI.

'You have to calm down sir, think of the consequences to these actions you are thinking about committing. Those strange energy particles are messing with your logical thinking and decision making.'

The tall 6'6" security guard stands three feet behind Jaden and asks, "Sir, you were asked to leave, can you please leave this bank?"

Jaden continues to face Tom, while Tom stands behind his seat.

"Mr. Tom, I'm asking you nicely one last time to bring my safety deposit box out here or someone might get hurt. If you don't want your insurance to get higher and severe damage to your nice safe, I would suggest you bring what belongs to me," Jaden says.

"Sir, I'm not going to ask you again!" The mid-thirties white male guard yells, but his voice sounds choppy to Jaden as if he is talking behind a fan.

Everyone in the bank is watching, even the tellers inside of a hard plastic and metal closed off area.

"Mr. Security Guard working for $12.50 an hour, if you don't want to wake up in the ICU or heaven I would suggest you stay out of my way and back away behind me," Jaden says while staring Tom   directly   in   the   eyes.

The edge of the seat behind Jaden's legs begins to slowly evaporate. The lights begin to dim and flicker. The guard reaches out with two hands towards Jaden's shoulders. His fingers, then hands are instantly disintegrated. Tom walks backwards with a petrified look on his face. The security guard begins to yell and scream in pain as he gets down on his knees. Blood begins to pour out of the end of his wrists. An rpm of 5100 shows up on Jaden's eyes screen. Customers begin yelling and screaming. Jaden walks over towards the door to where the tellers are in.

"We don't want any trouble!" Tom the manager yells while walking to help the security guard. Customers run out of the bank.

Jaden concentrates on his energy shield rpm around his body. The locked door's molecules strips away and he slowly walks through the door making a narrow oval shape. The lights go out in the building. The three tellers push buttons under their teller windows and quickly run out of the door on the other side. An alarm goes off. Jaden faces the safe and the nanoscanners scan the safe materials a second time. He charges his left hand and it glows bright blue. He extends it forward and a ring of blue light charges forward. It makes a one-foot circular hole straight through the safe.

"That worked somewhat. I like that weapon," Jaden says.

He increases his rpm shield speed faster and faster. The lights go completely out and the alarm stops ringing. A slight glow is seen going around him. His rpm shield speed reaches 110,000. He walks within three feet of the huge steel safe. One teller is still scared and hiding under a teller window. She cries and sits under the window looking at Jaden glowing.

"I would suggest you get out of here young lady, you might get hit by some debris. We wouldn't want your student loans not paid because you are in the hospital," Jaden says while his voice sounds like he is behind a wall talking to her. He has a smiling face and speaks with a southern accent.

She gets up and runs out the other door.

"Thank you," she says.

'Jaden you aren't thinking like your normal self,' AI says.

'I'm myself, I gave them another option, and they didn't want to choose the one I gave them. So now their insurance is going to have to suffer. I'm going to crack this piggy bank safe,' he says with a smile on his face.

His rpm reaches 150,000 and sounds of something charging are heard. The shield energy changes from being completely around him to on the sides of him. The shield generating nanodrones concentrate most of their energy on the sides around Jaden's body like an oval doorway shape. Jaden walks forward to within two feet of the safe. The shield begins to cut through the outside of the six foot round solid steel door, ripping away iron. The less thicker steel outside of the doors of the safe is cut right through. Jaden charges his right hand and a hundred foot circular white smoke extends around the bank. He snaps his right hand forward and a gravity shock wave is released. The loud sound of crushing and ripping metal is heard. The entire building shakes and rumbles like an earthquake. The steel door flings backwards with such force that it goes through another concrete wall. Debris and dust flies in front of his now full body energy shield. Smoke and debris particles make it impossible for his human eyes to see through. He closes his eyes and walks into the safe in the complete dark. He pulls out his safety deposit box and rips it open with his bare hands. The top of the case makes a rattling noise as it hits the floor. He takes out his money and puts it in his pocket. Jaden holds the letter in his hand and walks outside the safe with it, reading it. There is no one in the bank as the sunlight from outside shines in. There is blood on the floor as he casually walks by the desk he was sitting at.

'I think we should go out the back door. On second thought, there is a cop coming around back,' AI says

Jaden sees through a nanoscanner, that it is a black officer. The officer observes half of the steel safe door coming through some of concrete behind the bank.

'Okay, he is a black police officer, maybe he will hear me out. I'll explain to him, that this is my money and I was just taking what belonged to me,' Jaden says.

He quickly walks out the back door to a long alleyway leading up and down the side of the building. He looks up and down at the note written on typical letter paper. A concrete building is on the left side of the alleyway as Jaden walks towards the rear.

'I don't think that is a good idea, he looks edgy and nervous. His heart rate is somewhat high and he is hyperventilating. He has his hand on his gun holster. Your forward shields and gravity shock wave energy is very low. You have some reverse shield strength,' AI says while Jaden reaches the rear of the building.

"Freeze!" The officer shouts while pulling out his gun pointing it at Jaden, twelve feet away from him.

"Listen officer, there is a big misunderstanding here. I was just taking my money out of the bank and this note my father left me," Jaden says while taking another step forward trying to explain.

Suddenly the officer pulls the trigger of his gun and Jaden hears the click. Jaden's mind quickly goes into nanotime.

"Shit!" Jaden slowly yells.

Jaden's reflexes automatically activate the shield, but AI is already ahead of him. Nanodrones are slowly coming out of his back. Nanodrones around Jaden's heart quickly create a small internal forward moving one layer energy shield, that extends through his rib cage and around his arteries; another forms around his skull. Sparks slowly come from the gun as the empty cases fly from the gun. The first bullet comes in slow motion towards Jaden's neck he slowly moves his head to the left. His body isn't moving as fast as his thinking yet. His nanotime meter quickly accelerates from 1x to 10x and then 50x, due to his low energy. The next bullet is coming in lower and towards Jaden's chest. He sees it coming towards his chest. He tries to move to the right, but it hits his left arm. The force from the second bullet makes his left shoulder propel backwards. He groans as the pain travels towards his brain. The officer continues firing and a barrage of 9mm bullets continue towards Jaden. Another hits him in the chest and torso, ripping the note in his hand to pieces. Blood squirts out of his body as the bullet makes an entrance into his skin. The chemical messages in his nerves are slowly moving towards his brain. Blood gets on the ripped pieces of paper as it floats away very slowly. The reverse energy shield creates a slow moving force field around Jaden. But it is not strong enough to slow down the fast moving bullets. The bullets slow down from 850 mph to 500 mph. Nanotime goes off as his brain reaches the maximum time. Seven more miss him and ten hit him in the stomach, ribs, collarbone, neck, chest and arms. The bullet that came straight towards his heart penetrates his skin outside his ribs and is deflected back towards the ground. Three bullets pass completely through his body. The bullets shock his body as his brain is overloaded with pain. He loses his balance and falls backwards. His blood pressure spikes and throbbing pains are felt all over. He falls flat on his back coughing up blood.

Kimberly wakes up to the gunshots and look around the SUV. She doesn't see Jaden and panics. Her head is spinning as she suddenly feels nauseous.

Smoke is coming from the officer's gun after he finishes a full magazine. Jaden lays in traumatic pain as blood fills up his lungs. The gunshot wounds send a burning sensation to his brain. Tissue and cell repairing nanodrones try to coordinate the bombardment of chemical messages flooding his brain. They override the brain trying to make him blackout. The officer puts away his gun and gets on the radio.

"One suspect down, in the back of Halifax State Bank. Please send EMS and more units," the officer says while checking Jaden's pulse on his neck. The officer runs towards the side of the bank and looks inside.

The nanodrones around Jaden's skin quickly seal the bullet holes around his body to stop the bleeding. A clear seal appears around each bullet hole to keep the blood from escaping. Blood can be seen moving inside the clear seal. An army of nanodrones disinfect the eight bullets in his body very quickly. Jaden's lungs aren't breathing, but his heart is still beating. His internal injuries are quickly being repaired.

A few minutes pass by. The unknown energy is around the outside of Jaden's body, quickly moving towards his hands. Jaden's fingertips begin to change to a glowing black color. The exotic black energy quickly destroys the skin around his fingertips. The nanodrones quickly repair the skin around his fingertips and nails.

The officer walks back out where Jaden is and walks pass his body attempting to talk on the radio again. Kimberly is in front of the bank looking for Jaden as more police are seen coming down the street from a distance. She sees the guard screaming with missing hands and bleeding arms.

The bullets in Jaden's legs and arms push through the same clear holes. The other bullets gather together and push towards Jaden's new digestive tract. Damaged tissue cells and nerves quickly repair themselves around his body. Nanodrones temporarily replace fractured bones and torn muscles in his arms and legs. A nanoscanner flies down in an attempt to analyze Jaden's fingertips from the outside. The scanner gets too close to the black gloss and quickly dies. Jaden opens his eyes and tries to stand up as the officer has his back to him. Jaden's fingertips go straight through the grass and dirt, destroying it. Jaden looks at his fingertips in shock and sees this black stuff around it. The black shiny energy quickly goes away.

'What the hell?'

He stands up on his feet still in pain. Jaden sees on his eye screen that a nanoscanner is destroyed.

He looks directly at the cop.

"What kind of cop are you? You shoot an unarmed man trying to explain himself without giving him a warning to put up his hands?" Jaden asks in an angry voice standing while leaning to the side.

Jaden coughs up blood and two bullets.

"Holy shit!" The officer yells while looking at Jaden spit the bullets on the dirt ground.

The officer drops his radio. He reaches for his stun gun and quickly fires it towards Jaden, hitting him in his chest. Jaden doesn't flinch, but takes a step back from the force of the fast moving stun gun. He spits out three more bullets.

"300,000 volts huh? That's all you got?" Jaden asks him while the electricity goes around his body and then into his abdomen.

'AI? AI? Are you there buddy?'

"What kind of police officer shoots a suspect first with a gun and then Tasers him, Officer Anthony Winslow? Did you get your training in the *Police Academy* movie with your brother Michael Winslow?"

The officer drops the stun gun in disbelief and loads his gun with another magazine. The officer is panicking and doesn't respond to Jaden's questions.

"You shoot me again with your gun officer, and I'm going to make you eat your fired bullets," Jaden says with anger in his eyes and his face trembling.

The officer rapidly pulls the trigger with his gun pointed at Jaden's head. Jaden takes a step towards the officer eight feet from him. His reverse energy shield quickly begins to spin. The first bullet comes straight towards Jaden's head and it severely slows down in the gravity matrix. It stops near the middle of his forehead midair.

Kimberly quickly runs towards the bank after hearing more gunshots. Officers pull up across the street from the bank and jump out of their vehicles.

Jaden focuses his eyes on the bullet aiming towards his head. He walks into it and the hot bullet falls towards the ground. The other seventeen bullets are right around each other frozen in midair thirteen inches from Jaden's face. Jaden reaches up and grabs a handful of the hot bullets with his right hand as the shield disappears. They scold his hands. Kimberly is running down the alleyway as her long black hair bounces on her shoulders. A pair of

110

officers run thirty feet behind her and is yelling for her to come back, but she ignores them and run faster.

Jaden tackles the officer and they both hit the muddy grass. The officer screams as the wind is knocked out of his body. All the nanoscanners go inside the officer's motor cortex and medulla oblongata. They release some nanodrones and the officer struggles to get Jaden off him. Jaden puts the handful of hot bullets inside the officer's open mouth.

Officer Winslow begins screaming and hollering as the hot bullets scold his tongue. Kim sees Jaden over the officer and stops running.

"What are you doing to that officer? Get off of him," she yells while running up behind him trying to pull Jaden off the officer.

Two other senior officers approach behind her. They draw guns once they see Jaden over the downed officer. They see Kimberly trying to pull Jaden off the officer. Jaden has a smile on his face as he covers the officer's mouth with his right hand. She pulls on his bloody shirt and can't get a grip. She pulls him back by his arms.

Jaden ignores her and concentrates on the nanodrones making the officer gag and swallow the bullets. The bullets go down Winslow's throat as the nanodrones override his gag reflex in his nervous system.

"Take your medicine Mr. Winslow. I tasted your bullets, I want you know what it tastes like," Jaden says chuckling as Kimberly struggles to pull him away.

"Don't shoot him, don't shoot!" She yells while turning around.

Officer Turner on the left pulls her away, holding her, while Officer Payne on the right tackles Jaden off the choking Officer Winslow. He pepper sprays Jaden in the face and Tasers him in the back.

"Don't hurt him! Cooperate with them, don't resist!" She pleads while being held back. She begins to cry as she sees him being roughed up.

"Okay, okay. I give up, no need to keep kneeing me in my back," Jaden says while listening to Kimberly's crying pleads. He is lying on his stomach, not moving. The nanodrones finish repairing his skin and the clear plastic looking holes disappear. Officer Turner walks and pulls Kimberly by the arm up the alleyway. Jaden places his hands behind his back and the officer handcuffs him.

"You have the right to remain silent...."

Nanodrones and nanoscanners return into Jaden. Jaden sees his weapon systems are offline and his body needs to recalibrate itself. Winslow begins coughing on the ground. The officer walks over to Winslow to see if he is okay. They radio for the ambulance originally for Jaden now for Officer Winslow. Officer Payne removes the wrapped hundred dollar bills from his pockets and places them on the ground. Jaden begins to feel very tired. More officers come in the back along with the EMS.

'AI?'

Jaden thinks about the status of AI. The nanodrones in Jaden's brain run a diagnosis on AI's status. Jaden is stood up by the cops and they walk him down the alleyway towards the front of the bank. His dress shirt is dirty and is open in the middle. His chest shows and his tan pants are dirty with small holes.

"What is he charged with?" She asks while Jaden walks by her at the front of the bank being escorted by Payne to his police car. There is a crowd in front of the bank watching and pointing at Jaden.

"You can find that out at the local jail, ma'am," Payne says.

"They didn't want to give me my money out of my safety deposit box," Jaden says to Kimberly while the officer opens the squad door.

The officer puts Jaden in the police car.

"I'll see you at the police station," she tells him through the window.

Jaden has his head against the back of the seat. He suddenly falls asleep.

Pretzel Burger Frenzy – Pretzel bun, super Action Burger, double bacon, cheddar & pepper jack cheese, tomato, pickles, lettuce, onion ring & spicy mayo. Created by Vlane Carter.

Chapter 19: In Contempt of America

Jaden's body is drained and he desperately needs sleep to recharge his mind and body. He passes out. Officer Payne is driving while Turner is in the passenger seat of the police car on their way to the police station. AI is still not responsive. The nanodrones report AI SCAIN UNIT 5005 OFFLINE IN PROTECTIVE MODE.

"So are you going to tell us your name?" Payne asks Jaden.

There is no response.

"We will find out at the station then buddy," Turner says.

A few minutes go by. Turner talks to his partner Payne, "The captain is having Winslow checked for drugs and alcohol. He told the captain in the ambulance that he shot the suspect several times and the suspect went down. He said the suspect wasn't breathing and had multiple gunshot wounds. The suspect then got up and then he Tasered him with the maximum charge and this had no effect on him. Now get this, he said he shot another full magazine directly at the suspect's head and the bullets stopped in midair. He claimed the suspect shoved his fired bullets down his throat. There are no witnesses to back this story up. On top of that, the bank manager is in shock and can't speak now, and the security guard doesn't know how his hands were chopped off. Detectives and forensics are investigating the scene now. Winslow is definitely on something, talking like that."

Jaden is still sleeping with his head back. They reach the police station and open the door. He wakes up and they escort him inside. They place him in a room to take his pictures, then they take facial recognition scans and they take DNA with a Q-tip.

"Listen sir, you are facing multiple felonies, the best you can do is cooperate. Are you going to tell us your name?" A Sergeant asks.

Jaden is quiet and has a smile on his face.

"Take him to a cell. We will see if that smile is knocked off his face in a populated cell," the Sergeant tells the guard.

They walk Jaden across the station over to the jail side.

"I think you should put me in a cell by myself if you don't want anyone to get hurt," Jaden says.

The guard laughs.

114

"You must be a joker, first words that come out of your mouth make me laugh," the old white guard says.

They reach a door and a buzzing sound is heard and the door opens. A rush of musty air hits Jaden's face. The smell of mildew floods his nose hairs. He is led by the police officer to a medium-sized jail cell. The smell of old damp socks comes to mind. The guard puts Jaden in the cell and informs him to turn around. The officer removes the cuffs and Jaden walks into the cell full of other criminals. The guard locks the metal gate and Jaden stands by the door looking down. The cell is about twenty feet by fifteen feet. Concrete walls surround all three sides with the long metal gate covering the front of the cell. A biker gang of five sits and stands by the double bed in the corner. There are four skinny Hispanic men in their early twenties sitting on a long bench. They look fragile and don't look as if they did a serious crime. The guard goes around the corner and Jaden looks up towards the people in the cell. He walks directly over to the bed and climbs on the top bunk. The biker men with tattoos all over their bodies stare at Jaden, sitting on the top bunk.

"Hey there boy, these are our beds. I suggest you get your narrow dirty ass up and sit on that bench before you don't have a face," a big biker named Billy says.

"I think this city college boy is out of his mind and needs a country beat down," a medium-sized biker named Simon says.

"I don't want any trouble with you overweight biker hicks. There was no one sitting on this bed and all I want to do is sleep. I hurt enough people today, I think it's best you all leave me alone," Jaden says politely while his back is against the wall and legs folded on the bed near his chest. Sunlight from the cell window is shining on Jaden's body.

"I think we need to set an example, on how the Pirate BBS Gang does things," Simon says while standing in front of Jaden.

"Pirate BBS Gang? Are you hicks still dialing up into bulletin board systems with your 300 baud modem?" Jaden asks while chuckling.

"You got until the count of five, you half breed Negro. You think your kind can run this country? Your one term mulatto brother ran this country into deep debt and I'm going to beat his mistakes out of you," Billy says.

115

"Five!" Jaden yells while he kicks Billy directly in the face with his left shoe. He walks backwards losing his balance and the men on the bench quickly move out of the way, as he hits the concrete wall over the bench. There is a loud thump as blood comes from his mouth.

Jaden jumps off the bed and gets into his karate stance. Simon quickly swings towards Jaden's face. Jaden blocks it and grabs his arm, flipping him over his back and onto the floor near the gate. The third man grabs Jaden from behind wrapping his arms around Jaden's arms. A pulse of 50,000 volts leaves Jaden's body shocking the third man. He quickly falls down towards the floor mumbling and shaking. The fourth man tries to kick Jaden from the side. Jaden quickly catches his leg and gives him a straight punch to his chest. He flies into the concrete wall by the window. The other men that were on the bench try to get out of the way. Billy rushes towards Jaden, grabbing him tightly from behind biting his shoulder. The nanodrones quickly disrupt the gravity around Jaden. Jaden jumps up towards the ceiling while Billy is still holding on tightly and biting his shoulder. Simon stands up near the gate. Jaden leans his head forward as Billy's head rams into the ceiling. Billy goes unconscious and closes his eyes. As they come down, the nanodrones in Jaden's back become magnetized. Jaden's body and Billy's body quickly float backwards towards the steel gate. They crash into Simon on the way as they all ram into the steel gate. There is a loud crashing sound as dust falls from the ceiling. Billy and Simon fall towards the floor unconscious and bleeding. Jaden slowly walks towards the middle of the cell room.

"Anyone else with a suggestion or comment about the ex-president or want to get in the way of me sleeping?" He asks loudly. "Speak now!"

The other four men look in shock as they can't believe what they just saw take place.

"Okay then, the next person that bothers me, will get it worst than that BBS hugging sissy gang," Jaden says while jumping on the top bed and lying down with his hands behind his head.

Two guards quickly run towards the cell and the gate opens from down the hallway.

"What happened in here?" The guard asks the other men sitting on the bench together.

They don't say anything, while two shake their heads in denial. The guards check the pulse of the men.

"They were fighting each other! They were arguing on who had the most outdated dial-up modem at home. Then it got out of hand!" Jaden yells from the bed.

"Is this true?" The guard asks the young men with frightened faces.

They shake their head in agreement. The guards get on the radio and call for a few ambulances. Simon has CPR done on him. Ten minutes later the biker men are put on stretchers with neck braces. They are brought outside by several EMS workers and guards. Two of the four men in the cell ask the guard to be put in another cell.

"Sorry can't do that, you know you are here until Monday when you can see the judge," the guard yells.

Hours go by as the four men sitting on the bench stare at Jaden nervously while he sleeps. The sun begins to set as the remaining sunlight shines over Jaden's body. The nanodrones are still reporting AI as offline and in protection mode. Jaden's weapon systems are offline, recharging and being recalibrated. A guards drop off food in the cell. Jaden is wondering where Kimberly is and why she hasn't come to the jail yet. Jaden thinks about his father's letter he briefly read. He replays his memory of the letter and reads it back to himself:

'January 14th 2016

Dear son,

I've thought about you every day. I know deep in my heart that you are still alive and will return one day. The government said you stole a military airplane and you were shot down. I knew that story was such bullshit. You don't even know how to fly. They staked out our house for months and months afterwards, as if they were waiting for you to return. Your mother and I were harassed by the government for years after you left. Your disappearance put a strong damper on our relationship. Your mother couldn't bear losing another son and she had a nervous breakdown. Me and your mother's relationship first began to change when your older brother Douglas was killed in the war. We separated and then later divorced. She couldn't take the United States anymore, so she moved back to England with her family. I've been diagnosed with lung cancer and the cancer spread. The cancer center in Halifax is supposed to be treating me with some experimental nanoworms that can kill cancer proteins and tumors. So I'm leaving this letter here for you and my life savings in this safety deposit box. I hope I will be able to see you one day again my son.

Love,
Your father

P.S. Today is your 35th birthday.

P.S. Again- your girlfriend or ex-girlfriend Amy is claiming I'm the grandfather to her child. She has failed to show a paternity test and has really changed over the years.'

Jaden falls asleep thinking about his parents.

HALIFAX CITY JAIL SEPTEMBER 7, 2018 9:04 AM

"James Revis! James Revis on the top bunk. You have a visitor!" The guard yells through the cell bars.

Jaden thinks about that name and it sounds familiar. He figures it out and gets off the bed to walk towards the gate. The gate opens and Jaden follows the guard down the hallway. He wants to see who is visiting him, but his nanoscanners are recalibrating and are offline. He sits down on the other side of the thick glass with a telephone. He notices Kimberly walking through a door and towards a seat in front of the glass. Kimberly has a sad face as she picks up the phone. Jaden does the same. He smells her different perfume on through the glass.

"I figured out that James Revis was your ex-boyfriend and you were using that name because you knew I would remember, right?" He asks.

"Yes," she says in a sad face.

"What is wrong Kimberly?"

She doesn't respond. Her head is down and she doesn't look him in the eyes.

"Why didn't you come see me yesterday and why do you look so sad?" He asks.

"The police personnel said there were no visitors for anyone yesterday. That someone was hurt in the prison. Listen…" she says while she begins to cry, "I stayed at a hotel yesterday and my father came there. He talked to me for hours about you and everything that has been going on."

A tear comes from her left eye as she looks Jaden directly into the eyes and continues, "I can't see you anymore," she says while the tear quickly runs down her face and lands on the small grey desk in front of her.

"Why? Why not? What did your father say to you?" Jaden asks in a concerned voice.

Her eyes turn red and another tear rolls down her cheek, "J, I'm so confused with everything that has happened over the past few days with me and you. Just hear me out before you respond. I don't know what to believe anymore. My father questioned me about everything and he concluded that you are a professional con artist. He wants me to stay far away from you. I told him he couldn't feel what I felt with you, but he asked if I have ever seen you use any of your alien special powers. I told him no, I have never seen you do anything abnormal. My father suggested you used some kind of hypnotizing brain implant technique to upload all those images and feelings into my mind. You somehow copied my mind with some kind of advanced microchip in your hand. You manipulated my mind into thinking all of this is real. The airplane you jumped out of with a parachute, and the marshal guy was an actor or a friend of yours. That you set all this up to rob a bank and to hurt people. You had me tag along to be an accomplice with you. You already damaged my hard working career with that sexual harassment charge. My father looked on the Internet and said you murdered Ruffo the guard and threw him out the window…"

"Ruffo was a pedophile and that was self defense against his exoskeleton bionic suit. The rest of it is not true. Everything I showed you and what you felt is the real deal. How can I implant all of that in your brain, there is no technology out like that…" Jaden says while being interrupted.

"J, I've never actually seen your Gravhawk spaceship with my own eyes. Those images were not that clear in my memory, they were mostly distorted. I've never seen you throw a gravity shock wave. I've never seen your shield systems work. I've never seen you walk on the wall or defy gravity. AI could be an imaginary

119

friend in your mind for all I know. He could be another one of your personalities in your mind. A figment of your imagination. I never saw what happened at the back of the bank. The officers said you destroyed the inside of the bank with some kind of explosives. Your friend Lopez could have been in there to help you. The cameras in the bank were distorted with electromagnetic energy the detectives said. They said you assaulted a police officer by shoving bullets down his throat from his gun…"

"Those were the bullets he fired at me and I stopped them in midair with my reverse energy shields. I was shot over ten times," Jaden pleads.

"J, you are making this very hard on me without any proof. Show me some of your special alien powers. Show me something right now," she demands.

"I can't, everything is offline now and being recalibrated. AI is not responsive so everything is all screwed up in me. But I can use some basic magnetic nanodrones, watch this," Jaden says. The phone stays stuck to his ears, without any hands. His anti-gravity nanodrones are also offline.

'Shit, everything is offline. Why now?' He asks himself.

Jaden stands up.

"Please sit down sir," a guard standing by the door yells toward Jaden.

Jaden sits back in the metal seat.

"Watch this," Jaden says.

The seat and Jaden fall back on the floor.

"Did you see that? The nanodrones in my back pulled me towards the metal door behind me," Jaden explains while getting off the floor and putting the chair back up.

"I'm okay, I just fell off the chair," Jaden tells the guard.

"You just pushed the chair with your feet and leaned back towards the floor," Kimberly says. "J, you haven't showed me any real concrete proof. The only thing that you are proving to me is that you should have stayed in the psychiatric hospital."

"Okay, Kimberly, how do you explain my DNA?"

"You did something to strip the structure of your DNA and RNA. My father suggested you used some sort of modified nanoworms to destroy your DNA particles. The nanomoles you are claiming that are in the brains of humans could be some kind of isolated biological protein that could be the work of terrorists. My colleagues will use the 4D force atom microscope to verify what it actually is. My father had some valid points, the best point is I haven't seen any evidence with my own eyes. Why can't you just admit to me this was all a setup for you to rob a bank and you manipulated my mind with these detailed illusions?" She asks with tears running down her cheeks and she sniffs with a tissue in her hand.

"Kimberly..." Jaden pauses while his eyes turn red, "I didn't lie to you about anything. Everything, everything was the truth. Everything you saw and felt was real. I do have feelings for you, just like you have the same for me. Don't do this at a time that I need you," Jaden pleads while putting his right hand on the glass and holding the phone to his left ear.

She stands up and looks at Jaden while tears are rolling down her soft cheeks and connect together under her chin. Her left hand still holding the phone to her ear.

"I can't be involved with you. I have a life and a career. My father said the police are charging you with felony assaulting a police officer, aggravated assault on a security guard, felony bank robbery, and destroying property with an explosive device. You are looking at fifteen to twenty years in prison. They are still trying to identify who you are, I gave them your name as James Revis. I can't be involved with this, I don't know what to believe. Your ex-girlfriend Amy called you and left a voice mail on my answering machine a few hours ago. She said she is in New York City and she is going to the World Trade Center grand opening for the public tomorrow night. She said to bring her money there. I have to go now. Please don't contact me anymore. I'm sorry," she says while putting down the phone on the desk.

"Kimberly! Kimberly!" Jaden yells while hitting the glass hard with his hand. The sweat and tears rub off on the glass with his hand. She continues to walk away towards the door not turning around.

"Kimberly! I love you!" Jaden yells at the top of his voice while the guard stands behind him. His saliva squirts on the glass from his mouth. Both of his hands are flat on the glass. His eyes are red.

Kimberly stops at the door after hearing these three words. But then she quickly continues through it and disappears from Jaden's sight.

"Let's go Romeo, your visiting time is over," the jail guard says.

Jaden continues to stand there looking at the door she went through, as the guard taps him on his shoulder. He sees she isn't coming back, after a minute of waiting in the same position. Jaden turns around and the guard follows behind Jaden.

"Buddy, that good looking female was way out of your league anyway. You have to crawl before you can walk," the middle-aged guard says while chuckling. "The amount of time you are looking in prison, you should get used to liking men for now on."

The guard chuckles to himself while they reach a steel door with glass. The guard starts to open the door with a key and whispers behind Jaden's neck.

"I heard penetration hurts at first back there, for your first time, but over time you will get used to it and enjoy it. We are going to make sure you are in the most HIV infected prison in North Carolina for assaulting a police officer. Yeah, you going to get what is coming to you, young pretty boy," the guard whispers while opening the door.

"I'll be free by tomorrow," Jaden says with confidence.

"Oh, you aren't getting bail, criminal. There is no bail for assaulting a police officer in North Carolina," the guard says while walking to the cell.

He opens the jail cell door and Jaden walks inside. Jaden sees one of the three men sitting on his top bed. He quickly gets up and walks to the other side of the cell.

"Sorry man, I wasn't sure if you were coming back. I was just keeping the bed warm for you," the nervous young man says.

Jaden climbs on the bed and lies down. His body soaks up the sunlight coming in from the window. Jaden keeps thinking about Kimberly and all the things she said. He can't believe she doesn't believe him now. Jaden is so alone and keeps thinking about what happened to his friend AI. He sees: NANODRONES ATTEMPTING TO REVITALIZE AI SCAIN UNIT. 29 UNSUCCESSFUL TRIES TO RESTART on his eye screen. Jaden falls asleep thinking about Kimberly, AI and his daughter. He is wondering why his ex and daughter are in New York.

"You mean to tell me Jaden Marino disappeared without a trace. Dr. K. Chan, who was helping the suspect, suddenly disappeared from her apartment yesterday morning. The father was being followed, but your agent lost track of the father also. Your agent can only say he was heading south on the 95 expressway. What kind of incompetent agents do you have working for you Agent Mcright?" Robinson asks over the phone.

"My men are really well trained. They don't lose a tail that easy. Your drone aircraft and your satellite lost the father's vehicle. These people knew they were being followed and took evasive measures. My agent reported to me just now that Dr. Chan returned to her apartment in Rumford, Virginia. What would you like us to do?"

"Arrest her and charge her with aiding and abetting a terrorist. She probably knows where he is and what is going on. I'll interrogate her personally by video conference."

RICHMOND, VA, FBI HEAD QUARTERS 2:31 PM

Kimberly is sitting in a small interrogation room. The agents asked her several questions about Jaden and she refused to say anything. She knows anything she mentions about Jaden will either get her in a psychiatric ward or further in trouble. A flat screen turns on in front of her.

"Hello Dr. Chan, I'm the Vice President of the United States. I'm going to get right to the point. We know you had contact with Jaden Marino. We believe he is a terrorist and is part of a conspiracy to hurt Americans. You aiding and abetting a terrorist will have you in federal prison for many years. We know he used your Paylife at the airport in Albany, New York and you didn't report it stolen," Robinson says while an image of Jaden's other white face shows up on the screen.

"Like I told the FBI agents for the past hour, I don't know this man and I didn't realize my Paylife was used. I would like my phone call to call my father's attorney," Kimberly says.

"Do you know this man then?" Robinson asks while showing Jaden's original bi-racial face and body.

123

"Yes, that man is Jaden Marino and he was my patient at the hospital," she says.

"Listen you little Asian bitch. Just because your father is a multi-millionaire doesn't mean you are protected by the Constitution. We know about you joining the ANWO group back in college. We know you knew you were being followed from your house yesterday. We know you are working with this man. You will be in jail for the rest of your life and then we will deport your body back to Taiwan when you are dead. Tell us what we want to know! Where is Jaden Marino!?" Robinson yells while his voice echoes through the screen.

"I don't know where he is, last I saw him he was in the psychiatric hospital on Friday," she says in a nervous voice.

"This man killed a guard at your hospital. We believe he took this man's body somewhere at the airport..." Robinson is interrupted while Jaden's white face is shown on the screen again.

"How can someone take someone else's body? That doesn't make any sense," she asks with her arms crossed.

"I'm the one asking questions here. You shut your face when a man is speaking. This Jaden man, pushed two people out of an airplane and he jumped out with a parachute on..." Robinson says.

"Listen you cockeyed old man. I don't care who you are, you aren't going to talk to me like that. This is not the forties where you can disrespect a female like that. I paid and my family paid a lot of taxes to this country and I love this country. I told you what I had to say about Jaden Marino, if you are going to put me in jail or prison, then put me in prison. My father will have me out in a few hours. Just make sure you have proper evidence against me, because my father's lawyer will sue your government back into a recession. You can kiss my Made in Taiwan sesame chicken ass, you chauvinistic want to be President cockeyed pig. Now, I want to call my lawyer!" She slams her hands on the desk and screams at the vice president looking puzzled on the video screen.

There is complete silence in the room. Robinson's face turns completely red.

"Can't take a woman telling you what to do huh? I know you hate taking orders from a woman President. A woman telling you what to do really eats up men like yourself from the inside out. It is pig men like you who make it hard for women to have equal pay in the work force as men…" she is interrupted by an FBI agent behind her.

The screen goes off. Robinson is talking to special FBI agent in charge Andrew Mcright on the phone.

"Don't give her a phone call. Take her to Buckeye Maximum Federal Prison outside of Studley, Virginia. Make sure she is put in the special housing unit," Robinson says with a sneaky voice.

"Sir, you want to put her in the hole at a maximum federal prison for men?" Mcright asks.

"That is correct, she wants equal rights for women, and I'm going to give her the same rights men receive. She wants to defend a terrorist, we are going to treat her like a terrorist. Anyone asks at the prison, tell them the order came directly from the vice president."

"Yes sir.

Buckeye, VA, Buckeye Federal Prison 3:22 PM

Kimberly walks in handcuffs behind her back, being escorted by two federal agents through the front gate at the prison. Kimberly is wearing a blue skirt above her knees with white dots on it and a white blouse.

"Why am I at a federal men's prison?" She asks while walking through the courtyard.

They ignore her.

A man with a suit walks from the prison building towards them.

"I thought you were joking when you said you were bringing a female prisoner here. We can't have a female here, especially a female without a uniform on. These prisoners will get violent and out of control," the warden says with a southern accent.

Kim pleads directly to the warden as she walks by, "Sir, I didn't get my phone call. The government is violating my rights. I didn't even see a judge yet or get charged with anything."

"Ma'am I'm not talking to you."

"These are direct orders from my supervisor and from the vice president. You can call my boss or the vice president himself," the young agent says while continuing to walk towards the entrance to the building.

125

Armed guards with exoskeleton body suits in the four towers are looking and whistling at her. The warden gets on his cell phone. They walk her into the building.

"Yes sir," the warden says into the phone while walking towards the entrance of the huge prison.

She walks through a corridor area with a huge fence on both sides. Prisoners run up to the fence on the left and grab onto it. They line up to get a peak at Kimberly's beauty. They shake the gate together and yell through the fence.

"I didn't know Chinese food could be delivered inside the prison."

"I will lick every inch of your body with my tongue if you need a shower."

"General Tso's daughter is here to entertain the prisoners and to love us long time."

An old white man sticks his tongue through the fence and whispers, "We going to take turns on you just like we took turns on the women in Vietnam."

They bring her in another building and downstairs to the basement. The basement smells funky and moldy. The cold, damp air gives Kimberly an eerie feeling. Goose bumps go up and down her long skinny legs.

"I'm going to masturbate to your perfume and legs all night long," a man smelling the air looking through the food opening in the middle of the special housing unit. The guards put her into a six-foot wide cell by ten feet deep. The prison guard locks the steel door and instructs her to turn around. He removes her handcuffs. She walks inside the dark hole and begins to cry. Prisoners are shouting obscenities from other cells around and across from Kimberly's.

"We want real pussy! We want real pussy!" They yell together.

Kimberly sits on the floor in the corner and begins to cry and whine quietly to herself. She is cold, depressed, and feels very alone in the dark. She is thinking about how her father is looking for her now. She is thinking about what Jaden said before she left the jail. She is thinking about what he is doing in the jail at this moment.

Jaden is sleeping and suddenly wakes up sweating. The four men are still on the bench looking at Jaden with nervous looks on their faces. He is thinking about Kimberly and AI. Jaden misses talking to his alien friend AI. Jaden feels Kimberly might be in trouble.

His eye screen shows: MANUALLY RECALIBRATING OFFENSE AND DEFENSE WEAPONS 40% COMPLETE. AI STATUS UNKNOWN, STILL RUNNING DIAGNOSTICS.

He lies back down on the top bunk and falls asleep thinking about everything that has happened the past few days. He feels as if he is at his lowest point, now that he lost Kimberly, temporarily lost his powers and lost AI. He feels deeply depressed inside. He closes his eyes and remembers what his father told him back in 1999.

'Just remember, the people who run this country are very arrogant, money and power hungry and wants to eventually control us like animals. Our history proves this, cover-ups and conspiracies are the American government way. They betrayed Douglas and covered up his death. Eventually they will betray you son. Watch your back. If all else fails, save yourself and the people you care about....'

Thoughts of him leaving Earth and returning back to Xenos emerges. Thoughts of him finding his parents and leaving this primitive doomed planet are being entertained in his mind. He falls back asleep thinking about exploring this galaxy like the *Enterprise*.

BUCKEYE, VA, BUCKEYE FEDERAL PRISON 8:52 PM

Kimberly is sitting on the cold floor and crosses her legs and arms near her stomach. She is taking deep breaths and enters a deep meditative state. Her Buddhist religion has trained her throughout her life for handling her mind for situations like this. She finds her inner peace and is ignoring the screams and shouting from inmates around her. The toilet flushes by itself right next to her. Her mind is far away from the dark and dirty prison room. She has been ignoring her body's pleas to use the bathroom. Thirty minutes pass by and Kimberly comes out of her meditation. She opens her eyes and she feels as if she is blind. There is a little light coming from under the door and food tray hole. She stands up and feels for the toilet. Eerie feelings pass around her body as she touches sludge on the toilet seat. The feeling is grossing her out.

"Eww, this is disgusting. This is ten times worst than a gas station in Mexico. Oh shit, I don't feel any toilet paper anywhere," she says while standing over the toilet squatting with her skirt lifted up and panties pulled to her thighs.

She looks towards the door while she uses the bathroom and someone is standing there.

"I'll be your toilet sexy, I'll swallow anything your body doesn't want," a guard with a deep voice says. The guard is wearing night vision glasses as he stares at Kimberly squatting over the toilet. She covers between her legs with her skirt and hand.

She thinks to herself about replying, 'It seems there is no toilet paper in here for a lady, why don't you wipe me with your perverted tongue?' But she remembers all the prison movies she has seen over the years and knows he probably would do it, giving her a venereal disease in the process.

"I'm fine! But, if you could be a gentlemen guard and get me toilet paper?" She asks with a sweet voice while finishing up.

There is no answer while the man continues to stare at her.

"I didn't get a phone call or charged with anything, can you find out how long I'm going to be in here?" She asks while shaking back and forth over the toilet.

The guard walks away when Kimberly stands up and pulls down her skirt.

"I guess the one girl and a toilet show is over for him," she says while sitting back in the corner on the cold floor with her back against the dirty wall. She still hears profanity in the hallway from prisoners in other rooms.

"You are going to be in here for a long time, little terrorist helper," the guard says.

She begins to cry again, as she thinks about her family and friends. Her tears land on the top of her left hand.

An hour passes by and it is silent around Kimberly and the surrounding areas. She breaks out of another meditation. She hears tapping on the wall to the left of her. A low sounding Arabic man's voice comes from the room next to her. The sounds travel through a crack in the concrete foundation.

"Can you hear me?" He asks.

Kimberly ignores him and doesn't reply. The tapping continues.

"What terrorist group are you with? Are you a sleeper cell? American born terrorist?" He asks.

A minute goes by and Kimberly still doesn't reply. The man continues.

"What is your name? I'm Zaze Mohammad, but you can call me Zaze."

Kimberly listens but doesn't respond.

"I'm a part of the terrorist group that attacked New York City buildings in lower Manhattan with shoulder rockets on Jet Skis, back on July 4, 2015. I'm sure you heard about it in the news. It wasn't something I was proud of. I'm not really a bad person. I was brought over to America at a young age and I grew up in America. I had my citizenship and I loved this country as a teenager. My uncle owned a grocery store in Brooklyn that I worked at. I was also in college studying to be an engineer. I was saving my money to bring the rest of my family over from Afghanistan…"

The man sobs and then continues, "My family was running for years trying to stay clear of the U.S. attacks from 2001. My uncle and I sent them money to move from the refugee camp and to live in an apartment building. But in 2006 they died from a cluster bomb dropped on their apartment building. My two sisters, one younger brother, mother and aunts all died. The U.S. said there was a suspected terrorist in a nearby building. But the bomb took out an entire city block. The U.S. and NATO forces killed over 10,000 Iraqi and Afghanistan civilians over the years. That is just a low estimate. I had Iraqi friends who also died. The woman I was going to marry also died in an Iraq attack. My uncle suffered a heart attack and died after he learned of his sisters and family all dying. I vowed revenge on America and the UN for not protecting innocent people. The U.S. keeps attacking the cities not to keep the security situation stable, but so they can stay in Iraq and control the oil. Oil?"

He continues to cry and sob. The man bangs on the ground and a tear falls on his hand.

"Oil? I was studying to be an engineer that specialized in green energy. America always had the technology to get away from oil and gas. The USA always had the capability to have seventy percent of their vehicles running off solar, electricity, vegetable oil or water by the year 2000. Then there would have been no interest in oil or an interest to attack Afghanistan and Iraq. September 11, 2001 was staged so America could have a reason to invade a foreign country. Civilizations have been using this strategy for many centuries to invade someone weaker for something they might have. Who was held accountable for this?"

There is dead silence as the man continues, "The American government kept covering up in Afghanistan and Iraq how many innocent civilians were actually being killed by them. During elections in America, they would use airstrikes instead of ground forces to minimize their American military casualties. These airstrikes increased my people's death rates. So many innocent children and civilians' blood was on the street. The Americans kept criticizing Saddam for the mass graves. How many civilian graves did the Americans make in Iraq?"

Kimberly still doesn't respond, but continues listening to the terrorist's perspective. Sadness and sobbing can be heard in his voice as he continues.

"The U.S. lied and said Saddam Hussein had weapons of mass destruction. These weapons were never found and there was never any apology from any U.S. government. So many cover-ups and many Americans citizens didn't know everything that was going on over there. I had nothing left to live for in America. My anger for America's greed changed me as a person. So many civilians out of work and nowhere to go, many joined Al-Qaeda. I went to Baghdad in 2007 as a volunteer and joined Al-Qaeda where I was transported into Afghanistan. I trained for a year at a secret underground location in Afghanistan. I would return to America a year later as a sleeper cell and I would conduct a martyrdom operation. I would do anything, including sacrificing myself to bring attention to what the American military was doing to civilians in Afghanistan. An eye for an eye. American civilians needed to experience what Afghanistan and Iraqi civilians experienced for the past ten years. I fired my rocket directly at the UN building and it had my family's name on it. I was ready to join my family in heaven, when I rode up to a ferry boat and my Jet Ski didn't explode…."

The man moves his mouth from the crack in the wall and cries on the floor in the dark. The sobbing and crying can be heard vibrating against the entire wall. Kimberly continues to sit on the floor in a meditation position. She tries to comprehend what the man has told her. She blocks out his loud crying and meditates again.

"Hey you big cry baby man! Keep it down over there, some of us are trying to get off!" A man yells from across the hall.

HALIFAX, NC CITY JAIL 11:49 PM

Sleeping for hours, Jaden begins to dream.

He dreams Kimberly is in a black colored castle in a red princess gown. Jaden is in a white knight outfit, the same as in the virtual chess game he was playing on Xenos. He runs into the castle fighting pawns with his sword, suddenly the sky turns from day to night. Jaden looks up and the castle disappears from around him into a black darkness. The planet disappears around him and he is flying through space towards the moon using nanoeyes. He stops behind the moon, looking at a big mother ship facing Earth. The ship is camouflaged and cloaked into the abyss of black space. He feels evil vibes and evil intentions coming from the ship as it hides behind the moon. He hears a familiar voice coming from different directions in space.

'Jaden? Wake up buddy.'

He turns around and looks into the darkness and stars. It gets completely dark.

Jaden opens his eyes and sees the ceiling of the jail cell.

'Hey buddy, I'm back online,' AI says.

'What happened to you? I thought I lost you.'

'I went into what you humans would call a self induced coma. My operating system shut down after those unknown energies returned,' AI says.

'Yeah, I noticed a weird black shiny material on my fingertips. The skin was being destroyed under it.'

131

'I was looking at the data on that from the nanodrones in your fingertips repairing your fingernails and outer skin. I can't explain what is happening to you. I went offline after those bullets began to strike your body. I'm almost finished compressing your DNA in various areas around your body. You will have 10,000 DNA memo groups tightly packed together making your weapons and superhuman abilities work more efficiently. The DNA in the skin around your body will be stronger than Kevlar. I'm creating an artificial orbital hybridization bind with your skin cells. The technology is called nanotubes and it is in everything from bulletproof clothes, to the body of police cars.'

'Cool. As long as I don't feel strange, look different or feel a lot of pain. Do what you have to do. What time is it?' Jaden asks. 'I felt like I was sleeping for two or three hours, the sun is still out.'

'I knew you were going to ask me that, so I did a stellar motion on the stars a few hours ago, it is about 8:08 AM, September 8th,' AI says.

'It is 8 AM already? Shit,' Jaden says. 'I'm glad you are back buddy, I thought I lost you forever. I already lost Kimberly.'

'I was looking at the recordings; that was a tough emotional breakup. I hope you two get together again, I've sensed great chemistry between you two. It is funny that she never saw you do anything special with her own eyes. I never thought about that. Anyway, what was your dream about, I was trying to wake you up for hours, but your conscious was unreachable,' AI says.

'I was dreaming I was rescuing Kimberly in a castle, then I was looking at the Darclonians mother ship behind the moon. It was just sitting there and I felt evil. I know they are here already,' Jaden says.

'Fascinating, your dreams are enabling you to see things in the present and possible future I've been noticing. I'm still blocked out of them. I think the Darclonians want you to see them. We have to get out of this prison as soon as possible.'

'Something else, Kimberly said the images of the Gravhawk were very unclear in her mind, as if her memory or subconscious was trying to hide it. What do you think that could mean?' Jaden asks.

'According to psychology online encyclopedias, I believe something happened in her childhood or when she was younger.

132

Maybe something in a movie, an accident or something that traumatized her. There were some memories in Dr. Chan's past that are blacked out and hidden in her subconscious that we were unable to access. I don't know what it could have been. Maybe the next time you see her, you can find out.'

'Yeah, next time. I hope there is a next time. If I were her, I would leave the country for a while, with all she has been through the last few days. I wouldn't be surprised if she went back to Taiwan for a couple of weeks,' Jaden says.

'Possibly. The nanodrones have been reorganizing themselves so the task I was making them do, can be done automatically by you just thinking about it. They already began rerouting, and recalculating your weapon systems, pro-gravity and anti-gravity nanodrones. This is why they have been offline for the past forty hours. The negative side is your mind will have to do more calculations putting a strain on your mind. Your sleeping helped the nanodrones pull energy from the air, to manipulate and accelerate subatomic particles... I remember, save you the details on the big science words. Your brain neurons are at an even 200 billion. The next time you feel great pain or anger the nanodrones will create a microscopic shield around me or I can temporarily turn myself offline, to prevent any damage. Not one hundred percent sure that will work though. I wouldn't want to take the chance though.'

'Cool.'

'Where are we going after we get out of this jail?' AI asks.

'I was seriously thinking about just leaving this planet and returning back to Xenos. Let everyone fend for themselves here. I think I made a mistake wanting to come back to this planet. This was a big waste of time. I've tried to help people, warn the government and everything I do is a constant fight. The government probably doesn't believe there is going to be an attack on Earth, even after getting the message from deep space. I don't hear about any preparations or the government asking for my help. I don't see any special helmets being given out to citizens. The Andromedian elders were right, there isn't much one person can do,' Jaden says.

'What about your daughter? She is half you,' AI says.

'That snotty little bitch. I don't even know her. She is like a clone of her crazy mother.'

133

'There might be a side you don't know about your daughter,' AI says.

'Are you getting this from your psychology for dummies e-books?'

'No.'

The door opens in the huge cell and Jaden wakes up to look towards the door.

"Alright everyone let's go," the guard at the gate says.

Jaden gets out of the bed and walks through the gate. Three other guards help handcuff Jaden and the other four men to a long chain line. The four Hispanic men in their early twenties stand in a line behind Jaden. They look at him with nervous expressions on their faces.

'Anything you can do to speed up the recalibration?' Jaden asks.

'I'll see what I can do.'

"Where are we all going now?" Jaden asks the guard.

"Everyone has a court date to see the judge."

'How did a nanoscanner get destroyed?' Jaden asks.

'The black gloss that was around your fingertips completely destroyed a nanoscanner when it went to investigate from the outside. Whatever it is, nanoscanners aren't immune. Until we figure out what this is, they will have to stay away,' AI says.

They walk together in a line outside the building and towards a sheriff's van.

BUCKEYE FEDERAL PRISON 8:31 AM

Kimberly finally falls asleep against the dark wall while her knees are against her chest and arms around her legs. As the tears slowly dry against her face, her mind enters a dream state.

It is completely dark as Kimberly hears different voices all mixed together, right behind each other. The barrage of voices competes with each other. She tries hard to distinguish the familiar words, "Kids! Kids! Stop running...I'm your government appointed psychologist Miss Chan, What you saw was in your imagination...Do you want to see your parents again?... Mom, do you believe me?...I will hit you again if you keep making up

134

things...Are you okay?...Look at my hair floating..." Young *children begin crying simultaneously and then they fade away.*

Kimberly wakes up screaming, from her dream as images and voices locked away in her subconscious came out.

"I'll give you a reason to scream," a prisoner across from her yells towards her from the feeding hole.

WASHINGTON, D.C. WHITE HOUSE
COMMAND CENTER 8:50 AM

Robinson is upset that Max Miles suffered an unknown seizure and is on his way to a military hospital.

"How is it we are just finding out Jaden Marino was in a city jail in Halifax for the past forty-one hours and we weren't notified sooner?" Robinson asks Mcright over the phone.

"Jaden Marino is back in his original bi-racial body. The system had the white face and body in the face recognition system as his ID. His old face wasn't in the system anymore, when he had a new face scan on Saturday at the Halifax Jail there was no match. This is why we didn't find out anything until now. His fingerprints were also different. They had him in the system as James Revis. The dumb hicks at the jailhouse assumed their DNA scanner was broken since his DNA wasn't coming up. The court has been warned to have more court officers and sheriffs on duty. My agents are on their way," Mcright says.

"This is amazing, all this advanced technology the United States government has and we still get these slipups. I need this suspect killed or contained," Robinson says.

"Yes sir."

HALIFAX CRIMINAL COURTHOUSE 9:10 AM
MONDAY

There is a howling wind coming from the windows on both sides of the courtroom. The high ceilings show craftsmanship from the 1800's. There is a concrete statue of justice on the right of the judge's desk. There is an American flag hanging from a pole a few feet in the air to the left of the judge's desk. The cool morning

135

breeze flows through the courtroom kicking up dust from the walls. One of the Hispanic men begins sneezing, but he can't cover his mouth, so he bends his head down. Jaden is sitting in the front row of the courtroom still connected to the long chain, connected to the prisoners behind him by ankles and around the wrists. He can see the germs from the prisoner's sneeze floating in all directions. There is a big mug on the judge's desk. The steam from the hot black coffee slowly goes into the air. Jaden can smell the black coffee from where he is. He could really use some coffee this morning. Jaden turns around towards the seats behind him to see if he sees Kimberly. She isn't there and Jaden feels she truly wants nothing to do with him. There are many extra officers in the courtroom. Two court officers are wearing exoskeleton full body suits with guns on their waist by the door.

"All rise," a court secretary yells.

Jaden stands up with the rest of the prisoners. The court officer continues talking as Judge Katherine Spinelli sits at her desk. A court officer removes Jaden from the rest of the chain gain. He still has handcuffs on and chains down to his feet. Jaden stands in front of the judge. She has a metal electronic bow in her hair. Everyone sits down while the judge looks on her computer screen without a keyboard. People from the bank are in the courtroom seats.

"Mr. Jaden Marino, this is your name correct?" The judge asks while looking at Jaden.

'AI, what is going on buddy, they know who I am now. My eye screen is showing the calibration of my weapons and all nanodrones at ninety-nine percent finished. It has been stuck there for the past hour. My weapon systems' energy is at thirty percent,' Jaden says to AI.

"Yes it is," Jaden says to the judge.

'Your internal energy is fine and stable. There is a slight problem with the calibration, but we are working on it,' AI says.

'Are the nanodrones having a meeting or taking a break or something?' Jaden asks.

Four court officers in blue uniforms and with guns on their waists stand around Jaden.

'Something like that, you could say. The five nanoscanners will be online in less than a minute,' AI says.

"Mr. Marino, are you really Italian?"

"Yes, I'm half Italian."

136

"Interesting. I've never seen so many charges against one person before. Are you half Italian and half the devil?" The judge asks.

"Technically, half alien, one fourth Italian and one forth black is more accurate," Jaden says with a smile on his face.

"Do you think this is a joke?" She asks.

"Do you think you can ask me stupid questions and try to insult me? Let's get this over with, people are waiting behind me and I have places to go," Jaden says while the judge looks at her screen again.

A tall white court officer next to Jaden jabs him in the side with a nightstick.

"Show some respect in this courthouse you little prick," the middle-aged officer says.

"How about you show some respect for my nose by chewing some gum," Jaden snaps.

"Mr. Marino, you won't be going anywhere, but into federal custody without bail. You are charged with: felony assaulting a police officer, aggravated assault on a security guard, felony bank robbery, destroying property with an explosive device, aggravated assault on five jail inmates, second-degree murder of a security guard, destroying hospital property, identity theft... Should I keep going?" She asks.

"Yes keep going, this is interesting. I might beat the world record for the most criminal charges on a person," Jaden says while his nanoscanners go out around the room.

"...Opening an emergency exit while an aircraft was in motion, pushing two people from a moving plane, first degree manslaughter of a passenger and eighteen years of unpaid child support," she yells.

"Seventeen years, ten months and seven days to be exact of child support," Jaden says with a smile on his face.

"You froze your body in Europe for eighteen years to avoid taking care of your child? You let your child grow up without a father?" She asks.

"Well technically I didn't know I had a child. I didn't freeze my body, I was on another planet. So technically child support should only be for the amount of time I'm on Earth..."

Everyone in the courtroom starts to laugh.

"Are you crazy and a liar on top of it?" She asks.

"Judge, it seems you care more about me not paying child support over all my other foolish charges you just read. I must say this government is good with putting charges and made up charges on their citizens. It is too bad the laws and rules don't apply to me," Jaden says.

"Entertain me, Mr. Marino, how is it the laws and rules don't apply to you?"

"I'm not a *Homo sapien* like the rest of you humans, I'm what I call a BIO-Sapien. I'm an evolved human and the next level up on the species chain. I'm more of a modified human with alien technology, capable of doing things never thought possible with a human body. I'm here to help save this miserable planet from certain doom. But with all I've been through since returning to Earth last week, I think you people need to suffer your own Armageddon…"

The judge continues to look at her screen and ignores what Jaden says.

"I'm reading here that you shoved a magazine of a police officer's bullets down his throat in an attack?" She asks.

"No, I shoved the bullets he shot at me down his throat. They were very hot and burned my hands," Jaden says while chuckling. The audience laughs also.

"Sir…" the judge grabs her head as she feels pain.

"As you can see judge, there is a nanomole in your brain now, getting into position to over take your mind. There is a pending alien attack on Earth…" Jaden says while everyone in the courtroom laughs except the four Hispanic prisoners from his jail cell. They listen to him with their eyes on Jaden.

"Sir, Tylenol will fix this headache in the next ten minutes. I don't think the most advanced psychiatric hospital will fix your delusional brain. If you have magical alien powers, let's see you do something now," she demands.

"I know you are wearing some old pink grandma panties with a quarter inch hole in the rear, under your suit. Your old saggy breasts look as if they were allergic to bras the past forty years. I can read everything on your screen from here. Inputting I'm mentally disturbed on my profile isn't very nice. I'm sure you have that electronic device in your back by your spine because your husband left you a long time ago and it's been ages since a man

138

touched you. When I do something magical, your courtroom won't look the same when I leave." Jaden says.

"Are you threatening me and my court? Sir?" She asks. "You are already looking at three life sentences in prison, do you want to go for four life sentences?"

"Judge, would it really matter after one life sentence? I mean really, even though I can probably live over 500 years, another life sentence is like burying a dead body again in the same grave. I'll be walking out that front courtroom door in five minutes without handcuffs and without a guard escorting me. So you can add on as many life sentences as you want. Go knock yourself out, Judge Dredd," Jaden says.

The five court officers around Jaden begin to laugh together along with other people in the courtroom.

"OJ Simpson's lawyers couldn't get you off on all these charges against you. Not even Jesus himself can help you walk through that door unescorted in the next five minutes. You are completely delusional and entertaining to listen to along with my morning coffee," the judge says while taking another sip of her black coffee.

"Kimberly Chan is held in Buckeye Federal Maximum Prison in Virginia as an accomplice to the charges against me? Vice President Robinson is giving out these orders?" Jaden asks.

'I knew he had to be behind this. This is why everyone is after me,' Jaden says to AI.

"Yes, how did you know that?" She asks.

"I told you I'm watching your judge screen from here. I can see that the feds have me in the system as this face and my other white face. I'm on the terrorist watch list. I can also see that they consider me very dangerous and to be held until Homeland Security or the FBI arrives. Why do you think they consider me armed and dangerous even though I'm in handcuffs?" Jaden asks.

"You listen to me, you young teenager, I don't know what kind of tricks you are pulling here…"

"No you listen!" Jaden shouts and asks, "Why is my friend Dr. Chan is being held in a maximum federal male prison? She had nothing to do with this!"

"You are in contempt of my court!" She yells while banging her gavel as the audience talks amongst themselves.

Two UAV Predator drones fly by outside, along with a FBI helicopter hovering a few hundred feet from the courthouse. A local news-reporting agency is setting up on the steps of the courthouse.

"You are in contempt of America and I hope the feds put you deep in a hole where you belong, you mentally challenged terrorist traitor!"

'Good job and thanks for e-mailing this story to the local news in town, AI. I can see they are outside now,' Jaden says.

The court appointed public defender and prosecutor are being told to stay outside the courtroom.

'Thank to the free Wi-Fi in this courthouse building and in town,' AI says.

"Judge Spinelli, let me go now and a lot of people won't get hurt today," Jaden demands.

"Guards remove this mentally challenged man back to a holding cell, until the feds can take him into custody. I heard enough nonsense for my morning," she says.

Two guards grab Jaden's arm. They can feel his muscles bulging as if something is inside of them. They look at him with a strange look on their faces. Two other guards say, "Let's go."

Jaden stands in the same place, not budging. The courtroom lights begin to dim. Everyone turns to look at each other.

"I would suggest anyone who wishes not to get seriously hurt to please leave the courtroom now and stay out of my way. If you have a family or kids at home think of them now!" Jaden yells, while two court officers in exoskeleton body suits with helmets on walk down the court aisle from the entrance behind each other. Their metal feet make clanking sounds against the floor. The walking sounds behind Jaden remind him of Robocop walking. The tellers and some customers from the bank get up and run out of the courtroom. The four prisoners on the bench attempt to get up, but a court officer make them sit back down.

A guard's long hair begins to float in the air. Jaden's eye screen suddenly shows: OFFENSE-DEFENSE WEAPONS ONLINE 35% TOTAL STRENGTH, ALL NANODRONES, ANTI-GRAVITY, PRO-GRAVITY ONLINE.

Jaden sees small light particles moving inside his fair complexion, down to his wrist and ankles. Jaden turns around and looks at the door. Nanodrones destroy the metal compounds in his handcuffs. Smoke comes from the metal and all the cuffs drops to the floor. It makes a loud clinging sound. The officers look at the chains on the floor. The judge stands up to see what is going on. The lights go out in the courtroom and sunlight shines down from huge windows on the wall near the ceiling. Nanotime 100x shows on Jaden's eyes. He notices his body is moving faster along with his brain speed. Jaden hits the first guard with his elbow in the chest, and his body falls backwards on the bench. The other guards' hands slowly reach down for their guns. People in the rows of benches scream in a low growling sound as they try to climb over the benches towards the door. The judge slowly bends down towards her bulletproof desk.

Jaden grabs and removes three of the court officers' guns before they can reach it themselves. He tosses them straight into the air. The anti-gravity energy above him makes the guns slowly float towards the ceiling. Nanotime goes off and time speeds back to normal in his brain. Jaden does a roundhouse kick in the face of another officer and his body twists onto the bench other prisoners are hiding under. Jaden then fires a slight gravity shock wave with his right hand into the chest of the last guard standing near him. A dust of smoke is two feet around his body. The two officers in the bionic suits crouch to aim their guns at Jaden and fire at him. A nanoscanner is inside of the gun. Jaden can see the bullet loading into the chamber and quickly being shot. A barrage of 8mm bullets slow down to a crawl. Their guns begin to click as thirty-six bullets are four feet from Jaden's head. The last person runs out of the courtroom while the door swings back and forth. The bullets move down a foot and Jaden takes a step backwards. He fires a gravity shock wave towards the bionic court officers as they try to reload their guns. The shock wave takes the levitating bullets and a bubble of the energy shield with it. The bullets riddle their armor suits. The strong force lifts the officers off their feet as they fly through the courtroom doors and into a concrete wall twenty feet further. The left door hangs off its hinges as it looks as if it is about to fall off.

The first guard struck by Jaden aims his gun at him as he crawls over the benches towards the entrance.

"Save your bullets for a real criminal officer, I will have to make you eat those bullets you fire at me," Jaden says as the officer's hands shake. The nervous officer gets up and runs out of the courtroom.

Jaden puts his hands together in front of him and the guns thrown to the ceiling come down into Jaden's hand. The two other court officers that fell down run towards the door. Jaden turns towards the judge's bench. He hears the four Hispanic men making nervous whimpers.

"You see judge, if I was a terrorist, wouldn't I be killing and shooting innocent people also?" Jaden asks while walking closer to the judge's bench.

'We should go sir,' AI suggests.

The last guard in the room comes up behind Jaden with a nightstick, swinging towards the back of his head. Jaden quickly turns around, dropping the guns in his hand and stops his swinging arm with his hand. He catches the court officer by the neck with his right hand and begins to squeeze. He drops the nightstick.

"There is always a renegade officer who wants to try to be a hero. Didn't you just see me stop bullets in midair and blast two bionic dick officers thirty feet into a concrete wall? Why would you try to sneak behind me?" Jaden asks while still lifting him off his feet by a few inches. He gags and tries to remove Jaden's hand around his neck.

"You were trying hard to be in the newspaper tomorrow as the town's hero? GI-prick?" Jaden asks while lifting the 270-pound man.

Jaden lifts him by his body and tosses him high above the judge's desk. The American flag is hit and it falls from the wall. The man screams as he slams hard into the wall losing consciousness as he lands on the floor. The judge screams as the officer's body lands near her. Concrete debris and a clock falls onto the officer's body. Jaden sees words scrolling across his eyes and read it.

"Are you not entertained judge? Are you not entertained?" Jaden yells while turning around and walking towards the exit. The four prisoners lay trembling under the bench.

"That was three minutes and forty-five seconds with time to spare judge."

Smoke and debris floats in the air from behind the judge's desk.

Jaden walks out of the courtroom door and down the empty hallway.

'Where did you get that quote from?' Jaden asks.

'It was on the Internet under famous movie quotes. The movie *Gladiator*,' AI says.

'Cool. I know I missed a lot of movies from the past eighteen years.'

Jaden makes it towards the entrance glass doors of the courthouse building. A news reporter and cameraman walk through the front door to meet him.

"Are you Jaden?" The young small blonde hair news reporter asks.

"Yes I am. You are going to have to interview me quickly because, as you see, I just broke out of custody and the government is after me," Jaden says while the bright lights from the camera go on Jaden's face.

They walk back away from the front door.

"I'm Jan from Channel 3 News. Did you really travel to another galaxy and is there really a pending attack on Earth?" She asks in one breath, while putting a skinny wireless microphone to his face. A nanoscanner sits in front of the camera recording the interview also.

'Jaden hurry, soldiers are creating a perimeter around the courthouse.'

'I see them.'

"Yes, I left Earth in February 2000, you can research on the Internet Michael Morris government conspiracy 2000 for proof. I've traveled 2.2 million light-years to the Andromeda Galaxy to a planet called Xenos, where I met some friendly aliens that are about 70,000 years ahead of us. They uncovered a nanomole in my brain, implanted in human bodies hundreds of thousands of years ago. A nanomole is something that can control a human body with the right amount of energy from the mother ship. This is why these bad aliens called Darclonians are here to attack us for whatever reason I do not know yet. Their mother ship is here and hiding behind the moon watching us to plan their silent attack. I'm here to help the government to avoid this possible attack. I've been attacked by the government and police for the past few days..."

Suddenly Jaden's clear energy shield forms seven feet in diameter around the cameraman and news reporter. A three-inch circular hole is made in the glass door. It goes silent around them as a fast moving 4000 feet per second sniper bullet slows down towards Jaden's head. A ripple of white energy is seen around where the bullet enters the outside of the shield. The cameraman turns the camera towards the bullet slowly moving through the air and stops. Jaden walks up to the bullet still thrusting forward. He grabs the hot bullet with his fingers and shows it to the reporter.

"Did you really just stop this sniper bullet?" She asks while taking a step towards Jaden.

"Yes, I'm what you call a BIO-Sapien. Here is proof that your government is trying to kill the only person that can help stop this attack. Vice President Robinson is behind this attack on me. He has been trying to kill me ever since I found a UFO in 2000. These headaches and sudden unresponsive humans have been experiencing around Earth is all related to these nanomoles in their brains. The government has the instructions on how to block the signals in these nanomoles," Jaden says while dropping the bullet.

"Maybe this can explain why people are disappearing around the world at high elevations without a trace?" She asks.

"Yes, people should stay away from tall buildings and high elevation places."

"If the mother ship is here, why doesn't it just attack us?" She asks.

"They are much smarter than that. They would anticipate us to defend ourselves, they have something else in mind. They know a lot about us already. I would like to talk more to you, but I have to go save a friend. Make sure you play this story to everyone, even people in other countries," Jaden says.

"What are you going to do after you save your friend?"

"Go back to the Andromeda Galaxy or travel to another part of this galaxy. This planet isn't worth saving, I've had enough. I warned the government, so I've done my job. I saw some nice uninhabited Earth-type planets a couple of thousand light-years from here. Maybe I'll go there to start a family and start my own government," Jaden says while walking towards the exit doors.

"Good luck sir."

He sees SWAT people standing around different entrances while fifty men stand outside the building. Armed men are slowly walking up to the front of the courthouse stairs with their guns pointing forward. Jaden sees local police, state police, FBI,

Homeland Security, helicopters and drone planes flying by outside. Jaden fires a gravity shock wave at the front door as the cameraman continues recording ten feet behind him. An explosion and the sound of broken glass are heard. The glass doors quickly come off the hinges and fly into the air. The armed men on the stairs crouch down and look at the glass door flying over them and into a tree. The leaves on the tree fall quickly towards the ground with the door and debris. Jaden's body goes invisible as he runs outside the front opening and towards the left of the courthouse. The fresh warm spring air hits his body.

"Sir, the suspect disappeared from sight," a sniper across the street on top of a church says into the radio to a military commander.

He runs and leaps high into the air. The anti-gravity energy around him allows him to jump forty feet into the air as he slowly lands on the roof of a red church. He sees people across the street from the courthouse in a park where people are standing behind a yellow tape. Jaden jumps from the roof of the church and into a parking lot. Jaden continues to run down a side street. The nanoscanners show that the courthouse is being rushed by many federal agents and military personnel from all directions.

'They are taking the news anchor and camera man into custody,' AI says.

'I see, agents are taking their holographic disc from the camera now. Shit! That video is never going to see the light of day. I did the best I could do,' Jaden says while running down the street at 18 mph.

'All the roads are blocked off with heavy checkpoints. I have a creative idea on how we can escape out of town,' AI says while a helicopter flies by.

'Creative sounds good to me. Now I know how the predator and the invisible man feel,' Jaden says.

Chipotle garlic hot wings – Action Wings
smothered in Action Sauce.

BBQ Fusion wings. Best sellers. Action wings, bbq
sauce, action spices & special garlic sauce.

Chapter 20: The Prison In-break

Traffic is moving slowly on Highway 301 as a tractor-trailer pulls into a checkpoint. German Shepherds smell each vehicle and are walking with a state trooper. Federal agents are asking each driver questions.

"Sir, where are you heading and do you have a driver's license?" A FBI agent asks the truck driver.

"I'm heading to Roanoke, Virginia to drop off this load of books to a warehouse," the truck driver says while passing his driver's license to the agent.

"Roanoke? My mother lives on Cove Road in Roanoke, very nice town. Sir, have you seen these two men?" The agent asks.

"No, I haven't," the truck driver says.

An agent opens the passenger door and looks in the rear cabin behind the driver. He sprays a white powder in the cab with thermal glasses on.

"We are going to have to do a quick DNA cheek swab and we are going to have to look in your trailer also," the agent says while passing the truck driver a fresh Q-tip.

'AI, this isn't going to work, they are going to see me.'

The truck driver presses a button inside his cabin and the rear trailer unlocks. Dogs smell the back of the trailer and an agent climbs into the rear of the trailer. He sprays a white powder into the air and walks to the front of the trailer with thermal goggles, looking around. He looks at a shipment of books that read QUICKFLASH 2030, SCI-FI, SECRET AGENT, THRILLER. TWO BEST SELLER LISTS through the plastic on a crate.

The agent jumps down from the rear and says, "All clear."

Another agent on the roof of the trailer spraying a light white powder climbs down a ladder saying, "All clear."

The truck driver drives off and heads towards Highway 125.

'It worked, but the skin on my back is killing me. I'm also feeling a little dizzy,' Jaden says while the wind brushes against his body.

Jaden's back is against the side of the tractor- trailer.

'How didn't they see me with their thermal glasses?' Jaden asks while turning to the side to pull himself up to the roof.

147

'The temperature outside your body was matched with the temperature of the trailer. I also blocked any scents from leaving your body,' AI says.

'Good work buddy, now you are thinking. The driver said he was going to Roanoke right?'

'Yes, the west side of Virginia. We need to go northeast to Buckeye. I checked the path of the highway for the next one hundred miles by connecting the nanoscanners. There is another light checkpoint getting onto Interstate 95 in five miles,' AI says.

Jaden pulls himself to the roof of the trailer. He lies on his back on top of the trailer as his body turns visible again. The air is full of pollen and fresh oxygen from the trees around him. He is admiring the sky and clouds on this partly cloudy day. His body feels the gears shifting. He is thinking about Kimberly and his parents as the wind blows on his body. The engine constantly switching gears reminds Jaden when he was learning stick shift. Jaden thinks about being on another planet with Kimberly and starting a family.

They reach another checkpoint with two state troopers and the driver shows his ID. Jaden quickly goes invisible. The truck continues onto I-95. Jaden stands up using the pro-gravity nanodrones in his feet, fighting the strong winds as the truck reaches 65 mph. Cars are cruising at high speeds in the HSCCVL lane. He walks to the front of the trailer near the cabin. Jaden climbs onto the side of the passenger door and breaks the window. The truck driver swerves in the middle lane and cars to the side of him honk their horns while trying to avoid him. Jaden opens the door and climbs in. His body suddenly reappears as if he teleported there.

The truck driver begins to scream at the top of his lungs while trying to focus on the road and steering.

"Are you finished screaming like a little girl?" Jaden asks.

"How did you get in here? What do you want?" The frightened driver asks while looking back and forth

"For starters I would like your truck. Just to borrow it," Jaden politely replies.

The guy pulls out a stun gun from his visor and shoots Jaden with it. It jabs his arm and shocks his body.

"Wow, that felt good. But seriously I need your truck, you can pull over now or I can toss you out while it is moving," Jaden says.

"You aren't getting my truck," the scared man says.

'His heart rate is going very high.'

'I'm losing patience and I really don't care,' Jaden says.

The driver pulls out a knife, while pulling over and slamming on the brakes on the shoulder. Jaden leans forward and holds onto the dashboard.

"I'll stab you right now, if you don't get out of my truck," he says.

"You have a wife and two sons. Today is your oldest son's birthday. Do you really want to die on his birthday to protect your company's truck?" Jaden calmly asks while the truck completely stops.

The driver tries to stab Jaden in the left leg, but it doesn't penetrate his skin. His tough skin repels the knife like Kevlar in a bulletproof vest.

"Would you like to try again?" Jaden asks with his arms folded.

He stabs Jaden harder in the shoulder while grunting, the knife doesn't penetrate.

"What are you some kind of alien or cyborg?" He asks while stabbing Jaden in the head.

"You just made some of my hair fall out. It is men like yourself who leave people behind asking God why you had to die. All you had to do was jump out and say someone stole your truck. But you future dickheads want to do things the hard way!" Jaden yells while opening the passenger door. Jaden takes the knife and stabs the man in the leg with it. The man screams in pain while Jaden unbuckles his seat belt.

"There there, it doesn't hurt that much. Just remember, material things can't replace a life."

Jaden tosses the man out of the passenger door with one hand into the bushes about twenty feet away.

"Tell your company the BIO-Sapien Hulk stole your truck," Jaden snaps.

Jaden moves into the driver's seat and begins to drive. He switches gears. His hair begins to grow back in a patch in his scalp.

"Why must people do things the hard way, I don't get it… This isn't too hard, just like a stick shift car," he says while the engine stalls and the gears grind.

'Shit, I'm very rusty,' Jaden says.

149

'The driver is in a lot of pain and losing blood deep in the bushes,' AI says.

'The hell with him, he is lucky to still be alive. I'm having these evil feelings and thoughts of just killing anyone that gets in my way. I feel as if I'm turning into the Terminator or something. This is really strange, it is as if there is something evil growing inside of me,' Jaden says.

'I think those strange energies that come around you when you get angry or feel pain have something to do with the changes in your personality.'

'If it does, I'm sure you will figure it out. Every vehicle I see has GPS systems.'

Jaden inputs the address to Buckeye Federal Prison into the built in GPS screen.

"Drive forty-eight Miles on I-95," the GPS says.

BUCKEYE FEDERAL PRISON 11:57AM

Prisoners are moaning in surrounding cells around Kimberly. She can't go back to sleep because of the smell and prisoners yelling obscene remarks from their cells.

A man yells from his door with a scary voice, "It is snowing outside Chinese food, today is our lucky day. I'm going to fill you up with some warm protein, then top you off like a gas pump. I'm a certified serial rapist. They call me the Gyn-analyst."

She begins to cry again and doesn't know how she is going to get out of this mess. She keeps thinking someone is going to come in her cell any minute.

Jaden is two miles down the road from the prison in the tractor-trailer deciding his best strategy. He sees a strong prison guard presence throughout the prison with machine guns.

'What are these prison inmates doing to themselves in the basement?' AI asks.

'You don't want to know. Think of it as practice makes perfect or the death of millions.'

Jaden locates Kimberly in the cell in the basement on the other side of the prison.

'There is a prison guard holding his head screaming. It looks as if he was escorting a prisoner. Now the prisoner is kicking him and

150

hitting up with something…oh no, he is knocked out cold now,' Jaden says.

The prisoner is taking the guard's keys.

'His nanomole is affecting his brain. It is in between normal open and neutral. Most of the guards are coming towards the front of the prison with guns and exoskeleton body suits. There is only one other guard in the unit,' AI says.

'Shit, a huge machine is blowing white powdery looking flakes all over the ground and in the air around the prison.

'I guess we won't be sneaking in invisibly with that powder. You might need to do a full atomic solar recharge, if your shield strength gets too low,' AI says.

'I don't need to sneak in anyway. I'm ready for that atomic solar recharge. I remember when Bellona did it, that was so cool. I just hope it isn't too painful.'

'It won't work the same way, ours is configured differently. They can be deadly around humans. When the nanodrones explode at near the speed of light towards space, they make holes in everything in all directions. When they return to Earth, they carry a good amount of radiation energy from the magnetosphere. It can affect anything in a thirty foot radius until they return back into your body and are contained.'

'Okay. As long as my energy is replenished from it, I really don't care about anyone else. Damn, these guards in the towers have twin M2hb guns with fifty caliber rounds. Damn those are big bullets. They also have a weapon I've never seen before,' Jaden says.

'Those bullets fire over 4000 feet per second. That much power can penetrate your skin and quickly weaken your shield energy. They have a next generation nitrogen-cooled 15,000-rpm M134 mini gun in a tower. They also have bat bullets with little wings on each of them and nanorockets. Bat bullets turn in the air and hit the exact target it was aimed at, even if the target moves. Nanorockets are ten-inch mini rockets with C4 explosives,' AI says.

'Shit, let's do it,' Jaden says while there is a brief silence, 'I have a plan.'

'I have a plan,' AI says at the same time.

A few minutes pass by. The tractor-trailer is driving straight towards the gate of the prison. The driver's seat is empty. A prison guard sees the truck coming at 50 mph down the street and he gets on the radio. The guards in the three towers begin firing their huge powerful mounted guns at the truck as the truck bursts through the twenty-foot high checkpoint gate with barbed wire on top of it. The high-speed bullets look like flying sparks of light. The truck quickly catches on fire as Jaden is running one hundred feet behind the truck while invisible. The powerful bullets rip hundreds of huge holes in the trailer like paper. The tires go flat and the tractor-trailer changes direction and explodes. The books in the trailer explode in different directions as well. Jaden fires a shock wave at one of the towers. It cruises through the air making a hissing sound like a high-speed softball. It hits the tower ripping the top of it off. The guard in the tower feels an abrupt movement and then he experiences weightlessness as his body floats through the air with the tower. He grabs onto the walls around him. Fifty feet in the air, the guard suddenly experiences a direction change downwards and the weight on his body greatly increases. His body weight of 180 lbs increases to 520 lbs and his spine feels the sudden strain. He screams in pain as the glass and tower crash into the ground creating a huge amount of debris. The tractor-trailer stops against a huge wall and continues to burn. Black smoke quickly floats into the sky.

White powder completely covers Jaden's invisible body. He quickly turns visible and runs through the first gate. A secret weapon elevates out of the concrete on top of the wall. There are two square metal dishes right next to each other turning directly towards Jaden. Someone is controlling them remotely. The machines channels two invisible microwave beams towards Jaden's body causing him to fall and roll on the ground a few feet. The intense heat from the twin ray guns penetrates half an inch into his skin and turns off. The pain quickly stops as he lies on his back. The pain traveled all around his body as if he was being burned alive.

'Why didn't you use the shields Jaden? Why did you override me?' AI asks.

'I knew something was coming, I wanted to see what they were going to hit me with.'

A prison guard on a loudspeaker speaks to Jaden.

"Put your hands over your head and get on your knees. You are surrounded by two ray gun machines. If you step a foot into any direction you will feel heat greater than 150°F."

'Scan the machines with the nanoscanners when I get up so we can find out how this weapon works. Also analyze the waves' frequencies,' Jaden says.

'Yes sir.'

Jaden stands up and walks forward. A double burning sensation comes over his body as his body feels 155°F of microwave energy. He stops moving forward and the microwaves stop. Smoke can be seen coming off his clothes.

'Shit, now I know what an ant feels like when someone puts a magnifying glass on it in the sun,' he says while rubbing his hot navy shirt with holes in it.

'I have the configuration of the guns. There is a laser under the machine, heating up and ionizing the air. Then a plasma channel is created and electromagnetic waves go in the direction the square dishes aim towards,' AI says.

Jaden puts his hands over his head as if he was surrendering and rests on his knees.

'How can we use that type of energy?' He asks.

'The system works similar to the components of your molecule rippers by creating plasma energy. But to reproduce the same effect will require a lot of energy and not worth it. But, we can contain the wave energy by getting nanodrones to spin around in two directions to collect the electromagnetic waves and then redirect them like a mirror. Your hands will need to hold up the hot energy forces.'

'Sounds good, let's do that,' Jaden says.

Two officers in exoskeleton suits walk from the front steel gate surrounded by twenty-foot concrete walls. One of them has handcuffs in his hand. Jaden stands up and extends his arms in front of him.

"Get back on the ground and put your hands over your head, or we will hit you with a 180°F blast of heat. You will suffer second and third degree burns!" The man yells through the loudspeaker.

Jaden continues walking and yells out.

"Let's see what you got!" Jaden yells while his fingers are waving at them to come at him.

The two guards stop thirty feet in front of Jaden. The translucent heat wave molecules are disrupting the light waves between him and the ray guns. The vision looks hazy as the air quickly heats up. The intense double beams come towards Jaden at a high speed. The white powdery flakes floating in the air catch on fire between the ray gun and Jaden. They turn to smoke and disappear. He quickly turns his palms around towards the square dishes. The nanodrones are quickly rotating on the skin of his palms and try to contain the hot, intense beams in front of him. The force to contain the hot energy slowly pushes down on the palms of his hands and touches his skin. Jaden grunts and groans as his hands feel intense burning sensations up to 177°F. Jaden goes down on his knees from the forces on his arms and hands. The intense heat bombards Jaden's body and makes him perspire. His muscles bulge in his arms and shoulders. Smoke is coming from his shirt and hair. The operators of the machines believe there is a malfunction and increase the power. He slowly changes the direction of his hands and aims them towards the guards standing in front of him with confused looks on their faces. Jaden grunts aloud while sweat runs down his face. He redirects the hot waves of energy towards the guards in front of him. The ray gun waves redirect and hit the guards' suits, but can't penetrate the nanotubing fiber materials. The nanotubing material reflects the direct blast of heat. The waves quickly move in different directions around the exoskeleton suits. The heat cooks them from the outside and they begin to do a chicken dance and run back towards the gates.

"Do the southern fried chicken dance!" Jaden yells.

Jaden stands up with a smile on his face and runs behind the guards. He redirects the funneling energy back towards the dishes. The dishes turn glowing red and quickly turn off. His hands are smoking and suffer burns all over the skin. The guards in the two towers arm their big guns. Jaden can hear the loading of the guns from where he is.

He makes it through the second gate. He runs and jumps thirty feet into the air firing a blue tinted atoms ripper with his left hand towards the tower on his left. The atoms ripper creates a three-foot hole straight through the tower. The atoms ripper also makes a hole straight through the mini gun and the guard's body. Blood splats all inside the tower as if a tomato just exploded. Jaden runs into a small building where visitors enter through. He sees through the nanoscanners that prisoners are letting other prisoners out. The second guard is taken down and is beaten unconscious by crazed prisoners. Prisoners have their hands through the opening of their cells, yelling to the other prisoners to let them out. Kimberly hears the rioting outside her cell door and begins to pray.

"You are all mine, Chinese food. I'm going to put my duck sauce all inside of your sweet egg roll holes," the Gyn-analyst says through her prison cell opening while he jiggles keys.

He tries both keys but they don't open Kimberly's cell door.

"Monkey's cum! These keys ain't working!"

"You dickhead, let us out, we can help you," a man yells.

He opens the other prisoners' locked doors.

Jaden sees Kimberly is in trouble and quickly runs through the empty visiting area.

'It is a trap Jaden, I count: seven federal agents, fifteen prison guards, and six special ops military in exoskeleton suits carrying mini guns. They all have on gas masks. The men have twelve gauge shotguns, sniper rifles, bat bullets, nanorocket guns, and twin M2hb guns from the inside towers. There is an unmanned aerial helicopter gunship called a helidrone hovering above with Hydra II rockets,' AI says.

The hybrid helidrone has two wings on both sides that face down. There is a medium-sized rotary blade in the middle of each wing.

'Wow, AI you know your weapons.'

'I downloaded most government weapons and guns before we left town.'

'I don't have too much of a choice. It's show time, let's see what kind of a human weapon I am.'

Jaden opens the door into a huge courtyard area. He runs forward as white powder is everywhere and canisters of tear gas are exploding a few feet around him. The canisters explode as they hit the ground. Jaden holds his breath and closes his eyes. Thousands of fast moving bullets are shot at Jaden from the towers. Soldiers in exoskeleton suits a few dozen feet away fire their mini guns at Jaden as if they are a firing squad. Guards and agents on foot fire M16's and shotguns at Jaden. The fast moving bullets come from all directions and hit the outside of his shield with tremendous force. Bat bullets are coming at Jaden from rooftops. He has the rpm at 150,000 but the forward shield can't destroy the bullets fast enough. Nanorockets are being shot at Jaden from a distance. They twirl in the air from the towers and a huge explosion is seen hitting his outer body shield. Fire shoots upwards and Jaden's hands are holding the inside of the shield from jerking from the force. Fire forms around his shield as smoke flies towards the sky. The force from the four nanorockets with C4 knocks Jaden off balance and off his feet. The shield begins to enclose on him and turn grey as his shield gets weaker. The molecules from the bullets and energy from the blasts quickly move around the shield.

"We got him boys! Keep firing!" A guard yells, while they move closer to Jaden laying flat on his stomach with a grey material surrounding him.

Kimberly hears explosions and gunfire from a distance. She stands in the corner of the cell looking at the door. The roaming prisoners in the SHU area are running around yelling and screaming. One man runs into a small kitchen area that is behind the guard's office to steal food. A long corridor area behind the office leads to a steel door sealing off the SHU area from the rest of the building. Eight other men are trying to get Kimberly's door open with the two keys.

"Central we need help, two guards are down in the SHU2 area, prisoners are roaming freely," a guard at the checkpoint says on the radio while looking through security cameras.

"Sorry SHU2, keep the area sealed off, we are handling a serious threat," the warden says on the radio.

The prisoners talk amongst themselves.

"This is a special lock, the key is probably somewhere in the office," a prisoner named Tommy says.

The Gyn-analyst quickly pushes people out of the way and runs to the locked office where the SHU guards sit. He has a look of determination on his face to get Kimberly's cell door open. His hormones are driving him to find the key and be the first one through her door.

"The guards' room is locked. Someone help me find something to pick the lock," Gyn-analyst says.

A Mexican prisoner runs from the kitchen area behind the office with a small bottle in his hand.

"Look what I found! Some organic corn oil!" He yells at the men crowded around Kimberly's door.

"Alright! Good work man. Just what we needed!" A prisoner yells.

He pours it in a few of the men's hands as they rub it together in their hands. Drips of the corn oil fall all over the floor. Then they rub their hands in their orange prison pants. Tommy shines the guard's flashlight on Kimberly. He picks out the part of her body he wants to taste first.

"There is no MSG in this Chinese food!" Tommy yells.

"You are going to be Freddy Kruger's mother by the time we finish with you," the Gyn-analyst yells from down the hall while trying to pick the lock with plastic utensils.

"I'm first you dick," Tommy yells while they push each other.

Outside, the men continue firing over 3400 bullets at Jaden. The helidrone continues to float above, monitoring the situation. The glowing grey energy inside of Jaden's shield continues to crush his body. The pressure increases as his shield weakens more and he drops to his knees trying to fight back the strong forces pushing down on him.

'How much longer, AI? I feel as if I'm being crushed by a four hundred pound woman,' Jaden mumbles.

'Just a few more seconds. Continue fighting against the pressure,' AI says while doing calculations.

'What is all this grey shit around me?' Jaden asks.

'Advanced plasma fusion, it's recycling the kinetic energy and molecules in the bullets,' AI says.

"Keep shooting, he is still glowing!" A guard yells while all the men walk closer and circle Jaden.

Jaden is pushing his hands off the ground trying to lift himself against the strong pressure around his body. He strains and groans as he uses all of his muscle strength to push back. AI is doing advanced Andromedian calculus calculations for some nanodrones to return to Earth at slightly different angles and group together.

Trillions of energy storing nanodrones enter the glowing grey energy and quickly move around at high speeds. There is a bright flash of light around Jaden's body and a huge explosion is created.

Jaden's mind goes into 80x nanotime mode. The white powder flies in all directions. The energy-storing nanodrones, grey molecules and shield generating nanodrones explode in all directions at half the speed of light, creating holes in anything in their path. The men fly backwards into the air from the huge explosion as billions of microscopic holes are created in their bodies and guns. The military men in exoskeleton suits slowly fall backwards from the blast. Their impenetrable nanite-graphite armor has microscopic holes all over.

Jaden, still holding his breath, stands up with his arms toward the sky. He yells as his muscles strain and are in pain around his body. The fast moving nanodrones reach the strong energy from just outside the magnetosphere above the planet. They quickly slow down and change direction back towards Earth in groups. Jaden has no shields while the men land on the ground screaming in a low growl. The helidrone fires several Hydra 2 rockets at Jaden. A few of the men's bodies shake uncontrollably and bleed. Jaden's nanotime goes into 10x as the rockets slowly move towards him from above. The two towers to the left and right of Jaden 150 feet away begin firing their high-powered twin M2hb guns and nanorockets towards Jaden. The bullets slowly cruise in the air. The bullets quickly heat the air around them. Two soldiers in bionic suits struggle to stand to the right of Jaden. They are bleeding inside of their exoskeleton suits.

Nanotime continues, the first Hydra rocket get within seventeen feet of Jaden. He looks around at everything slowly coming towards him. The groups of nanodrones with radiation charged particles return from space at one quarter the speed of light. They come from all directions quickly passing through the guards laying flat on the roofs and the guards in the right tower. They also pass through the chest of a military man in an exoskeleton suit that just stood back up. They die instantly. The returning nanodrones return through the path of the bullets shot towards Jaden, destroying them also. The nanodrones return to Jaden's body and quickly start forming an energy shield around him. Jaden's sees on his eye screen that his full energy is at fifty-five percent. A 200-foot circle of gravity shock wave smoke is around Jaden as he fires it with his right hand towards the Hydra missiles. A great ball of fire forms as the first of four Hydra missiles explodes. The shock wave takes the explosive force and reverses its direction. The fire is circling inside of the shock wave like a tornado. Jaden's reverse shield forms around him at 275,000 rpm. Hundreds of bullets stop in midair to the left of Jaden. The first of two nanorockets from the left tower explodes at the outside of the energy shield creating an oval fireball around it.

Nanotime speeds up to 75x as the oval fire expands around Jaden's entire shield. The gravity shock wave fired towards the Hydro rockets continues to destroy the remaining three. The huge spinning fireball shock wave hits the helidrone before it gets a chance to move. The helidrone explodes from the force and explosion of its own rockets. It propels backwards out of control into the sky as a gigantic fireball. Jaden fires a gravity shock wave and an atoms ripper with both hands in front of him at the same time towards the left tower. The suspended bullets are quickly destroyed as a small bubble of the shield quickly moves with the shock wave. The bubble breaks up while expanding with the atoms ripping shock wave. It moves through the air like a huge spitball. The bullets and nanorockets vaporize before they can explode. The shock wave hits the tower with tremendous force, ripping the top of the tower off and causing it to spin. Trillions of molecules in the tower incinerate as nanotime goes off in Jaden's mind. The top part of the tower continues half a mile into the air and then straight into the ground.

The fireball that hit the helidrone continues a mile and suddenly changes directions straight towards the Earth. The last standing man in the exoskeleton suit tries to fire his mini gun at Jaden, but it doesn't work. The gravity shock wave nanodrones quickly return from different directions and into Jaden's body.

"You didn't learn anything from the end of *The Lawnmower Man* did you?" Jaden asks while walking over towards him. Jaden can see the fear in his eyes through his helmet. The man fires a stun gun from his left hand and the electricity goes around Jaden's shield.

"That's all you got?"

The man slowly walks away towards Jaden's left . Jaden picks up another huge 150 lbs mini gun lying on the white powdery ground.

"Please don't shoot," a robotic sounding voice comes from the soldier's helmet.

"Robocop voice guard, I just took out an army and you still going to try to shoot me? I see the fear in your eyes, bionic dick. Don't walk away, you should have thought of *don't shoot* when you were about to shoot at me again just now," Jaden says while the soldier walks towards the building on Jaden's left. He continues to aim the big gun towards the soldier.

'Don't shoot him, he is unarmed and we have to hurry to save Kimberly.'

'No, it is beginning to feel good, killing people. It's giving me some kind of high,' Jaden says in a low voice to AI.

"They say that graphite nanite plastic and nanotubing fiber materials are impenetrable to any bullet on Earth. I'm going to be your *MythBusters* host today. Seventy-five bullets a second, over 4000 bullets a minute, Robosoldier," Jaden says with a smile on his face.

'Jaden no!'

The loud mini gun's barrels quickly spins in circles, while bullets are shot at the soldier, who braces to cover his face. Hundreds of bullets riddle his exoskeleton suit in a few seconds. Shells from the gun bounce onto the ground. The noise from the ricocheting bullets echoes in stereo from all directions. The soldier falls face forward onto the ground.

"He is down for the count, Tyson knocked out his opponent in under three seconds. The crowd goes wild and people are demanding their money back," Jaden says while dropping the gun and putting his arms in the air as if he is the champion. Jaden makes crowd cheering sounds. Smoke comes from the barrel of the gun and the bottom of the soldier's body.

Jaden turns the soldier over and sees hundreds of bullets stuck inside the armor.

"The myth is confirmed, but the soldier's life isn't," Jaden snaps.

The nanoscanners show that the bullets didn't penetrate, but the bullets pushed the body armor inwards. Jaden quickly runs through the second building, which is a kitchen area for guards.

'Jaden, there are some chemical imbalances in your frontal lobe. Something is still changing your judgment.'

'Yeah, I think you are right. I don't know what came over me,' he says.

SHU 12:02 PM

"What is taking so long? I feel like I'm cooking a sausage in oil with all this back and forth friction," Tommy asks while walking to the door with his hand in his pants.

"I can't pick the lock," Gyn-analyst says.

"Idiot, how long you been in jail? These locks open with fingerprints and the warden has the only key for the door. Stop thinking with your brain in your pants," Tommy says.

"I've been in jail for twenty-two years. You are the idiot for just telling me now, you asshole. Come on, help me with this guard over here."

They run to the unconscious guard lying on the floor. Another man helps them lift and carry the guard to the office door. They press his fingers inside the door handle. The door opens automatically and they toss the guard to the side. They quickly find the key on a hanger.

"Give it to me, give it to me," Tommy demands.

"I'm first. I'm the Gyn-doctor," he says while holding the key in the air as if it is a treasure key. The rest of the men have smiles on their faces and cheer.

"Yo, this dude is carrying every STD in the book. We all going to have what he has, he should go last," Tommy says.

"How you know?" Another prisoner asks.

They push the Gyn-analyst down and take his key. Tommy pushes people out of the way as a mob of prisoners stand around the door close together.

"Stop rubbing your meat against me," a prisoner says to another.

The Gyn-analyst tries to push his way through the crowd. They unlock Kimberly's prison door with greasy hands as they yell amongst each other. They are pushing and shoving each other out of the way to get to the door first. The door doesn't open because men are in the way. A line of smoke appears on the floor around the prisoners' shoes.

"Move back you dickheads, I can't open the door!" Tommy yells.

161

"I just want to wear her skirt and panties," a small skinny prisoner says.

They open the door wide and Tommy runs inside first. The rest are pushing and shoving each other while trying to get in first. Suddenly there is a loud explosion. A second prison runs inside. A gravity shock wave force dismounts the holding area steel door down the hallway. The steel door flies down the hallway at a tremendous speed and down to the SHU cells. The fast moving door hits the third man from entering the cell and two other men in the hallway. Their bodies slam into a concrete wall and the door creates a new rectangular hole in the concrete. Sunlight shines through the hole over the horizontal steel door. Blood squirts in all directions. Jaden runs down the hallway as other prisoners lay on the floor with baffled looks on their faces. The Gyn-analyst is leaning flat against the wall across from Kimberly's cell, looking at the steel door in the concrete at the end of the hallway. Smoke and debris is floating in the air as Jaden runs through it.

Jaden turns and walks into Kimberly's cell. The Gyn-analyst looks at Jaden as if he is a ghost. Kimberly throws a straight punch towards Jaden's face.

"Hiya!" She yells.

He sees her punch coming towards him and quickly moves out of the way. She does not recognize Jaden covered in white powdery debris.

"It's me, Jaden," he yells.

Hazy light from the hallway is shining on her as she is standing in a karate stance with her panties on looking at Jaden with confusion. The two prisoners that ran into her cell are unconscious on the floor. Tommy's head is in the toilet and there is a crack down the middle of the toilet bowl. The other three men run down the hallway through the new hole that leads outside.

"You okay? They took your skirt off that fast?" Jaden asks.

The Gyn-analyst speaks behind Jaden, "Buddy, if you wanted a turn all you had to do was ask."

Kimberly responds to Jaden while putting her skirt back on, "I'm fine, I can handle myself. I took my skirt off so I could fight these perverts better."

"I forgot you took self defense classes and a few karate classes," Jaden says.

Kimberly sits back down in the corner of the cell with a sad look on her face.

"What are you doing? We have to get out of here," Jaden says.

"Hey dude, can you hurry up? This oil is heating up and I can't keep this hand in motion," Gyn-analyst says.

"STD-analyst man, step away from the door, before I take you off this planet. You have enough little crabs and lobsters between your legs that you can open your own Red Lobster. Smothering them in corn oil is animal cruelty," Jaden says while Kimberly chuckles.

The man stands there with an embarrassed look on his face.

"That was funny," she says.

"Kimberly, why did you sit back down? There is an army approaching the prison, we have to get out of here. I'm here to rescue you sweetie."

The Gyn-analyst responds while closing their prison door and locking it, "Screw you, you limp dick cocksucker."

It turns very dark in the cell as the closing door echoes in the small room.

"Why did you come for me? What do you want from me? How can I believe you are who you say you are?" She asks while beginning to cry.

"I care about you. I felt it was my fault you were put in prison in the first place. I thought breaking into a maximum security prison was enough proof to show I'm real," Jaden says.

"I'm still confused. I had this dream about my childhood this morning. So many things were corrupted in my memory, I need…" she says while stopping to sniffle and becomes more emotional.

'We have to hurry. The guards are leaving this building and the other prisoners that were down here are releasing the prisoners throughout the building from their cells. There is about to be a riot in here. The military and guards aren't coming this direction,' AI says.

'Okay, okay, AI.'

"…I need to know something," she says.

"What is it? Talk to me," Jaden says while sitting over Tommy's head in the toilet.

He breathes bubbles into the toilet, still unconscious.

"I need to know the truth from you.... I've been putting things together in my head for the past couple of hours. When I was seven

163

years old, I saw something traumatic that my subconscious made me forget until today. I was on a school trip in New York City on the tramway heading to Roosevelt Island. I saw this flying spaceship outside of the windows on the tramway. I've denied and suppressed this for years. I remember kids screaming and my hair floating in the air. I was the only person not scared of it. I felt something from the spaceship as if, as if my soul connected with it. I felt as if my life and future had a lot to do with that spaceship. If that was really you in that spacecraft, I want you to tell me what did the spacecraft do before it left?" Kimberly asks while holding back tears.

Jaden thinks and thinks.

'AI, help me out here, you were there too.'

"That was about a month ago, for me. I briefly remember hearing the conversation in the tramway. Your teacher…called you Kim," he yells.

"Yes, in elementary school until high school I was called Kim."

"That was the day I found the UFO… February… 15th 2000 right?" Jaden asks while standing up.

"Yes, it was. It was cloudy and rainy. But what did the UFO do in front of me?" She asks.

'Shit, I can't remember,' Jaden says to AI.

"Hmm.. You stood there and you weren't scared, I remember saying that."

"If that was you in there, you should know what you did," Kimberly says.

'There is a heavily armed Raptor jet fighter flying this way. I think they are about to bomb this prison. All the guards are way outside the complex. There are also thirty prisoners running towards this direction from the upstairs cells. Sorry, I don't remember what you did back in 2000,' AI says.

"The UFO ship did something that stood out before it left that I knew something or someone human was inside," she says.

A mob of men are at the prison door yelling inside their cell. Some look at the other prisoners' body parts splattered against the wall to the right of Kimberly's cell and run away screaming.

"We want some Chinese food! We want Chinese food!" They chant.

"Who has the key?" A big man asks.

"I got it right here. That bastard is hogging the Asian cuisine to himself," The Gyn-analyst says while he pushes his way through the boisterous crowd.

Jaden creates a shield around them to block out the loud chanting. It becomes romantically quiet around them. The chanting completely disappears. Jaden looks deep into Kimberly's crying brown eyes.

"I remember now. I got it. I was looking at you thinking how cute you looked with your brown innocent eyes. You were looking at me as if you wanted to come with me and you didn't have one nervous bone in your body. I made the outside shields look like a huge eye and I *winked* at you. The rain gave the shield a translucent look," Jaden says.

"Yes! Yes! That is correct!" She yells while jumping up and hugging Jaden.

'Jaden…' AI says.

"I'm sorry I didn't believe you before. I'll never doubt you again," she says while putting her arms around his shoulders. He puts his arms around her waist.

She tries to kiss him in the dark.

"That is my nose…that is my eye," Jaden says. She uses her hand for guidance and kisses him on his mouth.

"Hey! That's cheating," he says.

It is completely quiet as Kimberly's lips touch Jaden's. As her lips press against his, chemical signals travel all around his body. They connect for the first time emotionally and physically. They continue to slowly open mouth kiss.

'Her bacteria and cooties are entering your mouth…'

'So..her cooties and bacteria taste good.'

Time feels as if it is in nanotime for Jaden. He doesn't hear what AI is telling him. He feels her tongue rubbing against his. Her head turns side to side and their noses touch.

She pulls away and looks at him in the dark and says, "I think fate brought us together again."

"I think so, this is completely déjà vu. I felt similar feelings for you eighteen years ago as if you were someone I knew in another life or something," Jaden whispers to her.

'Jaden! There is a Raptor jet fighter two miles away that just switched to visual stealth mode and just fired a 5000-pound AGM-114Z Hellfire 3 vacuum missile. It is coming at this building at 1200 mph,' AI says excitedly.

"We have to go Kimberly, right now!" Jaden says while the door unlocks.

"Why? What is going on," she asks.

"Trust me, there is a powerful missile coming to blow this prison up," Jaden says.

"Why would the government blow up one of their own prisons?" Kimberly asks.

'What is a Hellfire 3 missile?' Jaden asks while charging a shock wave.

"Stand back sweetie," Jaden says while stepping forward. The loud chanting and yelling returns.

'One of the most deadliest thermobaric missiles. It will drop deep inside of a building before exploding. When it explodes it...'

Jaden fires a gravity shock wave at the door as it slowly opens. She feels the slightly increasing gravity by her feet. The door flies straight across the hall impaling eight men and ripping five bodies apart. The door goes into the cell across the hall and slams downwards into a concrete wall. There is blood and gore everywhere. Men begin to scream as they run towards the exit.

"Wow, I'm impressed," she says while seeing a new doorway.

"Well you did wanted to see some alien magic with your own eyes," he says while grabbing her hand and walking forward.

'...explodes it sucks all the oxygen out of a building, ripping lungs out, shredding internal organs, crushing the human body before engulfing the building in a huge fireball. There is also a powerful energy shock wave that can destroy nervous systems and brain activity in the body. Jaden! The missile is going to hit in twenty-one seconds.'

"Let me carry you, and close your eyes. This is going to get ugly," Jaden says while lifting her over his arms. She puts her left arm around his shoulder and holds his left hand with her right.

Debris is everywhere as Jaden and Kimberly leave the cell. Some men are yelling in the hallway with missing limbs.

"Good luck!" The terrorist man next to Kimberly's cell yells through his cell door.

"Can we let him out?" Kimberly asks.

166

"No time!" Jaden yells while jogging away.

"I'm okay, I'm going to meet my family in heaven soon," Kimberly's terrorist friend says.

Jaden quickly turns the corner with Kimberly on his back, while stepping over bricks, debris and body parts.

'Piggy-back ride will work better, you'll be able to run faster. You are going to need full body shields over 300,000 rpm. Remember the hamster wheel,' AI says.

"Are we going to make it out in time?" She asks in a nervous voice.

"Kim, piggy-back ride," Jaden says while she stands up and quickly climbs on his back. Her skirt is pulled up as half of her light pink panties are shown from behind.

"Whatever you do, don't let go and don't open your eyes. You can also pray to Buddha for both of us, " Jaden says while he jogs forward stepping over body parts.

'Run straight towards the small kitchen. There is a wall behind it, and past that, it drops off seventy feet to a river.'

A full body forward shield forms ten feet around Jaden, destroying the doors and walls to the SHU's. Suddenly there is a bright flash of light all around and a powerful blast is felt. The ground shakes like a magnitude 8.0 earthquake.

"Take a few deep breaths and then hold your breath. I have to remove all the oxygen in this shield," Jaden says.

"Okay," she says while taking a few deep breaths and then holding.

Jaden's brain goes into nanotime 90x as he jumps two feet into the air. Kimberly holds on tightly around Jaden's neck while her legs are around his waist. He feels her heart beating fast against his back. He lands on the inside of his shield as his feet are running in slow motion above the ground. The inner shield slows down to an easy running speed for Jaden. He is controlling the direction the shield is moving in. Air shock waves from the blasts reflect on all the walls. The prisoners are running about twenty feet in front of them. The sudden drop in pressure makes them scream as the oxygen is sucked out of their bodies as if they are in space. The air shock waves quickly destroy their nervous systems. They collapse to the floor as a strong explosion comes from all directions, igniting their bodies. The walls, floors and ceilings are collapsing all around Jaden and Kim. The shield is shaped like an octagon around Jaden. The force of the missile causes the shield to move inwards by six feet. The shield is counteracting the strong forces of the thermobaric missile and uses that energy to propel them forward. Anti-gravity nanodrones are circling inside the shield at full strength. Shock waves from the blast absorb into the outside layer of the shield. Fire is everywhere as the ceilings continue to implode around them. Kimberly's hair is floating as she feels no weight on her body.

Concrete, debris, shards of metal, fire balls, high pressures, and shock waves of kinetic energy bombard the outside of Jaden's energy shield. His rpm is at 450,000 while AI helps him with the shield direction and calculations. Jaden is fully concentrating on his running speed and the shield surrounding himself and Kim. The shield goes inwards another two feet as it counteracts the powerful shock waves pulling everything towards the initial blast zone. The pro-gravity nanodrones in Jaden's feet are keeping him from floating away. He is running on the inside of the shield as if he is on a treadmill. He passes the area that used to be the kitchen. The shield is rolling in the direction Jaden is trying to go. Kimberly opens her eyes and sees orange fire all around her within a few feet. She begins to scream in slow motion as she sees death is all around her. Her deep voice sounds like a movie playing in slow motion. She climbs a little higher as Jaden increases his running speed to 21 mph. Nanotime goes off and her voice speeds up into a high pitch scream. Jaden and Kimberly explode outside a concrete wall of the basement area in the prison. They go airborne. Kimberly is gasping to breathe. The zero gravity inside the shield allows them to continue floating forward. Trees are below them, as they glide over a river below. The fire around the shield disappears into the wind behind them and he stops running.

The shield disappears from around them and Earth's gravity pulls down on their bodies. The strong wind passes around their bodies and face, as Kimberly takes deep breaths of fresh air for the first time in a day. They glide down between some trees as the anti-gravity nanodrones circle around them creating an upwards counteracting gravity force. They land in a wooded area and Jaden braces his knees for the impact. Pieces of burning debris fall from the prison from all directions around them.

Dr. K. Chan Sandwich & Tots – Grilled chicken, egg, turkey bacon, honey mustard, lettuce, green peppers, tomatoes & double American.

Nacho Extreme

Chapter 21: Superlover
(PG-13 Parental Guidance suggested)
This chapter contains sexual references and romance scenes. If you are under 13 please skip this chapter.

"Are we safe yet? I can hear birds and crickets. Can I open my eyes?" She asks while continuing to hold on tightly to Jaden.

"Yes, we are safe now. Are you okay?" He asks while she stands on her feet with a confused look on her face. She straightens and pulls down her skirt.

"I'm fine, just a little shook. The inside of your shield felt like a plastic bag over my head, I couldn't breathe at all," she says while gasping and taking deep breaths.

"Sorry about that."

They look at the prison on top of a mountain across a small river. The building is completely destroyed. There are three UAV drone aircraft flying over the scene.

"I can't believe they destroyed the entire prison and all those prisoners inside. It doesn't make any sense," she says while holding her chest and still trying to catch her breath.

'That drone plane at 532 feet away is watching us,' AI says.

171

'Okay.'

"We have to keep moving, Kimberly," Jaden says while walking forward and extending out his right hand to her.

"I've never experienced anything like that. That was unbelievable, I mean, if this was a movie, that would have been one of the best rescues I've seen," she says while walking and grabbing his hand.

They walk down a slight hill with bushes, grass and leaves on the ground.

"What are we going to do now?" She asks.

"I was thinking we should leave the planet. I want you to come with me," he says.

"Leave the planet? What about trying to stop this attack and warning as many people as we can?" Kimberly asks.

"I've tried and I've tried. Nobody wants to listen, no one cares, the government thinks I'm a terrorist and I'm a threat. I've been put in a jail, a hospital, I've been shot at thousands of times and constantly chased the past few days. I don't need this, I'm the hero that was sent here to help save this planet. But I'm the villain, wasting time defending myself. I can spend the rest of my life traveling the galaxy or going back to Xenos. What is the point of trying to save our primitive, religious, homicidal, genocidal and self destructive race?" Jaden asks while she stops to look him in the eyes.

He turns to her and she says, "Jaden, there is a strong possibility there could be one or two people in the government making it difficult for you. Our race is all we have. If people knew what was about to happen, maybe more could be done…"

"It is too late, sweetie. That mother ship is here and the countdown is running out. I did an interview with a news reporter an hour ago and the government took the holographic disc. I'm the enemy of America, I think the rest of these humans should suffer the consequences. Humans were expecting the end of the world in 2012. Maybe Nostradamus was off by a few years and this is the end of human civilization," Jaden says.

"Come on Jaden, that's not true."

"The government can't comprehend that these Darclonians are the real enemies. Religions around the world all talk about rapture and Armageddon coming, well I think we shouldn't disappoint them. Maybe now is the time for change on Earth. Come with me

172

Kimberly, we can live on our own planet somewhere on the other side of this galaxy, just like Adam and Eve. We can start our own family and create our own first Bible and laws...."

'There are search dogs with guards and military personnel getting off a small boat near the river. There are more men coming from each direction around us,' AI says.

'I see them, shit, they don't give up,' Jaden says.

'You don't have a scent, but Kimberly does. We can't outrun them.'

'I have an idea,' Jaden says.

"Let's walk and talk Kimberly. What do you think about what I just said?"

"That sounds good, I've always wanted to travel to new planets and worlds. But, I can't leave my father here. He is older and I can't leave him knowing what is about to happen to the human race. My father and I are our only family here in USA. The rest of my family is in Taiwan. What about your family? What about your daughter, father and mother?" Kimberly asks.

There are UAV aircraft and helicopters flying by above. Jaden and Kimberly quickly walk down another small hill and over green leaves on the ground. Jaden leans against a huge tree and grabs Kimberly close to him. He puts his arms around her waist and looks deep into her eyes.

"My father, I don't even know if he is alive or dead. The letter he left me said he was being treated for cancer. AI used the nanoscanners to try to find him in Halifax when I was in jail with no luck. My mother is in London with her family. She should be okay, but I'll check on her before I leave Earth regardless. My daughter is a little bitch that deserves to have an alien take over her body, maybe she would have some better manners then."

"Don't say that, sweetie. Even though you barely know your daughter, you still love her. She is half of you and I'm sure there is a side of her that you can appreciate and learn to love. She is your flesh and blood. The Jaden I know isn't a quitter or someone who gives up. You are a fighter till the end, just like me. From the man who implanted his entire life in my memory has a good heart, love for his country and is a fighter..."

Kimberly pauses as she sees men and dogs behind the tree and Jaden.

"…there are guard dogs and military men with guns about thirty feet behind you coming this direction. My vision is blurry. Shouldn't we run or do something?" She asks while looking in other directions.

"They don't see us. I'm reflecting the light around us, making us look invisible."

"What about our body heat? They have heat sensing glasses."

"That is taken care of sweetie, nothing to worry about. The nanodrones are making the heat around our bodies the same temperature as the air. Your body scent molecules are being destroyed as they leave your body. Two nanoscanners copied your scent and are going to have fun with the dogs," he says while dogs and prison guards walk by kicking leaves. The dogs are barking as they smell the ground.

"You are so smart and creative to figure this out," Kimberly says while smiling, chuckling and watch the men walk by clueless.

"Well, AI helped out. So, continue what you were just talking about. Wait a second, turn around and watch the two groups of men with search dogs over there," Jaden says while pointing.

The dogs begin to quickly run and pull their owners. The dogs are barking loudly. A nanoscanner close to the ground is reproducing Kimberly's scent while three bloodhounds are pulling one guard. Two German Shepherds are pulling another guard from another direction. The German Shepherds are being manipulated by the other nanoscanner. Two soldiers are walking behind each of them. The nanoscanners pass by each other and all the dogs run into each other causing the guards to fall over each other.

"Oh shit," she says while laughing, "that was hilarious."

"Shh, they can still hear us," Jaden says while covering her mouth with his hand.

"Okay, okay," she says with a muffled voice.

"Can you continue what you were saying earlier Dr. Chan?" He asks while putting his arms around her waist.

She puts her arms around his neck.

"I was saying, you have a good heart and you are a fighter till the end. So what, the government is trying to kill you, there are always going to be a few bad apples. But there are a lot of good apples on this planet that deserve a chance at living their lives. There will be so many innocent children becoming victims in this attack. They need you…"

She looks up into his blue eyes and sees deep into his soul.

"…and I need you. I have just witnessed the impossible with that escape and rescue you just did. I have never witnessed something like that before, not even in a movie. I believe *we* can still help do something to prevent this attack on Earth. I want you to stay and fight to save our human race," she says in a sensual whisper.

She brings his head closer to her mouth. Her lips sets off a chain reaction through his body. They hear a commotion to the side of them. The guards unwrap themselves from the dogs' chains. The dogs quickly run into another direction as the nanoscanners guide them.

"Yeah, you are right Kimberly, you have some good points. I didn't really think about it that way. I have been doing the impossible lately and I shouldn't give up yet."

Kimberly looks deep into Jaden's eyes and he does the same. He spreads his legs outwards, so that he is at her eye level.

"You are a good man that I felt I've known all my life now. I have feelings for you and I know you will do the right thing. I love you Jaden Marino and I don't want you to leave me," Kimberly says while she kisses him gently on the mouth, he responds, but quickly pulls back.

"I love you too, my little Chinese food."

"Hey! Hey! Don't bring my mind back to that dirty, nightmarish prison," she says while Jaden quickly kisses her to be quiet.

Her arms wrap around his neck as they lock in a deep French kiss. She pulls him closer and his hands go to around the top of her ass. Her soft lips press against his as their heads go side to side. Their wet tongues greet each other and slowly wrestle. Their hearts begin to beat faster as their chemistry connects. He is staring deep into her brown eyes and she does the same. She unbuttons his navy blue dress shirt half way.

"I love your eyes and their shape, it is as if I can see deep into your soul. When I first saw your eyes when you were seven years old, I knew there was something special about you," Jaden says.

"You pedophile," she whispers

She rubs his back up and down slightly scratching it with her nails. She grabs his broad shoulders and rubs his muscles as she continues kissing him, making slight moaning sounds. Kimberly pushes Jaden to the right and off the tree. She turns and leans her back on the tree as she grabs Jaden's neck to pull him closer to her.

"Freaky and aggressive, are we?" Jaden asks.

"You should know," she snaps.

"That is so sexy…"

She pulls apart his button up navy shirt and the buttons fly in different directions. The buttons land on the leaves and ground around them. She pulls his shirt down to his arms and leaves it there.

The three bloodhound dogs are running towards a tree and the nanoscanner goes through it. The dogs run into the tree and tangle themselves around the tree.

"What is wrong with you boys today?" The guard asks the dogs. The dogs bark in confused tones.

Labrador search dogs from the military join the search and the dogs pull their master, while another nanoscanner joins the fun.

Kimberly is kissing and licking Jaden's muscular chest area. His shirt holds his arms in place. She stands back up to slowly kiss his neck. Jaden's head is looking up the high tree, as he slightly moans from the sensual pleasure he is experiencing. She pulls down the rest of his shirt and it hits the ground.

'This considered second or third base?' AI asks, while Jaden pays him no attention.

Jaden's hands go up her skirt and he rubs her smooth legs.

Jaden whispers, "Damn, your legs and skin are smooth."

She whispers in a flirting voice in his right ear, "That is the Asian secret. Only the chosen few are able to experience an Asian woman's naturally smooth skin."

"I guess I am lucky to have been chosen by you to experience the Asian secrets," he snaps.

"I'm risking being arrested when I return to Taiwan for espionage for giving away the Chinese secrets. That would make me a really, really bad girl," she says in a sexy voice.

Jaden lifts her up as she puts her arms around his neck. She wraps her legs around his hips as she leans against the tree. His pelvic area rubs against hers. Jaden put his right hand between her legs and on the outside of her panties.

"Whoa, your panties are soaking wet," he says while putting his fingers under her panties from the sides.

"You rescuing me and watching the police dogs run back and forth has really turned me on. I've never been turned on this much. The fact that they can't see us is making my heart pound. I feel as if we are in the wilderness and the world is watching us," Kimberly says while reaching down below Jaden's stomach and opening his pants.

"Wow. That feels perfectly wet, meaty and lubricated…" Jaden says while Kimberly places her finger over his mouth.

"Shhh…she is ready for an easy entry. Is your space shuttle ready to enter Earth's small tight window?" She asks while his pants fall down to his ankles.

"My new Orion space shuttle is ready. Do you like what you are feeling?" Jaden asks while she rubs her hand on it.

"What the hell?" She asks while looking down.

"What?" Jaden asks.

"What the hell is that? That third arm is about twelve inches long, three inches wide and as thick as my upper arm. Where do you think you are putting that?" Kimberly asks with a surprising look on her face.

"You don't like? Don't women like the King Kong size? I thought big was in?" Jaden asks in a confused voice.

"*Big* went out in the late nineties, women by the 00's wanted the average size and women by the two thousand teens realized the average size with a slight curve worked best," Kimberly says with a disappointed voice. "Jaden, I'm 5'6" 114 lbs, how did you think that would fit in my little body?"

AI quickly interrupts, 'Technically it should fit inside. This area and muscle are very stretchable. The average baby's head is one inch thicker than your reproducing tool down there, so…'

'AI, keep that info to yourself, she isn't having a baby now,' he says.

"Good question, I didn't really think about that baby."

"Very big, went out the last century. How you use it has been in for the past fourteen years."

"I'll make a note of that. But I have a solution," Jaden says.

"What is that? Putting your head down there instead?" She asks excitedly.

"I can do that, but I have a better idea. What size would you like it to be? An average Asian man's size, average white man's size or average…."

"How about an average eight inch size and average thickness? I think I can handle that," she says.

AI gets right to work. 'Reducing spongy tissue, corpora cavernosa and corpus spongiosum tissue in penis organ,' AI says while it quickly shrinks in size.

"Is this better sweetie?" Jaden asks as she inspects it.

"Shit, wow, that is amazing. You can control your penis size?" She asks loudly.

"Shhh."

Jaden just kisses her lips and then her neck. She is still leaning against the tree while her legs are around Jaden's lower hips. Kimberly closes her eyes and moans in pleasure as Jaden unstraps her bra with his left hand. He gently massages her breasts and kisses her nipples. Her pinkish brown nipples are pointing out. He pulls down her panties with his right hand while he continues to stare deep into her eyes kissing her. They stretch as she pulls her left leg towards her face and the panties come from around that leg. Jaden wraps the pink panties around her right leg as her left leg goes back around his lower waist.

He begins to kiss her left ear and sticks his tongue inside of it.

She whispers, "Wow, baby, you know my turn on spots."

He palms her ass cheeks with two hands.

"You know I like my ass grabbed," she moans in his ear.

His private part rubs up and down against her very moist, slightly hairy bush.

"How are you doing that without any hands?" She asks in a whispering moan.

"I can control it like a joystick in any direction. I have some extra small muscles down…"

"Shut up and put it in me," she whispers in a sexy voice looking at him while pulling his head closer to her face.

The area has search dogs and men running back and forth. Military men are looking around the area with advanced thermal goggles. UAV drone aircraft, hobby size UAV aircraft and helicopters slowly pass by overhead. Jaden and Kimberly remain invisible up against the medium-sized tree that is shaking on top.

"We got them boys, I know they are close by," a guard yells.

A nanoscanner guides the bloodhounds into the slowly moving river by the prison. The guard lets the leashes go as they jump into the water and they doggy paddle across the river. There is a loud pleased female scream coming from the woods. The guard by the river turns around and looks towards the top of the trees. Birds start flying into the air from the top of the trees. The military men and the two other search dog groups stop and look into the direction the scream came from. Jaden is covering Kimberly's mouth as he pauses inside of her. She closes her eyes and holds her breath. She is squinting and gripping his back very tightly with her hands and legs. Jaden feels sensual chills moving up and down his spine. He connects with her emotionally and physically. Kimberly feels Jaden's Chi energy passing through her body and combining with hers. She breathes from her nose and Jaden slowly removes his right hand.

"You okay?" He asks.

"Yes, just felt you going through my entire body just now and it's been awhile. Just give me a second."

'Aren't you going to use the condom in your pocket Jaden?' AI asks.

'That outdated condom? Do you feel how good this feels?'

'No.'

"Keep going, baby," she whispers, "But cover my mouth, I might get loud."

He continues to penetrate in and out of her. Muffled moaning and whimpering continues under Jaden's hand as his hand vibrates. The top of the tree branches shake and a few leaves slowly fall around Jaden and Kimberly. The leaves land on Kimberly's hair and on Jaden's back. He continues to kiss her neck and thrust himself inside of her. She continues to scratch his back with her nails. The men look in Jaden's direction, but they don't see anything. They continue canvassing the area.

'I know this is what men call going to home base or scoring, right? It is also interesting seeing how the chemicals in your brain react with this feeling of love you are experiencing. I understand better now with what the couple on the highway was actually experiencing and what you experienced in your past sexual

179

relationships. Your entire body's nerve senses are lighting up and sending signals all around your body,' AI says.

'You are messing up my concentration here...why don't you make yourself useful by counting the strokes,' Jaden says to AI, while he breathes heavily.

It goes completely quiet around Jaden and Kimberly. A clear energy shield forms around them and around the bottom of the tree isolating any sounds. The shield hugs and changes shape around the tree so that it isn't damaged. He uncovers her mouth as she moves her hips in sync with Jaden's thrusts. Her body moves up and down as she quickly moves her hips around in circles.

'You are eighty-five percent near orgasm and at 71,72,75 strokes...' AI says.

'The sperm is on vacation and won't come out right?' He asks.

'I've reprogrammed most of the sperm.'

"Hold on a second Jaden, I'm not on any birth control," Kimberly says while catching her breath.

"I noticed one thing didn't change in the future. Two people are still talking about birth control after sex has already started," Jaden says while chuckling. "I have a condom, but it expired fifteen years ago."

'Technically the condom wouldn't have been expired, it would have only aged a little over a month as you did,' AI says.

'Thanks for the technical analysis.'

"I have built in birth control, AI reprogrammed my army," he says.

"Damn you are amazing baby, that's cool. Baby, I have a question, when you first went inside of me, did your Orion space shuttle curve inside of me?" She asks.

"You noticed huh? Yes, my shuttle went straight for your G landing spot. You liked that, right?" Jaden asks while smiling.

"Yes, I did. That was amazing, it was like a shock all around my body. I almost came instantly that's why I screamed. It was like there was some electricity coming from your shuttle and curving upwards into my G-spot," Kim says.

"I bet the small device in your lower back can't do this..." Jaden says while thrusting himself deep inside of her and hitting her spot again. An electric spark leaves his body.

"Shit! Shit! Shit! Ahh!" She yells while her legs and lower body shake uncontrollably. She trembles against Jaden's sweaty chest and moans with pleasure. She breathes as if she has asthma, "Oh my God! I can't stop shaking. What did you do to me?"

Jaden has a smile on his face and looks at her breathing heavily with her eyes closed.

"I never had an orgasm like that, I don't think anyone woman has. That was unbelievable. I felt like I left my body for a few seconds there. That was like a super orgasm. You are milking me like a cow."

"On demand instant orgasms," Jaden says while chuckling.

"I'm keeping you baby. You are one of a kind. I need a little build up time, before I have a heart attack or can't walk the rest of the day," she says.

Jaden begins thrusting himself into Kim again. He stops suddenly, "Wait a second Doctor Chan, are you having sexual relations with your patient? You aren't supposed to be touching a patient, Doctor Chan that is unprofessional," Jaden says in a deeper voice sounding like Dr. Abraham.

"I'm sorry, sir, I was giving the patient a varicocele exam," she says while reaching down and grabbing Jaden's balls, "Now cough, Mr. Marino."

Jaden coughs and she says, "Okay the patient is fine Dr. Abraham."

Jaden changes his voice back to his voice. "Oh and Doctor Abraham I was just taking the doctor's temperature with my smaller Dragon spacecraft. Her internal temperature is 98.69°F sir, she is normal," Jaden says while laughing and she chuckles in a fake tone.

She grabs his ass and pulls it closer to her. "Now stop procrastinating, my back is beginning to hurt against this tree. Give it to me baby, I want to feel your duck sauce in my egg roll," she says. Jaden thinks to himself that she was probably in the prison too long, talking like that.

He thrusts himself deeper inside of her while he sucks her pointy nipples.

"Shit, shit, shit...I feel it in my stomach," she says while scratching deeply into his back.

"Oh shit, oh shit," he says while the tree branches shake from high above and green leaves fall around them again.

"Oh shit! Whoa!" Jaden yells while his body shakes.

He squeezes her ass tightly as he is about to climax. She moans louder as he curves himself inside of her. The German Shepherd search dogs stop running 175 feet away and begin to howl into the sky. The Labs do the same thing. Kim screams at the top of her lungs. Jaden moans as if he is in pain. They both climax and Jaden uploads ounces of sticky milk. They both breathe heavily as Kim's entire body shakes the top of the tree.

'Good work AI, manipulating my prostate and modifying my pituitary gland really gave me an out of this world orgasm,' Jaden says.

"You are the best baby, you are like a Superlover or Cockgod. Words cannot explain the feelings I'm feeling now. That was amazing, I missed the real thing," she says while trying to catch her breath.

"Baby, that was the best I've ever had also. I was so turned on," Jaden says while he lifts her down.

Kimberly stands up and puts her panties back on. Liquid is running down her legs.

"Sweetie, are you sure you are on alien birth control? That was a lot of fluid coming out of you, it completely filled up my insides. I felt like you were giving me a vaginal douche, it's oozing down my legs now," she says while wiping her legs with her panties.

"I'm sorry baby, I temporarily unregulated my pituitary gland for a better climax. Let me clean some of that up for you," Jaden says while bending down and using his navy shirt to wipe the fluids running down her legs.

They finish cleaning up the slight mess and they put their clothes back on. Jaden wraps the dirty shirt around his waist.

The shield disappears around them, and Kimberly takes a limping step forward. She moans in pain and can't take another step.

"Shit, I can't walk, my lower body is aching. My legs are still trembling," Kim says.

"Piggy-back ride? I'll carry you," he says while she hops on his back and he holds her legs up.

They continue walking invisibly through the woods and across leaves.

"Where are the dogs and military men?" She asks.

"They are over a half of a mile that way. The Labs and German Shepherds surrounded a house, so the military is searching it now."

"Very clever. Your AI friend wasn't watching what we were just doing right?"

"No, he was concentrating on providing the cover for us. He wasn't interested in what we were doing," he says.

"Cool. How does he communicate with you? What does he say to you? It wasn't too clear from your memories."

"He sits in an area of my brain reserved for multiple personalities. He sees everything I see, hear and feel. He can see most things in my memory from my past. We communicate internally with each other. AI or myself can control the nanodrones and nanoscanners in my body. He can't control my body, but he does help me out with a lot of things. Are you familiar with this area?" Jaden asks.

"Yes I am. That's very interesting. Hello AI, hope I wasn't screaming too loud for you," she says in his ear while kissing Jaden's neck. Jaden laughs.

"Keep walking that direction, there are some houses over that way. You find it funny when I kiss your neck?" She asks.

"No, I'm laughing at AI. He is messing with the dogs at this family's house. The military men are making a man get a cavity search because the dogs smelled his crotch. They thought he was hiding something of yours up there," Jaden says while chuckling.

'That is enough AI. You going to make his wife think the man was cheating on her with Kim,' Jaden says.

'Yeah you are right. I'll fix that,' AI says.

'But that was funny,' Jaden says.

"That is funny, I wish I could see," she says.

Jaden reaches over his shoulders and covers her eyes with the outside of his right hand. Nanodrones enter creating an artificial pathway behind her eyes. She sees through the nanoscanner.

"Wow, this is very clear vision. The details are amazing. I like all the wording on the screen," she says.

"Just keep your eyes closed or you might get double vision," he says.

"Cool. Ha ha, the police dogs are sniffing the wife's crotch area now. Cool... the nanoscanner passed through her body and the inside of her body looks animated like a cartoon," Kimberly says.

"The inside of an organic body looks cartoonish or animated. Regular materials and matter look as is," Jaden explains.

"Cool. Go up inside of the guards and state police crotches. I want to see what they are working with. I heard officers and men of authority have small private parts," she says while her arms are around Jaden's neck.

'She is almost as bad as you,' AI says.

'Yeah, you are right. At least she has a reason. I don't want to see though,' Jaden says while continuing to walk down a small trail.

"Yeah, I see you little pee wee, sleeping in your master's pants. Oh look at this one, the little Shenzou space shuttle is awake at a full five inches. The male officer is watching the wife get a cavity search from a female officer. What a pervert. Look at the female officer, her little private friend has a full beard. I can tell she isn't getting any…hey it is dark again, where did the images go?"

"Okay, that is enough for you, Miss Pervert. I thought I was bad," Jaden says.

"I got a little carried away. I did my thesis on penis size in relation to a man's work and vehicle. A big gun usually helps to make up for the size of his…"

"Hey! I don't care to know about this subject. You are a little freak aren't you? Looking at penis sizes. I don't remember this in your memories. I thought you were a quiet woman," he says.

"I'm sorry sweetie," she says.

"Don't be sorry, I like it. Now I don't feel as bad," Jaden says.

"You don't feel as bad for what?" She asks.

"Nothing," he replies.

"Tell me, before I tickle you in all your ticklish spots," she says while tickling him under his arms and down to his waist.

"Okay, okay, you win," he says while laughing, "Well I guess I can tell you now… I don't feel so bad for looking at your naked body dozens of times at the hospital when you walked around."

"I knew you looked at me naked. I was thinking about that when I was on the airplane flying back to Virginia on Friday. I knew it!" She yells.

"Are you upset?" He asks.

184

"No, not at all. If I were in your situation, I probably would have done the same thing. If I had x-ray vision and you were my doctor in the hospital, I probably would have looked you up and down also."

"I'm glad you understand like that. That is one of the things that I love about you. So me analyzing every part of your body at the hospital, doesn't bother you at all?" Jaden asks.

'Why don't you tell her about you counting her pubic hairs?' AI asks.

'AI buddy, that was you suggesting me to do that,' Jaden says.

'I was practicing my human sarcasm, I didn't really want you tell her that.'

"Nope. I see it as you wanting to analyze my body because you wanted to draw a picture of it in your mind. I think bodies are like art and we shouldn't be afraid to be in our natural human form," she says while playing with his hair.

"I had a naked body experience in an Andromedian city."

Kimberly rests her head on Jaden's neck and a few minutes go by. Her skirt softly lifts in the air as Jaden walks. They approach an area with houses.

"Now we just have to find a vehicle with some keys inside," Kimberly says.

"I already did, the black Cherokee at the third house in the driveway."

She climbs down from his back and they walk over to it and climb inside.

"I guess only in the south do people leave their keys in their vehicles," Jaden says.

"Yep, I also do sometimes," she says while Jaden starts up the SUV.

They back up and quickly drive off.

"They have roadblocks on the main roads," Jaden says.

"Let me drive, I know some back roads. We need to go to my father's house first and then my house. I have some clothes at his house and he has a car we could borrow," Kim says while he stops the SUV and Jaden opens the door. He walks around as Kim climbs over the center console and into the driver's seat. Jaden sits in the passenger seat and slams the door. Kim quickly accelerates and drives off-road.

'Did you notice she said she missed the real thing? What do you think she meant by that?' AI asks.
    'I don't know, but I'll ask her later.'

...............TO BE CONTINUED.

Written by: Vlane Carter

Creative art director: Vlane Carter

    Graphic artist: John Buurman
                   John Moriarty
                   Matthew Garofalo
                   Kwan Wilson

THE REBIRTH UNIVERSE SERIES:

BIO-SAPIEN VOLUME I   BOOKS 1-6

BIO-SAPIEN VOLUME II   BOOKS 7-12

BIO-SAPIEN VOLUME III BOOKS 13-18

BIO-SAPIEN COMIC BOOKS ISSUES 1-30

BIO-SAPIEN VIDEO GAME SERIES

<u>BIO-SAPIEN SPINOFF REBIRTH SERIES</u>

BELLONA SERIES BOOKS 1-3

ANDROMEDIAN CHRONICAL SERIES BOOK 1-3
ANDROMEDIAN CHRONICAL COMIC BOOKS 1-5
ANDROMEDIAN CHRONICAL VIDEO GAME
ANDROMEDIAN CHRONICAL CARTOON

BOMANI SERIES   BOOK 1-2

MARCO SERIES   BOOK 1-2

ROBOGODS & DARCLONIANS BOOK 1-2

TORAGON BOOKS 1-2

QUEEN VALASCA & THE ARACHNOSAPIENS BOOK 1-3

Atoms ripper – Is a molecule destroying energy similar to plasma fusion in the forward shields.

Bioparasites – Darclonians in microbial form. They wait to merge with nanomole to control a human body at high speed. Nanomoles protect bioparasites from human white blood cells. Bioparasites also control armies of microbots.

DEK – Dark Energy Knight.

DEQ – Dark Energy Queen.

DEW – Dark Energy Wraith – Mysterious dark energy that rides like a comet and fuels itself from the exhaust of a spaceship.

DHW – Darclonian Human Walkers. When nanomole and bioparasite merge. Darclonians are controlling human bodies at high speed. Making them super strong and slowly modifying the human body to turn them into super humans.

HBH – Hijacked brain Humans – See positive stage nanomole.

LRSB – Long Range Signal Beacon. It is put on UFOs just in case they get away from the US government. The top-secret technology sends transmissions through subspace.

Microbots – Darclonian robotic or organic organisms that can do a variety of things similar to the Andromedian nanobots and nanodrones. They prepare the human body to become super human.

Molevision – When the nanomoles are in a neutral stage they transmit different visions to other nanomoles when a human is suffering or experiencing pleasure from torturing someone else. It transmits and records dozens of emotions.

Nanoeyes – Invisible to the human eyes, range in size from a millionth to a billionth of an inch. Nanoeyes allow the host to hear and see things at a far distance. It can also pass through most materials. They can be controlled by host or on their own.

Nanoscanner – Invisible to the human eye and range in size between a millionth to a trillionth of an inch. Nanoscanners can do what nanoeyes can, and also analyze materials, scan through objects and determine their structure. They also have other capabilities especially in optic-warp. They can be controlled by host or fly autonomously.

Nanomoles – Are encoded particles sent to Earth over 100,000 years ago by the Darclonians. They sit hidden in the brain of humans. They reproduce in intelligent life from generation to generation, recording everything.

A Nanomole has three stages:

1. Negative - Mole is semi-hibernating and is recording and saving detailed information on the host.
2. Neutral – When the mother ship sends a high power signal to Earth to activate each nanomole in the brain. An 84 hour countdown begins. Humans go unconscious for thirty seconds before waking up, and go back into the negative stage. Some humans randomly go in and out of the neutral stage. The nanomole is expanding and preparing the neurons, axons and chemical messages in the brain to completely take over the human host.
3. Positive – HBH – Hijacked Brain Humans – The nanomole takes control of a human body and walks to upload areas. Bioparasites (Darclonians in microbes) merge with the nanomole and the humans become DHWs.
   * Humans are able to see, feel and hear everything around them, but can't control their own bodies and are prisoners.

Nanodrones – Advanced prototype organic nanobots that were specially made to work with Jaden's body. They work with his body in a collective of different groups and do many tasks.

Nanobots – Metallic, mechanical, microscopic robots that work with Andromedian biomechanical bodies and spaceships.

Optic-warp – The Andromedian species way of traveling through space at a fast rate. The ship approaches a local star at the speed of light, and then the ship breaks down into Quadrillion of molecules and slingshots through subspace at 6-90 second light-years.

Shield technologies –

Clockwise – Forward – 2 layers - First outside layer destroys objects by ripping apart its molecules and atoms. A part of plasma gasification. Second layer protects object or person inside the shield with solid energy force. Powerful projectiles can force through shield systems (gravity x force). The person, depending on the speed it traveled, can feel the force inside. The shield can change into any shape.

Counterclockwise – reverse – 3 Layers – First layer slows projectile and absorbs blast. Second layer gravity matrix analyzes material and stays in one place. It then recycles it into the shield whirlpool, which can be turned into a weapon for firing. Third layer protects objects or person inside with a solid force.

Gravity shockwave – It pulls gravity forces from ground level from all directions and leaves a smoky haze. The object caught in the pathway of the weapon instantly loses its gravity and propels forward at high speed. The object suddenly changes directions towards the ground at 3-4 times its body weight.

TC-100 – An instrument that scans through foreign material. It's like a high powered x-ray scanner that can see inside of aliens and foreign materials.

UF1-retrac team – The UFO police team that specializes in analyzing a
UFO and preparing it for transport to Area 51 for research. They analyze the ship, check for radiation. They work for the government in a special sector and are mostly civilians.

Wraithstalkers – Lightly armed Darclonian ships used for recon missions.

www.ingramcontent.com/pod-product-compliance
Lightning Source LLC
Chambersburg PA
CBHW071236130626
46556CB00003B/1039